Chase AFTER ME

New York Times & *USA Today* Bestselling Author

CYNTHIA EDEN

This book is a work of fiction. Any similarities to real people, places, or events are not intentional and are purely the result of coincidence. The characters, places, and events in this story are fictional.

Published by Hocus Pocus Publishing, Inc.

Copyright ©2020 by Cindy Roussos

All rights reserved. This publication may not be reproduced, distributed, or transmitted in any form without the express written consent of the author except for the use of small quotes or excerpts used in book reviews.

Copy-editing by: J. R. T. Editing

CHAPTER ONE

"Tell me again why you're naked."

Chase Durant glowered at his *sometimes* partner and friend. "Because, Merik, today the role of hot new neighbor is being played by yours truly."

Merik Stone nodded. "Of course. How could I have overlooked that? Hot neighbor role. Sure. Whatever." His bright gaze swept over Chase. "But I think I need more scene info to fully understand what's happening here. I mean, I'm not sure I buy what's going on. Do people normally move into new places and only wear jogging shorts while they do it? Isn't that kind of dangerous, you know, with the heavy lifting and what not?"

A long sigh escaped Chase. "Are you trying to piss me off?"

Merik shrugged. "Maybe. I'm a little bored, and it has been a slow day."

Damn straight it had been. Chase had started the new mission that morning, and they had moved in the temporary apartment very quickly—mostly because Chase wasn't moving in actual belongings. Just enough for the scene to look real. They'd made short work of the moving part, and he'd been sure that his prey would walk right into his path. It was a Saturday, after all. His target wasn't at work, and it should have been the perfect time to make her acquaintance.

Only...nothing. Hours had passed, and nothing had happened. Chase knew his target had left the building earlier that morning, but he'd figured she'd be back in a reasonable amount of time. Ha. No such luck. So far, four hours had passed.

"Look, have you considered that she's not coming home today?" Merik asked.

Not coming back? "She didn't take anything with her when she left. She was wearing shorts, a t-shirt, and tennis shoes." Yes, he'd been watching. *Spying.*

His head swiveled toward the only other apartment on the floor. They were on the fourth floor—the top floor—of the building. The place was located on the outskirts of Marietta, Georgia, and the old building had been converted and updated just a few years before. Exposed bricks and gleaming chunks of wood were everywhere, and Chase had the uncomfortable feeling that he might just be in one of those HGTV episodes because it seemed like the designer of the building had checked off every single box—

"If she's not coming home anytime soon, you could put your shirt back on," Merik offered.

Chase waved toward his abs. "I work hard for these."

Merik snorted.

"Moneymakers, that's what they are," Chase added, voice serious.

"Are you sure?" Merik appeared doubtful. "I'm not so—"

"They mean I'm strong enough to get the job done, *and* the ladies like them. Since my target is one lady in particular, I figure I'd start with my best asset and work from there."

"Okay." Merik crossed his arms over his chest. When he flexed, the long dragon tattoo on his left arm seemed to slither. "Let me see if I now understand this whole setup correctly. Your strategy on this case is to use your abs to woo your prey?"

"The abs are step one—an ice-breaker, if you will." Chase hadn't been kidding when he said he was playing the hot new neighbor role. When he'd been considering undercover personas for this case, it had seemed the easiest one to use. His target was the single woman on the floor—the woman who had not yet returned for their meet and greet. He had to get close to her. Had to sneak past her guard.

Then he had to learn every single secret that she possessed.

Sure, sure, normally, his job was to protect. At Wilde, the protection and security firm that he'd been employed at for quite a while now, they often took jobs where danger was just part of the game. They protected all sorts of clients—even royalty and rock stars—but they also took jobs that were under the radar. As in, *way* under the radar. Jobs that the government farmed out to them.

Those kinds of jobs were often Chase's favorites. Undercover missions had always been his specialty.

And Merik knew that—so why was his buddy giving him grief?

"I'm dying to hear step two." Merik nodded. "Do not leave me in suspense."

The man must be helluva bored. "Fine, if you must know—"

"I must," he cut in.

The elevator dinged.

Chase tensed. "Showtime." His lady had to be arriving. The whole reason he'd been killing time in that hallway with the *last* box of moving items on the floor between him and Merik? He'd wanted to be in the right place to run into his target.

He sucked in a breath. *Abs at the ready.*

The elevator doors opened.

And...

He saw her.

Her head was tilted down so that her loose, red curls fell forward. She stepped out of the elevator, moving with a stride that was slow and almost distracted. She still wore her tennis shoes, the t-shirt, and the shorts, and he couldn't help but notice the woman had killer legs. Long, toned.

Chase moved a bit to the left. It was a deliberate side-step because it would put him in her path.

But...

She didn't notice him.

His target was carrying a book, she was reading it as she walked, and she didn't even glance up as she made her way down the hallway and to her apartment.

Huh. That was...unexpected.

She was almost on top of him. The scent of vanilla teased his nose. He loved that scent. Reminded him of when he'd been a kid and his dad would take him to the local ice cream shop. He'd always ordered vanilla. It was his favorite.

She still hadn't looked up. Obviously, situational awareness wasn't high on her list of priorities. Strange, considering what he'd been told about her.

Maybe she's just pretending not to notice me.

Either way, he had to do something before she barreled straight into him. "Ahem."

She jumped, gasped, and her book flew from her hands to crash into the floor. Her eyes—a deep, dark green—widened as she stared at him. Her unpainted lips—bow-shaped and sexy—parted in a startled O-shape.

Chase gave her what he liked to think of as his winning smile. "Hi, there, neighbor."

She blinked. Frowned. Then bent and scooped up her book.

He craned to get a glance at the title of the novel. When he recognized the name of the author, his smile stretched a little more.

"I'm sorry." She gave a brisk shake of her head. "I think I was lost in a book."

"It happens." Dammit. She was even prettier than he'd expected. Creamy skin. Little button of a nose. And those eyes. Sexy as fuck.

Not that he was supposed to find her sexy.

She was the villain, after all. His job was to bring her down.

Red blossomed on her cheeks.

His head cocked to the right. She was blushing. Lots of reactions could be faked in this world. He'd seen some world-class actors in his time, but blushing? No, you couldn't fake that. It was an instinctive, physical response.

Her gaze darted over him.

Right. The abs. They would—

Her stare shifted over to Merik as he stood near their last moving box. "Nice tat," she told him with a quick smile.

What? She liked tats? If so, Chase would be happy to show her his. Except, well, it was in a rather hard-to-find spot on his—

Merik grinned back at her. "Thanks."

"Are you moving in, too?" Her voice was all warm and welcoming—as she spoke to *Merik*.

This shit could not be happening. "No." Chase realized his own voice sounded a bit too hard when her stare swung back to him. He cleared his throat. "My buddy was just helping me to move in." Now he extended his hand to her. "Hi, I'm Chase Durant."

She eyed his hand for a moment. Nibbled on her lower lip. Then slowly, her right hand extended toward his. Her left still gripped her book.

He didn't move. Chase was being patient and letting her take her time. This was all part of his strategy. She'd be coming to him, and he would be—

Her fingers touched his. A surge of heat whipped up along Chase's hand and flew through his entire body.

Her eyes flared, and he knew she'd felt the same surge.

An awareness. An intensity. A killer sexual attraction.

His hand closed over hers. "What's your name?" Her skin was so freaking soft. Meanwhile, he had calluses to hell and back on his hands, but they came from his workout regimen. Once a SEAL, always a—

"Vivian. Vivian Wayne." She tugged against his hold.

He immediately let her go. "Nice to meet you, Vivian." He liked the name. It was different. Sexy. *So is she.* He motioned toward his silent partner. "That's Merik."

Merik gave her a little salute.

She inclined her head—

"He'll have to leave soon." Chase beamed at his buddy. "Man, I sure do appreciate your help today, but I know you need to get back to your *wife.*"

Merik's lips twitched. He didn't have a wife. Or a serious girlfriend. Dude was a player to his soul. Chase kept warning him about that, but, so far, Merik hadn't listened to him. *I offer good life advice. Why don't people listen to me more often?*

"And you need to get back to your new place," Vivian said. Her voice was low, not quite husky, but definitely sensual. "I won't keep you."

He wanted her to keep him. That was the whole point.

She stepped around him. Made her way to the apartment on the other end of the hallway.

"I'm new in town," Chase called after her. "Maybe later you can point me in the direction of some good restaurants?"

She stopped. He saw her shoulders stiffen.

Hell. Had that question sounded as desperate as it felt?

Vivian looked over her shoulder at him. She frowned, making a faint furrow appear between her eyebrows.

Chase kept his winning smile in place.

Come on, come on...

"I'll be happy to help," she replied. She didn't sound particularly happy, though.

"And I'm happy to help you, too," he told her quickly. "That's what neighbors are for, right? So if you should need me for anything, just remember, from here on out, I'll be right next door."

She seemed to absorb that. Her green gaze slid from him to his apartment door. "I'll remember."

A few moments later, she was inside her apartment. The door closed almost soundlessly behind her.

He stood there a moment, just staring down the hallway.

"Did that go according to plan?" Merik sidled closer. "I am genuinely curious. When you came up with this scheme, did you secretly intend for her to compliment my tat, ignore your abs, and shut the door in your face?"

"She didn't shut the door in my face." Obviously. "I'm a good fifteen feet away from her door."

Merik laughed and slapped a hand on Chase's shoulder. "Tell me you have another plan."

He had lots of plans. Always did. And Merik damn well knew that. Actually, Merik already knew exactly what the next step would be because they'd had to discuss it and plan for that step *before* moving into the building.

Unfortunately, the next step would involve Chase having to play dirty. Shouldn't have been a problem. He'd played dirty on plenty of cases. In fact, he was very, very good at playing dirty but...

She'd blushed.

It meant nothing. He was sure that, under the right circumstances, even serial killers could blush. *Not* that Vivian Wayne was a serial killer. No, in fact, he didn't believe that she'd killed anyone. At least, not directly.

But she was dangerous. Very, very dangerous. And his job was to stop her. By any means necessary.

Playing dirty? Yeah, it was almost time.

So why did the idea of what he was about to do...why did the idea of it make him feel like crap?

***

Focus. Be friendly. Smile.

Vivian rolled back her shoulders, lifted her chin, and rapped her left hand against the closed apartment door.

Then she shifted her stance and went back to carefully cradling the covered dish in front of her.

She could hear the pad of footsteps. And then—

The door swung open.

He stood there. The new neighbor. The guy with the dark blond hair, the rough stubble of beard on his hard jaw, and the most amazing golden eyes that she'd ever seen. *Gold.* When she'd first looked up and into his eyes, the hallway had seemed to narrow. Her heart had thudded hard in her chest, she'd trembled, and when they'd touched, when his strong, warm fingers had curled around hers, she'd thought—

Oh, so this is what everyone is always talking about.

"Uh, Vivian?"

She blinked. Oh, God. Had she just been staring at him? He'd put on a t-shirt. A white t-shirt that stretched over his powerful chest and all of those wonderfully sculpted muscles.

Sexy guy, dead ahead. In her world, sexy men didn't just fall out of the sky and into her path. If only.

But...he had.

"Is everything all right?"

No, things were not all right. She was being an awkward mess, and she needed to take control of the situation, ASAP. He was her neighbor, and she could be friendly, dang it. Or, she could try. "I baked this." Vivian shoved the welcome gift toward him.

One eyebrow quirked. "Thank...you?"

Chase made it sound like a question. Probably because she was being weird. She *knew* she was being weird. Weird was her thing. Once upon a time, she'd tried to fit in with everyone else, but that just hadn't worked so well for her. She didn't usually waste time with polite chitchat. Why be polite when you could be real? Besides, when people were being polite, they were often lying.

White lies, sure, but they weren't saying what they really meant.

She hated lies.

Mostly because of her family.

Do not go there right now. She had enough to handle without a painful walk down memory lane.

Her new neighbor was staring at her. She hadn't responded to him. She had to correct that situation. "They may not be good. It's a new recipe."

"Possibly not good." Chase's other eyebrow rose. He lifted the top of the container to take a peek inside, then he asked, "So you brought me bad baked goods?" His attention shifted back to her. "Are you welcoming me or trying to scare me away?"

Oh, no. She felt heat burn her cheeks.

His eyes widened. "You're doing it again."

"Doing what?"

"Blushing."

"Of all the animals in the world, only humans blush."

"Huh." Chase seemed to consider her statement. "Suppose it makes sense."

"It's the nervous system doing it. The system sends a quick message to your facial muscles. The message tells them to relax, and when the facial muscles do relax, we have small veins that dilate in our skin. That dilation then makes your cheeks flush as the blood starts to—" Vivian stopped because he was frowning at her. She cleared her throat then plodded on, "People with fair skin have more apparent blushes. My mom was Scottish so..." She finally let her words trail away.

Oh, no. She'd done her thing again. One of her coping mechanisms. When she was nervous, she fact-shared. She had all these random facts in her head—mostly because she loved to read *everything*—and when she was stressed, some of the facts…escaped.

"You know a lot about blushing," Chase noted.

"Not really. I'm just good at memorizing random things." She had to get this situation back on track. She pointed to her gift. "Those are brownies."

"I thought they might be." His eyes gleamed.

Was he teasing her? "I think they are passably tasty, but you might have a different opinion. I just wanted to warn you so that you wouldn't be disappointed."

"I am not even a little disappointed." He wasn't looking at the brownies. He was looking at her. "So this *is* your way of welcoming me to the building?"

"Yes. I, um, didn't think I was being overly neighborly before, so I was trying again." Her hands twisted in front of her. "Am I doing better?"

His gaze seemed to soften on her. "You are doing a fantastic job."

Warmth bloomed inside of her even as a wide smile curled her lips. "Thank you."

Chase gave two fast blinks, then his gaze sharpened on her.

"Well, I'm sure you need to get back to your unpacking, and I have to run to the grocery store so…" She backed up. Stopped. "I hope we can be friends."

A slow nod. "I'd like that."

"Me, too." It would be nice having a friend in the building. She hadn't exactly made a ton of friends since moving to Marietta. The new job kept her busy and talking to strangers had always been hard for her.

Other people could strike up conversations so easily, but, not her. Probably because of that whole polite chitchat thing.

Vivian turned and headed for the elevator.

"I'll have to repay you."

Her steps faltered.

"Maybe you can tell me about a good restaurant, and I can take you there as a thank you."

She swung toward him. Had he just asked her out? Surely not.

"It would be a *neighborly* thing to do, wouldn't it?" Chase continued. "Taking you out for a thank you meal?"

Oh. Her shoulders relaxed. He wasn't talking about a date. He was just being nice. "There's a really good Asian restaurant on the corner. Maybe we can go there when you're settled in."

He smiled. "It's a date."

Her heart lurched. Wait, *was* it a date? But she didn't ask. That would have been way awkward, and she'd already been awkward enough, thank you very much. She hurried into the elevator. Hit the button for the ground floor. Turned around and watched as the doors began to close—

She could see Chase through the space between the closing doors. He was still in the hallway. He was staring after her, and for just a moment, his handsome face looked tense and hard and—

Then he smiled. In a flash, he went back to looking all charming. He even lifted a hand to wave good-bye to her.

The doors closed.

***

"These are freaking delicious."

"Stop eating my damn brownies," Chase growled.

Merik popped another chunk into his mouth. "Why? There are plenty here."

"Because she made them for me." He hadn't even gotten to taste one yet. Chase cut a big piece and popped it into his mouth just to see how they— "Fuck me."

"No, man, I'm good, but thanks."

Chase shot a dirty look at his partner. Then he took another brownie. It melted on his tongue. Passably tasty, his ass. It was like having heaven in his mouth.

Vivian Wayne was dangerous. Far more dangerous than he'd expected. He'd thought that he could waltz into her life, charm her, and seduce her into telling him what he needed, but...*no*. "I see what she's doing." He ate another brownie. Resisted the urge to moan.

Merik reached for more, too.

Chase bared his teeth at him and snatched the brownies away. "Go make your own."

"That shit is not cool. Friends share with friends."

No, they didn't. Chase put the brownies in his kitchen.

Merik followed him. "Uh, want to catch me up to speed? Because I feel behind. What—exactly—is your prey doing?"

"She is trying to seduce *me*."

Merik laughed.

"I wasn't making a damn joke. Isn't it obvious? First she plays hard to get..."

"I didn't see her playing hard to get. I saw her ignoring you when you were stripped down in the hallway."

"*Then* she comes sashaying over here, being all charming and cute with her brownies. Tousled hair, casual clothes, sexy eyes."

"Sashaying? Sexy eyes?" Merik peered longingly at the brownies. "I missed that part because I was inside moving around *your* boxes."

"The brownies were her genius move. She was trying to act all modest about them when she knew they were awesome. She knew I'd take a bite and want more." He could still see her in his mind. Standing in his doorway. Blushing. Telling him about the nervous system and facial muscles as she rocked onto the balls of her feet and her vanilla scent wrapped around him.

"So she's seducing you with brownies. Check."

"She's diabolical." Chase took one more bite. A small one. "But she's not going to fool me."

"Of course not. We both know you're the most diabolical bastard in the world." A pause, then, "So...are you ready to break into her place?

Because I thought that was our step two. You know, seeing as how we were going over the details until your diabolical neighbor knocked on the door."

Chase stepped away from the brownies. "I'm not breaking in. That's illegal."

"Uh, huh. Right."

"I'm just going to make it *look* as if someone broke in."

"Like that's not illegal, too?" When Chase cut him a glare, Merik laughed. "I'm messing with you. I know there's a Boy Scout buried deep inside of you, and I like to see how far I can push before he gets all twitchy."

"You are *not* funny." He exhaled. "Look, just go outside the building and make sure she doesn't return before I'm done." Her trip to the store was perfect timing for him. "I'll set the stage with the fake break-in." *Such an asshole move.* But one that was unavoidable. "When I'm done, you can vanish, and then..."

"Then you'll play hero. I know how this goes. You'll be there when she runs to you for help, and you'll be one step closer to getting her to trust you."

Yeah, that was the idea.

Merik turned and headed for the door. "She seems nice."

Chase stiffened. "I've met plenty of nice criminals. Some guys still had smiles on their faces right before they tried to put bullets in me."

Merik glanced back. "Guess I'm not as jaded as you yet."

"Give it time. You'll get there."

"Yeah, that's what worries me." Merik tossed him a wave. "Keep your phone on you. When she comes back, I'll text you."

"Will do."

Merik left, and Chase got his tools ready. It was a simple matter to reach Vivian's door and pry open the lock. If he'd really wanted to break in, he could have done so without leaving a trace behind. But the point wasn't to get inside without her knowing. The point was for her to realize that someone had broken into her place.

And for her to run to me for help.

He got the door open, and an alarm didn't so much as beep. He frowned into the darkness of her apartment. Seriously? No alarm? What was she thinking?

Even the villain could get robbed.

Shaking his head, he stepped back. He made sure to leave her door slightly ajar. Then he glanced down the hallway. There was a very, very small—almost miniscule—camera positioned to the upper left of the elevator. A camera that had arrived courtesy of his boss at Wilde. When it came to tech, Eric Wilde was the best. He'd had the camera installed there—and one on the bottom floor—so that Chase would be able to keep track of everyone who came to visit Vivian. Basically, the better for him to keep track of all the players in the game.

Chase strode back to his new apartment. He locked the door and booted up his laptop. In moments, he'd pulled up the security feeds from those two cameras. Now, it would all be just a matter of waiting until Vivian came racing to his door.

He was so ready to play hero.

And within thirty minutes, he got the text from Merik...

Evil Queen is heading back.

Chase frowned. Evil Queen? Since when were they going with that codename?

He glanced back at the security footage and saw Vivian heading through the building's lobby. She had a shopping bag cradled in her hands as she disappeared into the elevator.

He counted silently as he waited for the elevator to rise up to the fourth floor.

And then...

She was picked up on the second camera when she walked out of the elevator.

There you are. Chase smiled as he leaned forward. Yes, sure, he felt like a dick for staging the scene, but the woman was a criminal. She had to be stopped. He *wouldn't* fall for her tricks.

She'd fall for his. She'd see that open door and come running. She would—

She'd stopped at her apartment door. He saw the grocery bag drop from her hands. Then her fingers fluttered around the broken lock.

Yep, intruder alert. She turned her head, looking back down the hallway.

Chase tensed. *Come to me. That's what you're supposed to do. Remember, I said I was here if you need me. You can come to me anytime and you can—*

She pushed open her apartment door. Walked inside.

What. The. Hell?

Well, shit. As far as she knew, an intruder could have been in her place, and she'd just waltzed right inside to confront him.

So much for Chase's big, save-the-day scene. Time for him to improvise. He quickly locked his laptop in a desk drawer. Chase grabbed the empty container from beside him—the brownies had truly been awesome, so awesome that he'd eaten them all while he waited for her to return—and he bounded out of the apartment. He rushed down the hallway, frowning when he saw that two apples had rolled out of Vivian's abandoned grocery bag.

Evil Queen...Okay, fine, maybe the codename would fit her.

Her door was still open. He had to play this scene just right. "Vivian?" He raised his voice and pushed against the door. "Vivian, I was bringing back your brownie container and—" Chase let surprise ring in his voice. "Oh, no, did someone break your lock? *Vivian?*" He charged inside, very hero-like.

And then he immediately had to duck as Vivian came swinging at him with a baseball bat.

CHAPTER TWO

The bat thudded into the wall over Chase's head. Vivian's jaw dropped as she realized how close she'd come to hitting her new neighbor. "I'm so sorry!" She yanked the bat back. "I didn't mean to—"

His left hand flew up and closed around the upper part of the bat. "Easy, slugger."

Her breath heaved in and out. Her grip on the bat tightened. "Someone broke my lock."

"I saw that."

Chase held her brownie dish in one hand and his other was still gripping the bat.

"I thought the intruder might still be here, so I came inside," Vivian rushed to add.

"You did *what?*" He yanked on the bat, and, since she didn't let go of her weapon, his move had the effect of hauling her closer to him. So close that their faces wound up only inches apart.

"I thought he might still be here," she said even though Vivian was sure she'd been clear before. "So I—"

"Grabbed a baseball bat and went after him?"

Yes. Exactly. She nodded.

His eyes widened. "You should have come to me!"

That made no sense. "Why would I have done that?"

"Why? *Why?*" A muscle jerked along his jaw. "Because he could've had a gun!"

"Then I would have been putting you in danger. I couldn't do that to my new neighbor."

His eyes closed. Vivian thought he whispered, "*Fuck me,*" but she couldn't be sure.

He tugged on the bat again. This time, she let it go, and Chase propped it up against the nearby wall. Then he placed the brownie dish on the floor before he glanced around her apartment.

She followed his stare. "I don't think he's here. I searched through the rooms, but I didn't see—*ah!*" Her words ended in a startled cry because he'd just picked her up—scooped her into his arms as if that were a normal thing. It wasn't. "What are you doing?"

"Carrying you to safety."

"I am *safe!*"

"No, but you will be very soon." He'd taken her out of her apartment and was double-timing it down the hallway. Chase cradled her against his chest and moved wicked fast.

In the next instant—or so it seemed to her—they were inside his apartment. He put her onto her feet, nodded briskly, and said, "I'll check out your place. Stay here."

"Absolutely not." Why was he ordering her about? What was up with that? "Unless you're a cop or something, you're not supposed to be racing into danger. And I don't know why you're telling me what to do, but that needs to stop and—*is that a gun?*"

"Yes, it is. And I am an 'or something.'"

She frowned at him. "What?" He'd taken the gun out of a desk drawer, and he looked all dangerous and rough standing there as he held the weapon with a casualness that sent a shiver skating down her spine.

"I fall into your 'or something' category. Former SEAL, at your service. Though don't go telling that to the world because I really like to keep that particular part of my past on the down low."

She kept frowning.

"Real SEALs don't have to shout it to the world, and I normally don't, but I'm trying to reassure you that I can handle this situation so..." He shrugged. "Just so you get the full disclosure bit from me, protection is my business. I work for a security company. Please consider this your lucky day. I'll check out your place—free of charge—and be back in a flash." His golden eyes pinned her. "While I'm gone, please, stay here. I want you to be safe, and I also need to make sure no one is inside your home. Lock the door behind me, and I'll be back before you know it."

She wasn't used to someone helping her this way. Or...any way. "Thank you."

He gave her a quick smile, then was gone. She fumbled and locked the door and stood there with her heart drumming entirely too fast in her chest.

Someone broke in. When she'd peered around her home, Vivian hadn't seen anything out of place. But...

She was scared. The fact that someone had gotten into her apartment unnerved her. The minutes seemed to tick past ever so slowly as she stood there. Her whole body was tight and nerves had her stomach twisting into knots. Maybe she should go after Chase. What if he was hurt? Even SEALs could be hurt. Anyone could be hurt.

When she heard the scrape of a key in the lock, her body jolted. The door swung open, and Chase filled the doorway.

"Your place was clear. No one was inside. I didn't see anything disturbed. Everything seemed perfectly in order. Like, seriously in order."

So, ah, maybe she liked for things to be organized. Was that a crime?

Chase shut the door and stalked back toward his desk. He put the gun inside. Seemed to consider the situation before he mused, "Maybe he *didn't* go in. Hell, maybe he just picked the lock, and then something scared him off." He glanced over at her. "I could have scared him off. While you were at the store, I went down to my car, and then headed back up here with one more box. I came via the elevator. Maybe he heard me and rushed out by taking the stairs—"

"Or maybe you did it."

His amazing eyes widened. Then narrowed. "Say again?" He shut the desk drawer. Headed toward her with slow, almost predatory steps.

Vivian lifted her chin, straightened her spine, and refused to be intimidated. "I said that maybe you broke into my place. You're the variable."

Chase's head tilted to the right. "Explain."

"A variable is an element that can change or—"

"I know what a variable is," he growled. "Why am I your variable?"

Oh, right. "Because you're new. The only new person in the building. Because I've been here for over three months and nothing like this has happened before, but on the day you move in, right after I clearly tell you that I am leaving so my home will be empty..." Her mistake. She wouldn't be doing that again. "Right after that, someone broke into my apartment."

"You're right. Guilty." Chase nodded. "You got me. I broke into your place."

Now she squinted at him. "Are you being funny? Or are you confessing to the crime?"

"*Why* would I break into your place?"

He hadn't answered her. But she'd answer him. "Maybe you're crazy. Maybe you like terrorizing women. Maybe you collect underwear."

"*What?*" His jaw kind of hung open.

"Could be any number of reasons. You had the opportunity. You had the proximity. Like I said, you are my—"

"Variable, yes, I heard you the first time." He blew out a breath. "Look, someone just tried to get in your place. Do you want to call the cops?"

That twisting in her stomach got worse. Way worse.

"Because if you want to call them, we should do it right now." Chase nodded. "Get them down here so their crime techs can do their thing."

The police. "I want to see if anything was taken."

"*Before* you call the police?"

She wasn't sure that she was calling the police. She also wasn't so sure that she wanted to rule Chase out as a suspect. "I need some proof that you are who you say that you are."

He threw his hands into the air. "What does that even mean?"

"You told me you worked for a security company—"

He hauled a wallet from his back pocket. Dug out a white business card. Handed it to her. Their fingers brushed.

That weird lick of heat hit her again. The same heat that had surged through her the first time they'd touched. She'd even felt it when he did his crazy carry routine on her. When he'd scooped her into his arms, the heat had burned through her. Vivian cleared her throat. "I need you to stop that."

Both brows rose. "Stop what?"

"Making me tingle. I can't deal with that right now." She frowned down at the card. "What's a Wilde?"

"Eric Wilde is my boss. He owns a security and protection business. It's pretty big, you might have heard about it—"

"I haven't."

"Biggest on the East Coast." He coughed when she just stared at him. "You haven't heard about it. Got it. Well, you can call Eric. He'll vouch for me."

"But I don't know him. He could lie to me." She peeked at the card once more, rubbed her fingers over the embossed text, then glanced up. She found Chase staring at her, rather bemusedly. "What?" Vivian asked.

"How do I make you tingle? I almost missed that part."

Her cheeks burned.

"That is fucking adorable. God, I love it when your cheeks go pink."

"Kittens are adorable. If you like adorable things, you should get one of those."

A nod. "I will keep that in mind." He sucked in his cheeks a moment, as if he were trying not to laugh.

This was hardly a humorous situation. And she wasn't *adorable.* That was insulting. Especially because when she looked at Chase, she thought…

You're not adorable. You're sexy. You're gorgeous. Stupid hot. And I need to get out of here. "I have to see if anything was taken. Thanks, um, for your help." She brushed around him.

"That's it? You're just going to race back in there? What about calling the cops?"

Her shoulders stiffened. "If nothing is taken, there won't be much point in contacting them. The cops have plenty of other cases to keep them busy and, given that fact, a broken lock would hardly be a big priority for them."

"At least let me come with you."

She looked back at him. "Why?"

"Uh, for moral support?"

"What makes you think I need that?"

Chase shifted his stance. "Maybe *I* need it. I just moved into a new building, there was a break-in—or an attempted break-in—on my first day. My nerves are shot. Not being alone is helpful for me right now."

She spun to fully face him. Her hands flew to her hips. "Lies waste time."

"They do?"

"Yes. So just tell me what you mean from here on out and we can be friends."

He stepped toward her. "It's that easy with you? I just tell you the truth, and you'll be my friend?"

Her hand rose and trailed over the faint scar that cut through her left eyebrow. Her fingers trembled a bit as she said, "Having a good group of friends can help increase your lifespan, it decreases stress levels, and those friendships can also help to keep you mentally aware due to the fact that the risk of dementia decreases when you have—"

He held up one hand. "You spout facts when you're nervous."

Her lips pressed together. Yes, yes, she did. Her hand fell away from her eyebrow because he was staring at it—no, at her scar.

"I would like to be your friend," Chase continued carefully. His voice was almost tender.

Chase's tenderness made her feel funny on the inside.

"And as a friend, I don't want you to be nervous. So let me backtrack and try this again." He paused. "Please let me come with you as you check to make sure that nothing was stolen from your place." He extended his hand toward her. "And, I will try very hard not to waste your time with lies."

She stared at his hand. Then nodded. "I like that deal." Her fingers curled around his. "Thank you, new friend."

His golden eyes gleamed.

***

"I appreciate you installing the new lock."

It's the least I could do, considering I'm the prick who broke the old one. Chase glanced up as he finished tightening the screw on Vivian's new lock. He pasted a smile on his face. "That's what friends are for, right?"

No, friends aren't supposed to break your lock. They're not supposed to terrify you. They aren't supposed to use you.

A quick smile lit up her face. It was the first time she'd smiled since the break-in.

God, I am such a dick.

"Please tell Merik again how much I appreciate him stopping by the hardware store and rushing that lock over to us."

It was no trouble. He had the lock ready to go.

"Nothing was taken." She nodded. "So that's great. The intruder must have been scared off by someone—maybe by you—you know, like you told me earlier."

I think there is a reserved place in hell waiting for me. One that's extra hot. "Yes, that's probably what happened." Chase rose to his feet and gripped the screwdriver in one hand. "You need a security system."

Her eyelids flickered. "Yes. I should call around and get quotes—"

"I have connections. I can have one installed for you first thing in the morning."

"Because you work for a security company." Her lips pressed together, then she confessed, "While you were installing the new lock, I researched you online."

"You did?"

"I mean, I researched your company. Very well known. Lots of big clients. Celebrities and stuff." Her head tilted. "Have you ever protected someone famous?"

"Yes."

"What was it like?" Mild curiosity showed on her pretty face.

"The guy was a total ass." And one of the biggest names in Hollywood. "So it was basically a shit show."

Laughter sputtered from her. Rich, warm laughter. Chase found himself leaning closer to Vivian because he liked the sweet sound of her laughter so much.

"You're not impressed by famous people?" Vivian wanted to know.

Impressed? "Hell, no."

Her laughter faded. "I can't afford you."

"I can give you the friends and family discount. Trust me, you can afford our services." Especially since those services...shit, they were designed so that Wilde could keep an eye on her.

Her smile came and went again. It was truly a gorgeous smile, one that made her green eyes light up. "Thank you."

"Don't need to thank me." *Because when you do, your gratitude makes me feel worse.*

"I do, I have to thank you. I need to—"

"You can thank me by going out to dinner with me. Say, tomorrow night?"

Her gaze skittered away from his.

"I promise, I won't bite," he added gently. "It can just be a *friendly* meal." He was adjusting his strategy because Vivian was far too cautious. He had to play this game very carefully. He needed to be the nice guy for her. "We can even go to that Asian restaurant that you mentioned. I'll have my guys come by and set up your security in the morning, and then we'll hit dinner in the evening."

She shook her head.

Hell, *denied*. He would have to come up with a different—

"I can cook."

He thought of her to-die-for brownies. *Oh, hell yes, you can.*

"How about you come over here tomorrow night?" Vivian offered. "I'll cook dinner for us."

Chase held her stare. "I would like that."

"So would I." Vivian seemed surprised even as she said the words.

Chase had to laugh. "That's the thing about me. Before you know it, you'll be falling for my charm."

"I'll have to watch out for that," she replied seriously. Then she caught Chase off guard by giving a saucy wink. "But you should be careful, too. Before you know it, you might be falling for me."

"Huh." He stared at her.

She waited. And waited a little more.

Chase sucked in a breath. "Right. So, you gonna be okay here tonight? Because you're welcome to sleep with me."

Her eyes widened. "Excuse me?"

"Stay with me. *Stay with me*. You are welcome to stay with me." That was what he'd meant to say. The words had come out wrong. "You can take the bedroom. I'll take the couch."

"Thank you for the offer, but I'll be fine here. I have a brand-new lock, after all." She took a tentative step toward him. "You should get back to your place. When I was inside, I noticed that you had a lot of boxes left to unpack."

She was kicking him out. Understood. "If you need me, I'm right down the hall." He leaned a *wee* bit closer to her. His nostrils flared. She smelled so fucking delicious. "I love vanilla ice cream."

"I like chocolate. But why are we talking about this?"

His lips curved. "Because you smell like vanilla ice cream. It's my favorite scent."

"Oh, that's, um, body lotion. Vanilla bean."

His gaze slid over her face. Lingered on her mouth.

"You look like you want to kiss me," Vivian whispered.

She was direct. Maybe he should try being just as direct with her. "That's because I do."

The softest of gasps escaped her lips. "I thought you wanted to be friends."

"I want to be whatever you'd like me to be." His gaze lifted. Held hers. "If it's just friends, then I'll take that. But you said lies were a waste of time, so I figured that before I left, I'd tell you some truths."

"Go right ahead." Her voice had gone breathless. *Sexy.*

"If you want to only be friends, count me in. I could always use another friend. You can never have too many in this world. But, if you want more than friendship, if you want to see what happens when my mouth touches yours...*count me in.* I can be as much or as little as you want me to be. You decide."

She searched his gaze. "You just met me."

"And I already like you." Chase had to lighten the tension between them. He knew he was coming on too strong. *Be the nice guy. No pressure.* "I mean, how could I not like a woman who has such a killer swing? You should've gone pro."

Her gaze darted to the baseball bat that rested against the wall. Laughter spilled from her.

The sound warmed him. Chase felt like he'd just won some kind of freaking prize.

What is up with that?

"I should go. Lots of boxes." He nodded, stepped back, but had to look at her lips once more. Just once...

I want her mouth beneath mine. I want to see how she tastes. I want to make her moan for me.

Her mouth was going to haunt his dreams.

"Good night, Chase. Thanks for all of your help. And...I'm glad you're in the building." She offered her hand to him.

He took it. This time, he was prepared for the surge of awareness—of pure heat—that flew through his whole body.

"Do you feel that?" Her voice trembled. "It's more than a tingle this time."

"I feel it." His voice had roughened. He wanted to pull her forward. Wanted to put his mouth on hers. To taste her.

Instead, he let her go. "Have a good night. If you need me, you know where I am." With that, he strode toward his place, but Chase could feel her gaze on him. He looked back and found Vivian still standing in her doorway. Her head was tilted and her stare was sharp and focused on him.

Tension slid through Chase. Was she suspecting him? Was she figuring him out? Was she—

Her fingers lifted in a wave before Vivian retreated into her apartment and shut the door.

His breath left him in a rush. Damn. For a moment back there, he'd gotten off mission. He'd *wanted* her mouth on his so badly. Chase hurried into his place. Flipped the lock and—

"Friends leave brownies for friends," Merik informed him with a glower. His hands were flattened on the kitchen counter, and the dragon tattoo looked ready to breathe fire.

He hadn't realized Merik had lingered after dropping off the new lock. "You used your key."

"I totally used my key. I was waiting for you to come and check in with your current *partner,* but I guess things got all intense and involved over there." He tapped his fingers on the counter. "Is the Evil Queen on her way to ruin?"

"Don't call her that," Chase snapped.

Merik blinked. "My mistake. Jeez, someone needs to chill out."

"I am chill. The most chill."

"Whatever you say. So…is the target—the one suspected of selling classified intel, the one who could be potentially risking the lives of dozens of good men and women—is she on her way to ruin?"

Chase winced as he made his way to the fridge. He yanked out a bottle of water and took a long gulp. "She doesn't seem bad."

"Oh, shit." Merik had turned to follow Chase's movements. Merik's eyes squeezed closed. "She's getting to you. It's day one, and she's sliding under your skin already." His eyes opened. He glared.

Chase took another swig of water. "No, she's not." *Yes, she is.* "I feel bad, okay? I broke the woman's lock. Scared the hell out of her."

"Because you're a jerk."

He put down the water bottle. "No, please, don't pull your punches."

"I'm not. I don't ever. You just pulled a dick move by sabotaging the lock, but it needed to be done. We both know it. Sometimes, the end justifies the means."

"I hate that saying." With a deep, burning passion. "And I still feel like shit. She was upset, man. If she's innocent, then I feel like—"

"*If she's innocent? If?* Did you just use the word *if?*"

He had, yes.

Merik's glare turned into a gape. "She's not innocent! You read the evidence! I read the evidence! She is stealing secrets. No, correction, she *stole* secrets. And we have to find and recover the intel before she passes the data off to the bad guys who are out there. There is no *if* with this woman." He stalked toward Chase. "You and I both got our orders from Eric. Uncle Sam pulled us in because our particular brand of crazy was needed on this case."

"Things feel fucking crazy about now." *He* felt crazy. Her laugh had just sounded so—

"Are you thinking with your dick or your head?"

"*Watch it.*" Chase wasn't in the mood to play.

"She's sexy, I'll give you that. I always had a little thing for redheads so I get the attraction."

Chase's hands fisted.

"But she is dangerous," Merik added grimly. "The point was for you to play her, not the other way around."

"I know what I'm doing." He did. "It's just...dammit! She seems innocent." The way she spouted off her facts when she was nervous—he'd picked up on that tell right away. The way she blushed. The way she rubbed the faint scar over her eyebrow when she— "How'd she get that scar?"

Merik waved his hand in front of Chase. "Focus."

He was focused. He'd read the background file on Vivian. Read it over and over. There had been no mention of a scar over her left eyebrow.

It was white, faded, so she must have gotten it long ago. But how? He didn't like the idea of her being hurt.

Shit. Merik is right. I need to focus.

"Chase, buddy, pain in my ass...this is what I'm hearing...You're saying she's all innocence and light."

Yes, he'd basically said that. "I left out the light part. Just mentioned more that she could be innocent. It's an instinct, all right? My instincts say she's not some—some Evil Queen."

"Let's back up. Reassess. Did she do *anything* tonight to raise red flags with you?"

Chase glanced away.

Merik whistled. "She *did*. Okay. What was it? Tell me."

"She didn't want to call the cops." But... "She was right. I mean, they wouldn't have been able to do anything and—"

"We both knew she wasn't going to call the cops even before you touched the lock. With the kind of extracurricular activities that Vivian Wayne has going on, the last thing your sexy neighbor would want is for uniformed cops to be poking around in her place."

Chase leaned back against a nearby counter. "I told her that Wilde would put in a security system for her first thing in the morning."

Merik's smile flashed. "Now *that* is the kind of progress I am talking about! We'll get some listening devices in there, and we'll—"

"I know what we have to do." Didn't mean that he liked it.

"It's just another case, man." Merik backed away. "I get that she's got pretty eyes and she bakes killer brownies, but you need to remember that even Ted Bundy had no trouble luring prey to him. Bad guys—and women—can be charming. They get you to see what they want you to see." He headed for the door. "We both know she's smart as hell. She's also as dangerous as they come. Don't forget that." At the door, he paused and pointed at Chase. "You can't believe anything she says. You're playing her. She's playing you."

"Huh."

Merik's expression darkened. "Do *not* pull that 'huh' BS with me. She *is* playing you. So stop feeling guilty, Boy Scout. Do the job. If you can't do it..." A shrug. "I'll step in. After all, she liked my dragon."

Chase immediately stiffened. "No stepping in necessary. I've got her."

"Be sure that you do. Be sure that *she* doesn't have *you*." With that, Merik yanked open the door—

And almost mowed right into Vivian.

Because she was standing in front of my apartment door.

"Thanks for bringing me the new lock, Merik," Vivian said into silence that stretched a bit too long. "Tell me how much it cost, and I'll be happy to pay you back."

"Forget money. You can pay me with brownies," he told her easily. "A pan that Chase doesn't get to touch." He looked back at Chase. "Don't forget what I said, my friend," Merik told him with a teasing smile that didn't touch his hard gaze. "I look forward to seeing you play the game."

You are such a bastard. "Good night, Merik. Appreciate you helping me get settled."

Merik tossed his hand into the air and was gone. Chase had to admit, he was glad to see Merik vanish.

Vivian lingered in the doorway.

Chase stalked toward her. "Did something happen?"

"Yes." She nodded.

But didn't say more.

He looked down the hallway. Her apartment door was closed. "What? What is it? What—"

"I like conducting experiments. Variables are my thing."

A smile wanted to pull at his lips. "I thought I was your variable."

"You are." Her gaze was on him. "That means I should see what happens." Her shoulders squared. "You said you wanted me."

He *had* said that. He probably should have kept his mouth shut, but that confession had been raw and honest.

"I want you, too. So let's see what happens when we kiss."

When they—

She stood onto her tiptoes. Her hands pressed to his shoulders. "Kiss me, Chase."

He wasn't a damn fool. His head lowered to hers. He took her mouth.

CHAPTER THREE

The kiss was hot. Sensual. Consuming.

Chase kissed with finesse and raw power. With a focused intensity that had her toes curling in her tennis shoes and her nails pressing into the soft fabric of his t-shirt. A moan built in Vivian's throat as her mouth opened even more for him. His tongue stroked so skillfully over her own.

This wasn't a sloppy kiss. Not too wet. Not too rough. It was a kiss of seduction. A kiss that promised so much more. A kiss that told her—

The man is going to be trouble. The kind of trouble that a woman would enjoy endlessly. But…

"Tell me that you aren't a bad guy," she whispered against his lips.

Chase stiffened. "What?"

She kissed him again. After all, if you were going to conduct an experiment, you had to be thorough. Her tongue slid over Chase's lower lip then dipped into his mouth.

His hands curled around her waist, and he hauled her closer. There was no missing the unmistakable—very large—physical reaction he was having to her.

Only fair, since she was certainly reacting to him. Her heart drummed frantically in her chest.

Her nipples were tight and aching. Her body was eager, heat filling her, her sex was—

His tongue rubbed against hers. His kiss was just as focused as before. Sensual command. Expert care. So good that she could kiss him for hours on end.

"What the hell did you mean," he growled against her mouth, "about being a bad guy?"

With an effort, Vivian pulled back. Her breath was coming out in quick pants. "You're a very good kisser."

"So are you. Best ever." Said simply. "Get back to the bad guy part."

Oh. Okay. "I was just double checking, before anything else happened to make sure that you really were as, um, good, as you seem to be. Sometimes what you see isn't what you get. I don't want to be burned that way again."

His brow furrowed. "I'll need you to explain more about that."

Her head tilted down. Vivian's hair fell forward.

His hand lifted. Carefully touched her cheek. Then pushed back a lock of her hair, tucking it behind her ear. "Viv?"

She liked that. The little nickname. It seemed personal. Tender.

You just met him. You can't trust him. "I want to make sure you're as genuine as you seem. I've had lies before, and I don't like them." She wasn't talking about lies from a lover, but he wouldn't understand that. She needed to tell him more, though, because when she looked up again, she found him staring at her with an intense, brooding gaze. "I don't want to make a mistake with you. I was curious to see if the attraction between us would be as strong as I suspected." She backed away. "The tingle was new for me. I've never met someone, touched, and instantly…felt that."

He nodded. "The attraction is strong. Glad we both feel it." He put his hands on his hips. Kept standing in the open apartment door.

"You asked if I wanted to be friends or if I thought we might be more. Seemed like a good idea to try and figure that out. Why waste time?" Her voice was too husky.

"What are the results of your experiment?"

The result was that she wanted to kiss him again. She felt shaky and uncertain and turned on. Very turned on. More experimentation would be required.

Stop it. Stop being so clinical! But she did that to protect herself. "I don't want to make a mistake." She could still taste him. Feel him. "You're not some secret criminal, are you?"

Chase gave a slow shake of his head.

She started to smile—

"Are you, Vivian?"

Her smile froze.

"Are you some secret criminal?" Chase asked her, and his voice had roughened. "Do you have deep, dark secrets I need to know about?"

Her hand rose. Her fingers smoothed over her left eyebrow. "There was this study conducted a while back. It said the average person was usually keeping about 13 secrets, and of those thirteen, there are about five that those people will take to the grave."

"Thirteen, huh? Seems like an unlucky number."

His words sparked her interest. "Do you have triskaidekaphobia?"

His eyelids flickered. "Fear of the number 13? No, I'm good. Actually, I don't fear very much. That's something you should know about me."

Her heart drummed in her chest. She was spouting off her weird facts, and he wasn't looking at her like she was crazy. Instead, he was still gazing at her with a hot, hungry lust in his eyes. A lust that had made his golden eyes burn even brighter.

"Something else you should know…" He leaned close to her. "I'm not bad. I'm not the villain in this story. Believe it or not, I'm supposed to be the good guy."

She could believe it. Or maybe she just *needed* to believe it. "I'm glad." She wanted to kiss him again. Because she wanted it so badly, Vivian retreated a few steps. There had been more than enough experimentation for one night. "I hope you get settled all right." She turned toward her place.

"Are we still on for dinner tomorrow?"

"Yes." She looked over her shoulder at him. *That stare of his…* Need surged through her. "Come over around six?"

"I'll be there."

She hurried back to her home. Put her key in the new lock. Rushed inside. When she shut the door—and locked it—Vivian put her back against the wood. Her breath came in fast rushes. Her heart kept racing.

I'm supposed to be the good guy.

Chase was good, but he was sure making her want to do all kinds of bad things with him.

***

"Yep, definitely a place in hell for me." Chase reached for the water bottle that he'd left on the counter. "Good guy, my ass."

He wasn't good. He was lying. He was using her. He was going to find evidence to lock her up and send Vivian to jail.

Vivian...in jail? Trapped behind bars?

No, that didn't feel right.

His hold tightened on the bottle.

He hated this case.

Chase took the water and headed toward his desk—and the locked briefcase that waited beside it. He put down the water bottle and lifted the case onto the desk. A quick flick of his fingers, and he'd set the correct combination on the briefcase's lock. The case popped open, and Chase reached for the file that waited inside.

A file he'd read dozens of times.

Vivian Wayne. She was a civilian contractor currently working in conjunction with the CIA. She'd gotten the proper clearance to do her job. Jumped through all the right hoops.

She had her Master's degree in engineering from Georgia Tech, and she'd been brought to the covert CIA branch in Marietta to work as a Digital Forensic Engineer. Doing contract work at first, but the plan had been for her to eventually transition over to working fully with the agency.

Except something had gone wrong.

Classified intel had gone missing. Initially she hadn't been the only suspect, but the agency had done a good job of narrowing down the field until she was the primary target. Now they wanted concrete evidence against her. They wanted her caught in the act of selling the intel to enemy agents.

Despite the evidence pointing only at Vivian, the agent in charge at the CIA—some fellow named Dexter Ryan that Chase hadn't met yet—he'd decided that she might have a mystery partner working with her at the agency. Someone who had managed to avoid detection. So Dexter had made arrangements to take the investigation *outside* of the agency. He'd pulled some strings with Eric Wilde, and suddenly...

Chase had been assigned to the case. His current mission was to bring down Vivian Wayne.

His gaze slipped to her picture. It was the ID photo from her job. She wasn't smiling, just looking straight ahead. The rich red of her hair was obvious in the picture as the locks tumbled over her shoulder. Her green eyes stared straight ahead, and her full lips were slightly parted.

He'd looked at her picture over and over again since Eric had assigned him to the case. Undercover ops were usually a cake walk for him. Hell, half the fun in his life came from the opportunities he had to *be* someone else on his cases. When Eric had first told him about the job,

Chase had thought this would be easy. He'd even been eager for the new assignment.

Until he saw her picture for the first time. Until he stared into her eyes.

She didn't *look* bad. But then, the dangerous ones never did. If you could see the darkness, the world would be a much safer place.

When he looked at Vivian, he didn't see any darkness or danger.

Not when she blushed.

Not when she told him her random facts.

Not when she kissed him as if she was desperate for his mouth.

As desperate as I was for hers.

But the evidence was hard to refute. A security recording had even been recovered showing her accessing secure servers that had been beyond her clearance level.

The material she'd allegedly taken? The real names and locations of CIA operatives all over the world. If she sold that material, if she gave that data to the wrong people, then the operatives would die. That was why he was supposed to catch her in the act. Dexter Ryan had somehow picked up chatter of an in-person exchange. Except no one knew when or where that exchange would be.

So, yes, Chase was being a bastard. He'd broken the lock on her home. He was lying to her. He was doing his job.

Anything necessary. Lives were on the line. He couldn't let an attack of conscience stop him from completing the mission.

A pretty pair of green eyes couldn't derail him. She was the job, nothing more. He'd tell her whatever she wanted to hear, and soon enough, he'd get her to tell him all of her secrets.

All thirteen of them?

She'd looked so serious when she'd told him that people usually had thirteen secrets. *And five that they carry to the grave.* Vivian had seemed genuine. Real.

He'd found himself leaning toward her. Smiling as she talked. He'd found himself being freaking *charmed* by her—

Shit. *Be the player, not the one who gets played.* Chase slammed the file shut, tossed it back into the briefcase, and marched for the bedroom. This case could not end soon enough.

***

He slipped down the hallway. It was three a.m., and the building was dead quiet. Gaining access to the place had been easy enough, especially for someone with his particular talents. Then, instead of riding the elevator, he'd headed up the stairs—it was easier to stay hidden that way. Lots of shadows were in the stairwell.

Now he crept toward his target. He lifted his hand, the key at the ready.

Then he stilled. *What in the fuck?* The lock looked different. It was shiny and *silver*. It had been bronze before, he was sure of it. When he jabbed the key into the lock, it didn't fit. Sonofabitch. When had she changed her damn lock? And why had she done it?

His fingers fisted around the key he'd brought. This should have been so simple. But, no, she'd just had to make things harder. He almost drove his fist into the door.

Can't do that. That might wake her up.

He didn't know how to pick a lock. He hadn't *needed* to pick it, not when he had a key, but now, everything was screwed up and—

A male voice shouted, "Hey! What are you doing at Vivian's door?"

No one else should have been on the floor. The other apartment was supposed to be empty. But some bastard was yelling at him.

He yanked his hood closer to his face.

"*What are you doing?*" The jerk's voice was even louder. "Get away from there!"

Great. Just what he needed. *Some asshole is playing hero.* Before the asshole could get a look at his face, he turned and ran back for the stairwell.

"Hey!" A snarl. "*Stop!*"

No way. He wasn't stopping. He was escaping. His hands flew toward the stairwell door. The key fell even as he shoved the door open. *Dammit!* No time to pick it up. His steps clattered as he raced down into the shadows.

CHAPTER FOUR

"Hey! *Stop!*"

The shouts had Vivian's heart racing as she threw open her door. She rushed into the corridor and her body slammed into something big. No, not something. Someone. Chase.

He caught her and twisted their bodies as they fell. She braced for a hard impact with the floor, but Chase landed on the bottom, with her sprawled across him.

His chest was bare. And probably harder than the floor. All of those muscles were like rocks and—

His gaze held hers. Blazing. Electrifying. Panty melting.

"He's getting away!" Chase lifted her up. Put her on her feet. "Go inside. Lock the door!" Then he raced for the stairwell.

She raced after him. Just as she reached the stairwell door, her slippered feet hit something.

Something shiny.

She bent and scooped up a key. Then she flew down the stairs as she hurried after Chase. Who was getting away? What was Chase talking about? She'd woken to the sound of his yells, and she'd hurried out, thinking he needed her.

He'd helped her before. Wasn't it her turn to help him?

Vivian reached the bottom floor, and she shoved open the door. The lobby was empty. Completely quiet, except for the sound of her frantic breaths. She looked to the left and the right. She hadn't been *that* far behind Chase. Where had he gone?

The lobby's entrance door flew open. "Lost the bastard!" Chase charged forward with his face locked into tense, angry lines. Then he saw her. He staggered to a stop. "What the hell are you doing?"

Her shoulders stiffened. "Backing you up?"

He shook his head. Marched toward her. "You're supposed to be in your apartment."

"But why would I be there? Something was obviously happening down here. You might have needed my help."

He halted right in front of her. She'd realized he was tall, but this was the first time that his size had felt intimidating. Engulfing? Maybe because he was towering over her. And the waves of his anger seemed to fill the air.

"I told you to stay up there for your safety," Chase gritted out.

"I can protect myself. I came down here to help protect *you*."

His expression grew even darker as his gaze swept over her and then lingered on her shark slippers.

"I have training, okay? I can handle some trouble."

He squinted at her slippers. "You're wearing Great White shark shoes."

"Great Whites can have about three thousand teeth in their mouths at a time."

His head lifted. His gaze met hers.

"Not my slippers," she mumbled. "The real Great Whites."

"I figured that." Chase raked a hand over his face. "You can't run into danger."

"Wasn't that what you were doing?"

"I know how to handle it when shit gets bad!"

She surged toward him. "I do, too! I told you, I have training! It was required for my job!" She'd excelled at the training. Even though she was only doing contract work for the CIA so far, she'd been pulled in for initial operative training sessions. She didn't plan to do any field work, but Vivian had always believed in being prepared. Side note, she'd also never met a class she didn't like. Getting to learn hand-to-hand combat? Having the opportunity to figure out every weak spot on her opponent's body? *Yes, please. Tell me more. Teach me everything.*

His brows flew down. "Exactly what kind of job do you have?"

"I..." *It's classified.* "I work with computers." That was a nice, safe, and true answer.

"Of course, you do." Chase shook his head. "You believe your computer training qualifies you to rush after bad guys in the middle of the night." He put his hands on his lean hips.

Her stare dipped down to his hips. Bad move. Wrong move. She forced her gaze back up. "It's not computer training," she told him heatedly. "It's—" Nope. Vivian caught herself. She wasn't supposed to tell anyone that she was doing contract work for the CIA. Then she realized exactly what *else* Chase had said. "Wait. Hold on. You were chasing a bad guy?"

A jerk of his head. "I heard some noise in the hallway."

"I heard noise, too," she retorted quickly. "It was you, screaming for help. That's why I ran out to you."

A muscle flexed along Chase's jaw. "I wasn't screaming for help. I was telling the asshole who was trying to break into your place to *stop*. I ran at him, I would have caught him, but you stepped in my path and stopped me." His gaze pinned her. "Why the hell would you protect him?"

What? "I wasn't protecting him! I was helping you!" How did he keep missing that? And her voice had risen. That wasn't good. She glanced around the lobby. They were the only ones there. The lights shined faintly overhead, but plenty of shadows filled the area...*because it was three a.m*. Okay, she needed to reassess. "Someone was trying to break into my place?"

"He got away." Chase sounded disgusted. "By the time I reached the ground floor, he was gone. I hit the street, but there was no sign of him."

Her hand tightened around the prize that she still gripped in the palm of her right hand. "He was at my door?"

"Yeah, and I stopped him from getting inside."

"He must have been the guy who tried to break in earlier!"

Chase licked his lower lip. "Um..."

"I have to see...I think I know..." Her words tumbled together as she whirled and ran back for the stairwell.

"Vivian! Vivian, dammit, wait for me!"

She didn't have to wait. He was right on her heels as she double-timed it up those stairs. Once she reached the fourth floor, Vivian threw open the door and beelined straight for her apartment. When she got there, she shoved the key toward the lock.

Doesn't fit.

"It's the wrong key," she said, voice excited. Or maybe she was just panting too much from the run up the stairs. *Mental reminder, do more cardio.*

"Uh, what?" Chase was right behind her, and he didn't sound even a little out of breath.

"I found this key when I was running after you. It was right near the stairwell door." She grabbed for the set of keys she'd hurriedly put in the pocket of her pajama shorts earlier—the set that included a key to the new lock *and* still had her old key on there. She put the old key next to the one she'd discovered at the stairwell door. Her eyes narrowed as she studied the shapes of the keys. "They're a match." Her heart kept thudding frantically in her chest. "He was using a key to my old lock." Her head whipped toward Chase. She caught him studying her with a hard, assessing gaze. "What?" Vivian asked because she couldn't decipher his expression.

"You're telling me the intruder had a key to your old lock?"

"It looks that way." Her shark slippers shifted a bit as she retreated a step. "That makes *zero* sense to me. I mean, if he was the same guy who tried to get in earlier, *he* broke the lock."

Chase glanced back at the stairwell.

"If he wasn't the same guy, then why would two people try to break into my home within a twenty-four-hour period?" But even as she asked the question...

Oh, no. No, no.

His attention slid back to her. "Because there is something important in your home. Something people must want very, very badly." The edge of suspicion was there. She could see it. "What do you have that people want so desperately?"

Her lips parted. Fear slithered through her. "Nothing." Her voice broke on the word.

"This is where I tell you that you need to call the cops."

If I'm right, the cops can't help me. "And this is where I tell you good night."

"What?"

She unlocked her door. "The...the security system will be installed first thing in the morning?"

"Damn straight it will be."

"Excellent news." She forced a smile. "Good night, Chase."

"What in the hell? Vivian!"

Very softly, but very firmly, she shut the door in his face.

Oh, God. I am in trouble.

***

Chase stared at the closed door. "What in the hell?" he demanded again. He lifted his hand to pound against the wood, but then stopped.

Check the security footage. Check in with your team.

He backed away from her door and hurried to his place. He yanked out his keys from the front pocket of his jogging pants and made his way inside. It only took a few moments to pull up the security feed from the camera in the hallway.

I see you. You didn't come from the elevator. You took the stairs up. And when the fellow had exited the stairwell, he'd already had the dark hood of his sweatshirt pulled up around his head. The perp went straight to Vivian's door. Chase leaned forward as he watched the footage. The perp was pulling out a key, his gloved fingers were wrapped around it, and...

The key didn't fit.

The fellow stood there a moment, seemingly confused, when the key didn't slide into the lock on Vivian's door. Then Chase saw himself appear as he rushed after the would-be intruder. Next up was Chase's collision with Vivian as she came barreling out of her place and then—

He slowed down the video feed. Sure enough, the perp had dropped something shiny near the stairwell door. The key.

Chase switched security cameras and studied the earlier feed from the lobby. The guy came in easily, accessing the building by quickly typing in a key code on the exterior security panel. When he hurried into the lobby, the hoodie was in place, but he didn't know about the camera that had been installed down there. The guy turned and—

"Gotcha," Chase said smugly. He hit a few buttons on his laptop then reached for his phone. His fingers did a little tap as he waited for Merik to answer—

"You are messing up my beauty sleep."

"There's no rest for the wicked."

"What in the hell is that supposed to mean?" Merik's voice sharpened.

"It means some joker just tried to break into Vivian's place."

"What?"

"Though there wasn't a whole lot of breaking involved. He had a key. If I hadn't ever-so-helpfully broken her lock earlier—and then given her a new, better lock—he would have gotten inside to her."

Silence.

"Hello?" Chase prompted. "You there?"

"Did you just give yourself credit for breaking that woman's lock?"

"I did save the day," he modestly replied.

"It is too late for me to deal with your brand of crazy."

"What are you talking about?" He printed out the picture he'd captured of the perp. "You can never deal with my brand of crazy."

A rough laugh came from Merik.

"I got the bastard," Chase supplied with no small amount of glee. His fingers flew across the keyboard. "Caught his image on the lobby's security camera. I'm sending it to you and to our techs at Wilde. Let's get this fellow ID'd ASAP."

"On it."

"The would-be intruder could just be a thug hired by the big player in this game. You and I both know the bosses don't like to get their hands dirty on cases like this."

"Yeah, guys in charge always let others risk everything."

Because the hired goons were expendable. Still, a key to Vivian's place indicated a personal connection in Chase's mind. "While you ID him, I'll stick close to our target."

"Uh, just how close are we talking?"

As close as necessary. "She said the cops couldn't help her."

"Yes, well, that tends to happen when you try to sell classified intel to bad guys. You step into some serious shit."

"If the cops can't help, then I need to show her that she has other alternatives. I can be what she needs. And..."

"And what? Don't leave me hanging. You know how I hate being kept in suspense."

"I think she has the material we need inside her place. If this guy was trying to break in, then he must have thought so, too." Using a key to her place meant he'd been very well prepared. This was no average crime. "That means I have to get in and take a nice look around."

"I thought her place *had* already been searched. You know, by the CIA guy who brought us in on this case? And he found nothing."

"Maybe he didn't look in the right places."

"Fine. Maybe he didn't. But can't you just search when we install the security system tomorrow?"

"Why wait until morning? She needs me now."

"Hold up! She needs you? Is this about you helping her or catching her?"

Chase considered the question. "Huh."

"*What does that mean?*"

"It means I said the wrong thing." Jeez. Someone was grumpy in the middle of the night. "Chill your ass out and ID the perp, will you?"

"Do *not* blur the mission goals! Do *not* let that woman get to you! Do *not*—"

"Man, you're breaking up. Bad connection. Talk to you soon." He hung up the phone. Grabbed a t-shirt. Shoes. Yeah, he'd forgotten to put shoes on when he'd rushed after the perp. He'd grabbed keys before heading out of his apartment, but stopping for shoes hadn't seemed important.

He had a quick flash of Vivian and her shark slippers. Fucking cute. Why was the villain of the story so cute?

Because the cuteness disarms me. It makes her seem less threatening. No one seems dangerous wearing shark skippers.

But...

Maybe it's all an act. Maybe she's far better at the game than I realized. He'd thought it would be easy to play her. Instead, she was playing him. Throwing him off-balance. Kissing him.

Trying to trick him.

Not going to happen. It would take more than a few moments of cuteness to get Chase off mission. Hell, *nothing* had ever gotten him off mission.

He threw some supplies in a backpack, slung it over his shoulder, and then in no time, he stood in front of her apartment door. He knocked a few times.

She didn't open the door, but he heard creaks from inside her home.

"You need a peep-hole," he told her as he raised his voice a bit. "Or a doorbell that lets you see video footage of whoever is outside your door. I'll be taking care of that tomorrow."

The door opened. "Why are you back?" She peered at him, all suspicious-like.

He offered a charming smile to her. "Because I'm here to be your knight in shining armor."

"I don't want a knight in shining armor. Didn't request one at all." She gripped the edge of the door.

She was still wearing those damn slippers.

"Women could also be knights," she added as her hold tightened on the door. "There was an order in Catalonia, The Order of Hatchet, that was for women."

Chase felt his grin expand a little more. "I love when you teach me new things. I did not know about Hatchet."

Her lips parted. She also let go of the door and backed up.

He took that opportunity and eased inside. "If I'm not a knight, how about I play the role of friend?"

"You were mad at me. When you left, you were mad."

"What makes you say that?"

"Your expression. Your voice. Pretty much everything about you."

He shut the door. Flipped the lock. "I was worried. I didn't want you hurt." That was true. It wasn't about her just being a target. It was…hell, he didn't want anything bad happening to her.

"Huh."

"You figure something out?"

"Working on it."

Her lips pursed. One of the sharks tapped against the floor. "You locked my door."

"Well, sure. I didn't very well want a bad guy rushing in behind me and getting the drop on us both."

Her arms crossed over her chest. She wore a soft, white cotton t-shirt and loose, blue, silky-looking shorts that skimmed the tops of her thighs.

"You have fantastic legs," he told her. "But I'm sure you realize that." His gaze lifted to hers.

She frowned at him. "Why are you in my home right now?"

"Because I'm going to sleep on your couch."

"Why?"

Chase let out a long-suffering sigh. "Because I'm worried about you. Because someone came close to getting into this place while you were sleeping. Because you won't call the cops—which, by the way, seriously means you have something to hide. Not that I'm judging, I'm just saying. And, oh, yeah, I'm crashing on the couch because if I don't make sure you're safe, I will never be able to sleep." He paused. "Are those enough reasons?"

"You have a hero complex."

"Maybe."

"You're an ex-SEAL, you chased after the bad guy tonight, and you work for a security company. I'd say it's more than a maybe."

He shrugged. The movement made his backpack dip. He'd almost forgotten about it. "Not to sound immodest, but I'm a fucking fantastic bodyguard."

"I looked up Wilde. Considering your client list, your rates must be astronomical. I can't afford them, and as I told you, I can protect myself. I have training."

"Computer training," he pushed, deliberately.

Her chin notched up. Her green eyes seemed to darken. "I'm not at liberty to discuss precisely what kind of training. Just know that I can defend myself."

"Good. Excellent." He nodded. "Will you let me crash on your couch so that I can actually sleep?" He could see her indecision. "You checked out my company earlier, didn't you? You verified I'm one of the agents?"

"Of course, I verified it." Now she seemed annoyed that he would even question her checking. As if it were a given for her.

He controlled the curl of his lips, and said, "Then you know you can trust me. That's great." He eyed the couch. It was nice and comfy-looking with overstuffed cushions. Much better than some of the spots he'd used for sleeping on other missions.

"I don't trust many people. I just met you. I have *no* reason to trust you."

Yes, that was the problem. If she didn't trust him, then he couldn't learn her secrets. Time to play some hardball. "He might come back tonight."

Her tongue swiped over her lower lip. "I have considered that possibility."

"Have you considered the possibility that if he gets in here, while you are sleeping and you don't hear him until he is over you with a gun or a knife...have you considered that your training won't do much good?"

Vivian swallowed. "The thought did cross my mind, and that's why I'm glad I get a fancy new security system tomorrow."

"*Why* don't you already have it?" The question tore from him, but it had been bugging Chase.

"I was saving my money for something else. Thought it would be okay. This is a safe part of town."

"No place is one hundred percent safe."

Her long lashes—thick, dark—flickered.

"If I'm on your couch, the bad guy has to get past me before he can come to you. So you'll hear the two of us fighting and you'll wake up and—bam, your survival chances have just increased."

"I don't want you hurt."

That was good to hear. "I don't want to be hurt. But don't worry. I'm an extremely light sleeper. Occupational hazard. I've got great reflexes, and I can disarm an attacker in about fifty different ways, all in under five seconds."

"Are you being immodest again?"

This time, Chase didn't fight his smile. "You want me to stay. Or at least, you're thinking about it."

"I met you *today*."

"Actually, yesterday, because, you know, it's after midnight and all."

The tension didn't leave her body.

Right. "You checked my references. If you want, I even have a detective on the Atlanta PD who will vouch for me. Want to call her? Actually, I know the mayor of Marietta, too. The mayor can—"

"Stop."

He waited.

Vivian shook her head. "Why do you want to help me?"

"Because I like you."

Her lips parted. "You just met me. What could you possibly like so far?"

Actually, lots of things. He closed in on her. "You make insanely delicious brownies." He could smell her sweet scent. "You smell like vanilla." *And I want to lick you up.* "You are a fantastic kisser." His stare focused on her mouth. "Those are a few of the reasons I like you." Then he admitted, "And I really, really *don't* like it when some asshole tries to terrorize a woman. Pushes all my buttons."

She leaned toward him. "I think you are a fantastic kisser, too," Vivian whispered.

"I try." He wanted to try again. Right then. His head dipped toward her.

Her hand pressed to his chest. "Do you just want to stay so that you can seduce me?"

"No, sweetheart," the endearment slipped out. He didn't intend for it to happen. It just did. "I'm staying to help keep you safe. But if you want to try your hand at seducing me..." *Go for it.*

Vivian searched his gaze. "You're one of the good guys?"

"If that's what you want to call me. I don't like labels." Especially since, in this instance, he was lying his ass off to her. "Though we definitely have to talk about the issue you seem to have with bad guys."

She leaned even closer. "I don't want bad."

He wanted her mouth. "I can be very good."

"Bad breaks your heart. Lies to you. Wrecks your life."

Aw, hell. He *was* lying, and by the time he was done, he would wreck her life. But breaking her heart?

That will only happen if she falls for me.

Wasn't that the point of his undercover persona? To get her to trust him, to confide in him, to even *fall* for him? All so he could learn her secrets.

She's selling out CIA operatives. "You never know who is bad," he rumbled. "Sometimes, the worst kind of evil hides beneath the sweetest facade."

"Yes." Their lips were almost touching.

I want her mouth.

She stepped back. "I'll get some extra pillows and covers for you."

"Because you're letting me stay?"

A nod. "And...thank you. I appreciate you looking out for me." She turned and hurried toward the bedroom.

You don't have anything to thank me for, sweetheart. Quite the opposite. When he locked her in jail, she wouldn't be thanking him.

Vivian would be cursing his name.

CHAPTER FIVE

"Morning, sunshine." Chase smiled at Vivian when she entered the kitchen. The smell of fresh coffee teased her nose, and Chase...with his hair all rumpled, his golden eyes sparkling, and that faint stubble coating his jaw...

Hello, sexy sight in the morning.

He lifted a mug toward her. "Got this ready for you. The Wilde crew should be arriving within thirty minutes."

She took the mug. Her fingers curled around the warm ceramic surface. Vivian savored a bracing sip. "You put cream in here. Honey. And milk!" Just the way she liked it. "How did you know I took it that way?"

Chase turned away and reached for his own half-full mug. "That's the way I take mine," he said.

She smiled a little as she took another sip. They had the same taste in coffee. She didn't know why, but that little bit of randomness made her feel good. After last night, she could use all of the good feelings that she could get.

"I have a question for you." His shoulders seemed a little tense. "I should have asked before, but it was after three a.m., and I wasn't exactly thinking at my best." He turned back to face her. "Who have you given a spare key?"

"No one." She took another sip. She'd dressed in her running shorts and t-shirt. Her shoes were laced up and ready to go. Normally, she took a three-mile run on Sunday mornings. Speaking of it being Sunday... "I can't believe you got a crew to come out here on such short notice, especially on a Sunday! I'm starting to think you're my guardian angel."

"Something like that," he muttered. He was staring at her. No, correction, frowning at her smile.

Her smile slipped. "Is something wrong?"

"You're *sure* you didn't give the key to someone? Maybe to a boyfriend?"

She put down the coffee. "If I had a boyfriend, I wouldn't have kissed you yesterday."

His hold tightened on his mug. "Good to know."

"You don't, ah, do *you* have a girlfriend?"

He stared straight at her. "I wouldn't have kissed you if I did."

So they were both single. And his gaze had heated. And this scene was tense. The air had even seemed to thicken. "Glad we cleared that up."

"I'm available. You're available." He shrugged. "Two good things to know." His stare didn't leave her. "You still planning to make dinner tonight?"

Dinner?

"Because we could go out. I could take you on a date. Wine you. Dine you. Let you see me for the amazingly charming man that I am."

"I—"

"The installation could go long. Maybe it would be better to have that date *out* of your place."

"Okay."

He smiled at her. It was a wolfish grin.

There was a sharp knock at her door.

"They arrived faster than I thought." He put his mug in the sink and headed to answer the door. "I'll get the team settled. Hey, by the way, noticed your outfit. Are you planning to go for a—" Chase opened the door. "Run," he finished flatly. His body stiffened. "Who the hell are you?" Chase demanded.

Sunday morning. Vivian plunked down her coffee and rushed for the door. "Luc, you're right on time."

Luc Coderre beamed at her. He was wearing black running shorts, one of his typical wicking shirts—he *always* ran in those—and his water bottle was gripped in his hand. "Ready to get sweaty with me?"

"*What?*" Chase snapped.

"Let me guess." Luc pointed his water bottle at Chase. "New boyfriend?"

Chase puffed out his chest. "Listen—"

"Chase, Luc's my running partner." She caught Chase's arm and pulled him toward her. "Luc Coderre runs with me sometimes, and he's a co-worker."

Luc raised his brows as his gaze darted to her hold on Chase, then back up to Chase's hard face. "And you're the new boyfriend?" A faint French accent slid under his words.

"Damn straight, I—" Chase began.

"No, he's my neighbor," Vivian explained quickly.

Chase's muscles stiffened beneath her touch. "Yep, that's me. The friendly neighbor."

Luc craned his head to see into the apartment. "You're here very early, friendly neighbor."

"That's because I stayed here last night, friendly jogging partner."

Luc's mouth tightened. "Are you ready, Vivian?"

"I can't go." She winced. "I'm sorry. Something came up last night, and I have to stay here today."

"Something came up," Chase repeated. "You know how it is."

Luc frowned at her. "But you never cancel."

"She's canceling today, buddy," Chase told him flatly. "Deal with it."

She cut him a glance. He seemed…extra. Why all the hostility toward Luc? Trying to ease the tension, Vivian explained, "I have a security team coming to install an alarm system for me. I need to be here." She motioned toward Luc. "Please, go without me. Sorry I didn't call." Getting a call from her at three a.m. probably wouldn't have been ideal. To be honest, she'd forgotten that he was coming by until he'd rapped on the door. She'd put on her jogging clothes because that was her Sunday routine, but she hadn't even thought about Luc. Not until he'd knocked on the door.

She wasn't normally so forgetful.

Then again, people didn't normally try to break into her home.

Luc frowned at her. "Is everything *bien*?"

No, things were not *bien*. "Of course. I'll see you tomorrow at work."

"*Au revoir*." He popped an ear bud into his left ear as he turned away. His right hand still clutched his water bottle.

Chase's gaze narrowed as he watched the other man head for the elevator. "You run with him every day?"

"No, just sometimes on the weekends."

He shut the door. "And I just have to know...you said he was a co-worker, right?"

She nodded.

"Does he also have that specialized training that you mentioned?"

She swallowed. "I think he has more training than I do." Luc was a full-fledged operative. "But he hasn't discussed that with me. We're just jogging buddies."

"Huh."

Her head tilted. "You did that thing again."

"What thing?"

She smiled. "You said 'huh' just then." She liked it when he did that. "You figure something out?"

"Yeah, good old Luc wants to be more than jogging buddies with you."

Doubtful. "I don't think so."

Chase laughed. "Trust me on this. I know what I'm talking about."

"And how do you know?"

"Because I'd sure as hell want to be more than jogging buddies with you. The dude didn't like it when he found me in your place at this time of the day."

"He seemed fine to me."

"His accent got thicker. Seen it before. It's a tell for some people when they get angry. Your Luc was pissed."

They needed to back up. "He's not my Luc."

"Wonderful to know." Chase tapped his chin. "Luc doesn't happen to have a key to this place, does he?"

"Why would he have a key?"

"Can't think of a reason." His hand fell. "Out of curiosity, do you keep your keys locked in your desk at work?"

"I keep them in my desk, but it's not locked. I work at a *very* secure facility."

"What is it?" Chase wanted to know. Then he teased, "The FBI?"

"No." But he was close.

She worked at the CIA.

***

"I don't trust him. Dig up every piece of dirt that you can on Luc Coderre," Chase snapped into his phone.

"I told you already," Merik fired back, "he's supposed to be on our side. I told you this stuff *this morning* when you called me all huffing and puffing about the man. He's—"

"He's trying to screw my target, so that makes him a person of interest for me. Dig deeper. A lot deeper. Use a freaking shovel." The day had passed in a blur of activity. It was almost time for his big date with Vivian. Time to wine her. Dine her. And get every bit of intel out of her.

Why the hell was his stomach knotting? *Just a job. Just a job.* He'd lied plenty on other undercover operations. You did what was necessary to get the job done. "I don't trust him," Chase repeated once more.

"Dude, are you sure that you're not just jealous and—"

Vivian's apartment door opened. She stepped into the hallway, and the black dress that she wore floated around her thighs. As he watched her, she paused to lock her door. The security team had finished up an hour earlier.

Just a job. Except she didn't look like a job. She looked like the sexiest woman Chase had ever seen in his life.

"You aren't even listening to me," Merik muttered. "Hello?"

"I've got a date, buddy." Deliberately, Chase raised his voice. "So, got to let you go. Just take care of that business for me, would you? Thanks. You're a rock star."

Vivian glanced toward him.

Just a job.

A smile lit her face.

Fuck me.

"You are a bastard," Merik told him.

Tell me something I don't know. "It takes one to know one." Chase laughed. "Talk soon." He shoved his phone into his pocket. Then he headed straight for Vivian. "I was about to come to your place."

"I..." She faltered. "Does this make me seem overeager? That I came to meet you? Because I'm not really good at following dating rules. I never understand all the games people are supposed to play."

He shook his head. "Screw the games. All I want is for you to be yourself with me."

Her wide smile came again. The one that made her eyes light up. The one that made his chest ache.

The one that made him feel like a total ass for lying to her. *Yeah, I'm saying no games when I'm playing her for all that I'm worth.* Chase cleared his throat. "You are beautiful."

Her cheeks pinkened. "And you look very handsome."

He offered his arm to her. She took it, and he felt the burn of her touch all the way through his body. They walked toward the elevator together, and he slanted a quick glance down at her heels. Two-inch heels. Sexy as hell.

If she was trying to seduce him, Vivian had definitely brought her A Game.

***

"I want one of the thirteen secrets." Chase leaned back in his chair and locked his eyes on Vivian. He'd just paid the check. They'd laughed and chatted easily—too easily—through the meal, and he'd almost forgotten to do his damn job because he liked being with her.

She doesn't seem like the type of woman who would sell out her country.

She lifted her water glass. Took a sip. Her eyebrows rose questioningly.

"You told me that most people had thirteen secrets," Chase reminded her. "Tell me one of yours."

She put down the glass. "Only if you share one of your secrets with me."

He'd play, and they'd go dark with their secrets. No light and fluffy BS about him secretly loving long road trips or being soothed by a sunset. They'd cut straight to the hard and painful parts of life because he didn't have time to waste. Her place had been searched—both by him and by the Wilde security team—and no one had turned up the intel they needed. If he didn't gain her confidence, fast, lives could be lost. Time to form a bond with her. Time to break through her walls. "My childhood was shit."

The faint smile that she'd been wearing slipped.

"My father was an alcoholic. My mother cut out as fast as she could. Left me with him when I was just a kid. Not that I blamed her, she had to look out for herself." All of this was true. He'd found it was easier to stick to the truth as much as possible on assignments like this one. Too many lies could trip you up later.

Vivian's hand flattened on the table.

"Didn't want people to know what it was really like at home for me. So I got good at pretending." It was why he loved undercover work. "Happiness is easy to fake. Hell, most things are easy to fake, if you have the right motivation."

Her lashes flickered.

Holy shit, were there *tears* in her eyes? Was she about to cry for him? Was she *that* good of an actress?

"Sorry." Chase cleared his throat. "Probably not the secret you wanted to hear. Supposed to keep first dates light, aren't we? How about I try again?"

"No." Her hand reached across the table. Her fingers curled over his. "I like seeing who you really are."

That was the point, wasn't it? To make her think she was truly getting to know him?

Even if she wasn't.

"Secret one." Chase turned his hand over and threaded his fingers with hers. The electric surge was still there when they touched—the awareness that told him sex with her would be absolutely phenomenal—but there was more, too. Something almost intangible. Something deeper. Her touch had made him feel better. It seemed to soothe a part of him that had been hidden deep inside.

Okay, stop this shit. Get back to business. "I gave you my first secret. Now it's your turn."

Her tongue snaked over her lower lip. "Secret number one."

Chase nodded even as desire surged through him. That little pink tongue of hers was—

"It is only fair that I give you a secret. Okay." She squared her shoulders, but didn't pull her hand from his grip. "My childhood was also less than ideal."

From what he'd read, that was a serious understatement. She was holding back. Way back.

"Vivian, I'm not going to judge a single thing you tell me. That's not who I am."

She seemed to pull in a bracing breath. "My father was a criminal. I didn't know him very well because during my childhood, he was in and out of jail cells. Not some sort of petty criminal, either. He was a very smart man, and he viewed his criminal activities as a sort of challenge."

"I'm not sure I understand." He did, because he'd read her file.

"My father liked to collect things. Unfortunately, those things belonged to other people."

According to her background info, her father had been a world-class thief. He'd made easy work of getting past the security systems of the rich and famous. He'd stolen almost for sport.

"Getting those items was a challenge for him. He stole incredibly valuable things. Unfortunately, he took some things from the wrong people."

Russian mafia counted as wrong, yes.

"And he was killed. Then it was just me and my mom, but she passed away the summer before I turned eighteen."

"I'm sorry." His grip tightened on her hand.

Her long lashes swept down. "Thank you."

Sadness seemed to surround her.

He leaned forward, brought their joined hands to his mouth, and pressed a careful kiss to her knuckles.

Her lashes immediately flew up as she sucked in a quick breath. Her eyes locked on him.

"I didn't mean to make you sad," he told her. "How about I give you a different secret to make up for it?"

"You didn't make me sad." She blinked quickly. "We can't change the past or what happened to us back then, but it's the future that matters now. We can change what happens in the future. We can make anything happen that we want."

Her hand was close to his mouth. He wanted to press another kiss to her skin.

"I promised myself I'd never be like my father. I enjoy challenges, too." A faint smile came and went on her face. "But I don't plan to break the law or spend my days trapped in a jail cell."

He didn't let his expression waver. "I promised myself I'd never get lost in a bottle. That I would never treat my family the way my father did." Shit. He'd just slipped up and gotten dead serious with her. Chase found that he couldn't look away from her eyes. In that moment, he felt more connected to her than he ever had to another person.

He pressed another kiss to the back of her hand and let her go.

She lifted her water glass. "Here's to keeping our promises."

He lifted his glass.

Fuck. Am I playing her? Or was Merik right? Is she playing me?

***

Vivian stepped into the elevator, and her heart was racing. The dinner had been so nice. Easy. Talking with Chase had felt like the most natural thing in the world. There had been no awkwardness at all. Not like the way it usually was for her with people.

They'd had so much in common. The things he'd said...it was as if he already knew her.

He'd just *gotten* her.

"I think this was the best date I've ever had," Vivian blurted out the truth.

She saw his shoulders stiffen as Chase pressed the button for the top floor. The doors began to slide closed as he turned toward her.

"Thank you," she told him softly. "It was nice."

His expression hardened, and some emotion that she couldn't quite name flashed in his eyes as the elevator began to rise. "You don't need to thank me." His voice was low and growling. Rough.

Sexy.

He stepped toward her.

She crept closer to him.

His arms rose. His hands curled around her waist.

Vivian put her hands on his chest. Leaned toward him.

His mouth came toward hers and—

The elevator plunged into darkness and jerked to a shuddering halt.

CHAPTER SIX

Vivian's breath choked out. "Did we stop?" It sure felt as if they'd stopped. The elevator had gone pitch black for an instant, but now she could see a faint, red glow coming from near the control panel.

"I'm sure it's just a glitch." Chase's hands were warm and steady around her waist. "Nothing to worry about."

Oh, if only. Her heart thundered in her chest.

"We'll be moving in no time, I'm sure," Chase added.

She waited. Thanks to the red glow, she could make out his features and—

The red glow winked off.

Darkness. Complete and total.

"Secret number two," Vivian whispered. "I don't do well in tight, dark spaces." Not well at all. When she'd been a kid—six years old—her father had told her they were going on an adventure. That adventure? Turned out, he'd wanted her to slip through an air conditioning duct. He'd wanted her to help him on one of his heists. She hadn't known...hadn't realized that the adventure was actually against the law and wrong.

But a guard had come by. Her father had slipped away. He'd left her in there and told her not to make a sound. It had been so dark. So tight.

She'd felt as if she couldn't breathe.

"Vivian." Chase's voice was even deeper. Rougher. "It's okay. I'm not going to let anything happen to you."

Mentally, she knew everything was okay. A temporary stop, nothing more. But try telling that to the six-year-old who liked to sneak from the corners of her mind and whisper old fears to her. Easing away from Chase, Vivian pulled out her phone and used the light to help her find the control panel. Just the illumination from her phone had her feeling better. At least, for a moment. She located the big red button on the bottom of the control panel—the emergency button. She hit it, then yanked open the door that hid the elevator's emergency phone. Yes, she'd examined this panel before. Better to be forearmed, right? After talking to the building's manager, she'd even learned that the elevator phone called straight to the maintenance company that handled all repair and emergency issues. She grabbed the elevator phone, put it to her ear, but—"I don't think it's working."

"I'm calling for help now."

Vivian glanced back at him. Her phone light swung toward him. Chase had his phone to his ear.

"Yeah, hey, buddy, I need help." Chase's voice was grim. "We're in the elevator of my building, and it stopped working. Vivian and I are trapped inside." A pause. "Sure, sure, as fast as you can. Appreciate it." He shoved the phone back into his pocket.

Vivian realized that she was shining her light in his eyes. Whoops. She immediately lowered the light even as she kept the death grip on her phone.

"Merik isn't far away. He'll get building maintenance and we'll be out of here in no time."

Time seemed to be passing extra slowly for her.

"Or maybe the elevator will start on its own," Chase continued in a reassuring tone, and she knew he was trying to be optimistic.

Building maintenance. The building manager. Of course. "I should have contacted him right away." They didn't have to wait for Merik. "I've got Jacob programmed in my phone." She called him quickly, and the phone rang. Once. Twice. Three—*voicemail.* Gritting her teeth, Vivian said, "Jacob, I need your help. It's Vivian. Vivian Wayne. I'm stuck in the building's elevator with Chase Durant. Call me as soon as you can— or even better, please get us out!" Her voice had definitely risen at the end. She took a steadying breath, lowered her phone—

And the elevator lurched.

Lurched *down.* As in, it felt as if they dropped a foot. A startled cry escaped Vivian as she tumbled forward, and her phone fell from her fingers.

"It's okay." Chase's hands closed around her shoulders. "I've got you."

She was back to being in darkness. Her phone's light had turned off. The darkness was thick and closing in and she was *not* okay. "I hate being trapped." It was the worst part for her. "I was trapped as a kid." Did this still count as secret number two? "I couldn't move. Couldn't make a sound." She sucked in a hard breath. "I *hate* this."

"We're getting out of here. If I have to pry open the door, I will get you out."

But even if he managed to get the elevator open, they could be trapped between floors. Prying open the doors may do no good and— "Distract me." She was holding too tightly to him. So what? "Kiss me."

She shouldn't have said that. She should get her shit together and be strong and stop freaking out because she was—

He kissed her. His lips pressed against hers in a tender, soft kiss. Her lips were open. His were open. The kiss was careful. Gentle.

Her tongue slipped out and licked along his lower lip. Her body pressed closer to his. She didn't want to feel the darkness surrounding her. She only wanted to feel Chase.

He was strong and warm and the kiss deepened. His tongue thrust into her mouth as he tasted her. He kissed with a restrained passion, with a careful control.

She wanted to shatter that control. *She* was out of control. Her heart was racing. Her whole body trembling. With every touch of his lips, every lick of his tongue, desire burned hotter within her.

His hands were around her waist, and hers were locked on his shoulders. Her nails bit into the fabric of his dress shirt even as a little moan built in her throat.

"Vivian?"

"Don't stop," she whispered against his mouth. Whispered. Pleaded. Whatever.

The next kiss was rougher. Deeper.

Less controlled.

It turned her on even more.

The darkness stopped feeling thick and suffocating. She stopped feeling the dark at all. His hands were huge, circling her. He was so warm. She rose onto her tiptoes. Caught Chase's lower lip and nipped lightly.

This time, he growled. A savage, hungry sound.

He lifted her up against him. Held her with an easy strength. She kicked off her shoes and locked her legs around his waist. The long, hard length of his arousal pressed against her, and she rubbed her sex against him. Her dress had hiked up. She could feel the fabric bunching at the top of her thighs as she kissed him with a wild and desperate hunger.

This wasn't her. She didn't do this. They were on a *first date*. She didn't lock her legs around a guy and hold on tight and kiss him like there was no tomorrow on the *first date*.

But she was. She was clinging to him, her heart was pounding, and she didn't want to let go.

He did this sexy little rubbing thing with his tongue, and she moaned. Then his mouth was leaving hers and he was kissing a path down her throat. Vivian tipped back her head, keeping her eyes squeezed tightly shut. He licked her. Sucked her skin. Gave a gentle bite.

Her sex pressed against him as she squirmed to get closer. *My panties are getting wet*. Because she was turned on like crazy.

Reality seemed a million miles away. Her control—her *ordered* life—was gone. She was living in the moment. Feeling, not thinking. When she thought, she became afraid. She didn't want to be afraid. She just wanted to be with him. She wanted to keep feeling this good. To feel the need and desire surging through her.

"The lights are back on. Fuck, we're moving."

They were what?

It took a moment too long for his words to register. Her eyes stayed squeezed shut and then she heard a ding. A ding?

"Ahem."

Her eyes opened. She stared straight at Chase. His golden gaze blazed at her. His face was locked in savage lines of lust, and all of that lust was directed straight at her.

Do I look like that? So hungry? So wild?

She sure felt that way.

"Ahem." That loud throat clearing came again—from behind her.

Her head whipped around. The building's maintenance manager, Jacob Webb, stood just beyond the open doors of the elevator. He had a tool belt wrapped around his lean hips. His brownish-red hair was tousled, and he had the sleepy-eyed look of a man who'd just been hauled out of bed.

Chase's friend Merik waited next to Jacob. He gave Vivian a friendly wave. "Hi, there. I'm here to rescue you." His head cocked. "Though you both look busy, so maybe we should come back."

You look...

Oh, sweet hell. Her legs were still wrapped around Chase's hips. Her shoes were on the floor. Her dress was hiked up. And her hands were gripping Chase's shoulders as if she'd never let go.

"I am going to kick your ass later, Merik," Chase promised. His voice was a thick, deep rumble of dark intent.

"That is *not* the way you say thanks," Merik responded with a grin. "Not at all. We have got to work on your manners." Merik clapped a hand on Jacob's arm. "Found the maintenance manager. He got things working in no time."

Just how much time *had* passed? It had seemed like only a moment, but...Merik was there. Jacob. Obviously, a lot more time had elapsed than she'd realized. Once she'd started kissing Chase, Vivian had gotten lost.

In him.

"Please put me down," she whispered as her gaze swung back to Chase. Embarrassment burned through her.

A muscle jerked along Chase's jaw. Slowly, he eased her to her feet.

Vivian swiped out with her hands and grabbed her shoes. As she bent to put them on, Chase stepped in front of her, shielding her with his body. "What in the hell happened?" Chase demanded to know. "Why did the elevator stop?"

"Looked like a short caused the problem. Normally, I'd have to call the elevator repair company—they have a guy they send out for this kind of work," Jacob explained in his slow, I-take-my-time-with-things voice. "But I knew enough to fix it. Didn't exactly want to leave my best tenant stranded."

Chase glanced back at Vivian. "You're his best tenant?"

That was news to her.

"I don't jump out of bed for just anyone," Jacob said. "Definitely best. I mean, have you tasted her cinnamon rolls?"

Chase stiffened. "That had better not be some kind of fucking metaphor."

What?

When Chase then proceeded to surge toward Jacob, Vivian leapt to grab Chase's arm. "He's legitimately talking about cinnamon rolls," she rushed to explain. "I gave him cinnamon rolls when he helped me to move into my apartment."

Chase's gaze narrowed on Jacob.

She needed to add more details to her explanation because Chase obviously had the wrong idea. "It was very nice of him. He saw I was moving in alone and helped out."

Jacob grinned. His slow, sly smile. "I am a helper."

"I just bet you are," Chase replied. He didn't smile. His eyes *did* narrow.

Okay. Enough. Vivian was ready to get the heck out of that elevator. She hurried forward. "Thank you, Jacob. And, um, Merik."

They backed up when she passed, and she realized the elevator doors had stayed open during their conversation because Jacob was keeping them open with a raised hand. After Chase filed off the elevator, Jacob headed inside of it. "Gonna do a few tests. Just to make sure everything is running smoothly again. I'd hate for another tenant to get stuck." He inclined his head. "Night."

The elevator doors slowly closed.

Vivian shifted a bit, moving from high heel to high heel. Merik's stare was darting from her to Chase, and he seemed concerned.

Well, they *had* been stuck in an elevator. That was a cause for concern. "It's a very good building," she blurted.

Both men frowned at her.

Vivian winced. "I know—you started your first day with my break-ins, and now this is happening on day two, but I swear there wasn't any trouble here at all..." Her voice trailed off because she hated to say the rest.

But Merik smiled at her. "Let me guess, there was no trouble at all...until Chase moved in?"

Unfortunately, yes.

Merik nodded. "Sounds about right."

Chase cut him a dirty glare.

"Buddy, we need to talk," Merik told him. "Since I'm here and all, how about we knock out the last bit of our project work tonight? I've got the data you needed, and I can go over it now. That way, we can hit the ground running tomorrow."

Chase's eyebrows rose. "I'm on a date."

"Yeah, I did notice that." Merik winced as he gave Vivian a look of apology. "I hate to wreck the party."

"No. It's okay." She backed away, sidling toward her place. "Go ahead. Take care of your business."

Chase surged toward her. "Vivian, wait!"

She froze. "I had a great time."

He closed in on her. "Don't fucking lie. You were just trapped in an elevator, in the dark, with me." He yanked a hand through his hair. "That is not how I saw this night ending."

"I'll bet," Merik muttered—loudly—from behind him.

Chase didn't look back at his friend. He appeared to focus completely on Vivian. "Are you okay?"

Her heart was still racing, her breaths were coming too fast, and she was turned on. Okay wasn't the right description. She'd *never* been turned on so much in her life. "You made me forget to be afraid." Her voice carried only to him. "I could only think about you."

His gaze sharpened on her. "Vivian—"

She leaned onto her toes and brushed a kiss against his cheek. "Thank you." Then she stepped back. Gave him a weak smile. "And I think I still owe you a dinner. One that I cook." Nervousness flooded through her. "Maybe we can make plans for that?" *Yes, I'm asking for a second date.*

"Count on it." His gaze seemed to scorch over her.

With an effort, she turned away and hurried down the hallway. When she got inside her home, Vivian flipped the locks, kicked away her shoes, and then sagged against the door. "*OhmyGod.*"

***

"Romeo, you need to get your ass under control," Merik mumbled as he eased up beside Chase.

Vivian had just gone into her apartment. Chase didn't know why the hell he was still standing there staring after her. *I'm staring at a shut door.*

"This is where I have to ask—*again, because I brought this shit up before*—are you thinking with your dick or your head?"

Very slowly, Chase turned his head toward Merik. "I know what I'm doing."

"Does that mean the answer is dick or head?"

This was the only warning he'd give. "Keep pushing me, and you'll regret it. There's a line you don't want to cross." Partner or not. Chase marched to his apartment, threw open the door a moment later, and knew that Merik would tail him inside.

"Thank you, Merik," his partner said loudly once they were secure in Chase's temporary home. "I appreciate you hauling ass to save me."

"I didn't need saving." Chase crossed his arms over his chest and faced off with his partner.

Merik's brows climbed. "Oh, obviously. What you probably needed was two more minutes. No, scratch that. I'm sure those extra minutes were what you *wanted* so you could screw the target but—*whoa! Calm your ass down!*"

Chase had charged toward him. But he stopped before he actually grabbed Merik. Chase locked his muscles. "I told you to not cross the line."

"Dude, you're the only one crossing lines! You were supposed to get close to her—"

"I *was*."

"It looked like you were about to fuck her!"

I was. But...hell, wanting her had nothing to do with the case. Everything that had gone down in the elevator had just been about Vivian. "She was afraid in the dark."

"Oh, was she now?"

"Yes," Chase gritted. "She was trapped as a kid. Made her claustrophobic. Being trapped in an elevator was like her worst nightmare. I was distracting her."

"Is that what we're calling it now?" Merik tapped his chin. "So hard to keep up with the lingo these days."

"Stop being an asshole."

"Then *you* stop falling for the target! I thought you were supposed to be the undercover expert—"

"I am!"

"Oh, so falling for her is part of the strategy?"

"Getting *her* to fall for me is."

Merik shook his head. "That's cold, man. I mean, I get that she's the Evil Queen—"

"*Don't* call her that."

"But you think breaking her heart is fine to do? As long as you get the intel you need?"

Chase didn't want to break her heart. "I think we're wrong about her." There. He'd said it.

Merik squinted at him. Waited. Didn't speak.

"I think we're wrong," Chase said again. "She's not the villain." *She's not the fucking Evil Queen, so stop calling her that.*

"Beg to differ." Merik exhaled. "Did you hit your head in the elevator? Like, when the lights went off, did you fall or something?"

"No," he gritted.

"Then please tell me why you're being a dumbass."

"Because she's not cold. Because she doesn't want to wind up like her father. She doesn't want to go to jail—"

"Too bad! If that's what she wanted, then the woman shouldn't have stolen classified intel!"

"I don't think she did it. I think it was someone else."

"And you're basing this on...what? Your dick's reaction to her?" As soon as he said the words, Merik immediately lunged back. "Do *not* take a swing at me!"

He'd been about to do just that. Hands still fisted, Chase snarled, "I'm basing it on my gut instinct. I know people. I know her. She's not cold-blooded. She...she freaking bakes, man."

"You'll need more evidence than her brownies to convince our boss that she's innocent."

He knew that.

"Is that what you're trying to do now? Because, like, I'm seriously trying to understand what's happening here. After one date—*one*—you want to convince everyone that Vivian Wayne is innocent?"

"I want to investigate. Fully." Tension still knotted Chase's body. Tension. Desire. When he'd held Vivian in his arms, he'd gone wild for her. At first, he'd tried to hold on to his control, but when she'd started moaning, when she'd pressed against him, used that sexy little tongue of hers...

For a while there, he'd forgotten everything but her.

The job had vanished from his mind. It hadn't been about playing a role. It had just been about her.

"If you don't think she's the guilty party, then who is?" Merik wanted to know.

"Luc Coderre."

Merik shook his head. "No. That's what I wanted to talk to you about—it's the business I said we had to discuss."

Chase released a bitter laugh. "And here I thought you just wanted to end my date."

Merik nodded. "That, too." He rolled back his shoulders. "Coderre has dual French and American citizenship. He's forty years old, he's a triathlete who exercises religiously, and the guy volunteers at a soup kitchen every holiday. He's worked at the CIA for years. Spotless record. His bank accounts have been checked. No big deposits or withdrawals. No suspicious trips. He looks clean as a whistle."

"Her accounts were clean, too."

Merik inclined his head. "But *she* was the one with the access, the one with a biological father who was a master thief, the one with connections to the Russian mafia because her dear old stepdad just happens to be—"

"I'm not so sure Vivian knows who he really is," Chase had to say.

"What? Why do you think that?"

"Because she told me about her father's death today. Told me about her mother. Never mentioned at all that her stepfather was the man who'd taken her dad's life." And that was the kind of detail that would seriously mess with a person's head.

Merik didn't appear convinced. "So she didn't mention it. Big deal. Not exactly surprising. I mean, that's hardly the kind of trivia you drop on a first date. Little dark, don't you think? I thought first dates were supposed to be all about charm and fun."

Their first date had been about learning secrets. "Vivian told me her father was a thief who stole from the wrong people. *That* was dark trivia."

Now Merik appeared suspicious. "How'd you get her to share so much on the first date?"

"Because I know how to work targets." Shit. He was such an asshole.

I can still taste her.

"You...you're not falling for her, are you?" Merik's voice was halting. Worried.

Chase turned away from him. "Never been in love." He closed his eyes. *Felt her.* "I want to fully investigate all of our options. You say Luc is clean, but what the hell was he doing at her place on a Sunday morning?"

"Uh, going on a wild hunch here, but...getting ready to jog?"

"He could jog anywhere." Chase spun back around. Opened his eyes. "He wants her."

Understanding flashed on Merik's face. "And you have a problem with that."

"I have a problem with suspicious situations. The guy looks clean on paper—at least he appears clean to you—but you know what I heard when you were rattling off about him?"

"I am dying to know." Merik crossed his arms over his chest. "Enlighten me."

"All those years of CIA service—could be that he's a rock star."

"Could be," Merik agreed.

"If that's the case, it means he has skills that we don't know about. A top-of-his-game agent is a deadly opponent. If he goes dark—if he *has* gone dark—then he can take the whole world down with him. If he's our adversary, then we're stepping into a nightmare. I don't like that he was at her door so soon after the break-in. Maybe Luc was her jogging partner or maybe he was coming by to pick up intel."

"But we searched her place, and there is no sign of the data. She must have it well hidden."

"Or she doesn't have it at all." Simple. "Because she was framed by someone like Luc who knew exactly what he was doing. Someone with plenty of international connections because he's worked all over the globe."

Merik fell silent. At least he appeared to be considering what Chase was telling him.

"Then there's the maintenance manager." Someone else on Chase's suspect list.

Merik's eyebrows shot up. "The guy who got you out of the elevator? What problem do you have with him? Oh, wait, was it the cinnamon roll bit? Because I could tell you weren't thrilled with that part."

"Too big of a coincidence."

"What? Her baking for him? Nah. Maybe the woman just likes to—"

"First the break-in, then the elevator stops with Vivian inside of it? She just happens to become trapped in her own worst nightmare? I'm supposed to buy that she's randomly having the weekend from hell?" Chase shook his head. "Nope. Someone is targeting her."

Now Merik straightened. "All right, I wanted to say you were full of crap and still thinking with the wrong brain, but I get the coincidence part. I don't like coincidences."

Who did?

Merik scratched his temple. "You believe maybe the people she was going to sell the intel to...do you figure they've decided it's easier to come after her?"

"I think she's in danger." And it infuriated him. "If someone is coming for her, then they'll find us waiting."

Merik smiled and straightened. "Oh, I get what you're saying. We'll spring a trap on them all at once. Then we can bring down the whole ring!" He pointed at Chase and wagged his finger. "Sorry I doubted you. It was crazy to think you were getting all emotionally involved with a woman you just met. Especially when she's the chief suspect! I mean, come on." He turned for the door. "Not like you're some green agent who doesn't know better."

"Absolutely crazy," Chase echoed as he followed Merik out. "Insane."

"Get you some sleep, buddy. Who knows what will happen tomorrow." Merik saluted him and headed for the stairs, not the elevator.

Good choice.

Chase lingered in the hallway.

It was crazy to think you were getting all emotionally involved with a woman you just met.

Chase didn't get emotionally involved with anyone. Why bother? No relationship lasted forever. Nothing was permanent. When times got hard, when anything got hard, people left.

And why in the hell was he staring at her door again?

Because she's in danger. Because someone screwed with the elevator.

As if on cue, the elevator dinged, and the doors opened. Chase's head whipped down the hallway toward the sound.

Jacob Webb leaned out of the elevator, looked around, then slid back inside—

"Wait!" Chase rushed toward him.

Jacob threw up his hand and stopped the doors from closing. "You need something?"

Chase studied the other man. Before moving into the building, he'd gotten a dossier on Jacob Webb. Only Jacob wasn't just the maintenance manager. He owned the entire building. That info had come via some deep digging. Jacob liked to keep his assets very hidden.

"Yes, I need something." His narrowed gaze swept over Jacob. Thirty-five. Fit.

"Well, what is it?" Jacob prompted. "I've got a bed waiting. Can't just stand here forever."

"Did you hear about what happened at Vivian's place last night?"

Jacob's gaze flickered down the hallway, toward Vivian's apartment. "Yeah. Talked to her this morning. Told her I'd put on a new lock, but you'd already beaten me to it." His jaw hardened. "I'll have cameras put outside the building. The owner likes to give his tenants privacy, but I know he'll want them to be as safe as possible."

"Great to hear that about the *owner*," Chase muttered.

Jacob's lips thinned. "Vivian is a nice lady. I'd hate to see something happen to her." His hand dropped. The doors began to close.

Is that a freaking threat?

Chase shot forward. His hand flew up, and he stopped the doors from closing. "I'd hate that, too. First the break-in, now the elevator trouble…"

He caught the faint stiffening of Jacob's shoulders.

"You said it was a short? That's what caused the elevator to stop?"

"Just some wiring trouble," Jacob replied with a shrug. "It happens."

"But there had been no other trouble today with the elevator? It only happened when Vivian was in the elevator?"

"Vivian and you."

Chase's gaze assessed the other man. Jacob's posture was too hard and stiff. "Let's hope there are no more accidents."

"It's my job to make sure there won't be more. Now, could you move your hand? I'm ready to get my ass to bed."

He didn't move his hand. Not yet. "Why'd you help her move in?"

Jacob rolled his eyes. "Same reason you had your mouth locked on hers when the elevator doors opened. She's sexy as hell."

That surge he felt—the one that made anger churn inside of him—it wasn't jealousy, was it? Chase heard himself growl, "That ship has sailed for you."

"Got it. Now move the hand?"

He moved his hand. The doors closed.

Chase lingered there a moment. What in the hell was happening? He wasn't jealous. He was never jealous. Not of anyone or anything. You had to care to be jealous. He didn't get close enough to care.

Vivian was a job. She might be innocent. His instincts certainly said she was, mostly because Vivian just seemed too fucking *nice* not to be innocent.

Not nice. Perfect. She seems freaking perfect.

But he knew—all too well—that appearances could be deceiving.

CHAPTER SEVEN

Vivian released a long, slow breath. She didn't have a choice. Desperate times could call for the most desperate of measures. Her hand lifted, and she determinedly knocked on the apartment door.

She could hear the pad of steps from inside and then the door swung open.

"Well, hello." Chase smiled. The smile that made her insides feel extra warm. "This is a surprise. I didn't expect to—"

"I'm in trouble."

His smile froze. In an instant, his eyes went from warm and welcoming to hard and cold, and his expression...

Lethal.

She'd had trouble imagining him as a SEAL. SEALs were supposed to be fierce and deadly. He'd seemed so easy-going to her before, but right now...*Yep, I can see him as a SEAL.*

"Is someone after you?" He reached for her, and his slightly callused fingertips slid over her wrist as he pulled her into his home.

"I...maybe?"

Chase's brows pulled together even as he shut and locked the door behind her. "Maybe?" he repeated.

She licked her lips. Paced. The apartment was still full of boxes—he obviously hadn't gotten around to unpacking. *Because he had to spend one night at my place. Then he had to get a crew to install my alarm system and then—* "This is a mistake. I'm sorry. I've already put you out enough." She turned to head back for the door.

He stepped into her path. "We're not a mistake."

She stopped. It was either stop or run into him. Her head tipped back so that she could stare up into his eyes. She'd gone straight to his place after work. She still wore her heels, the dress pants, and the white blouse that she'd put on that morning.

"Viv, tell me what's going on."

Her instinct had been to go straight to Chase. He was the one with security experience. The one who'd helped her. And, yes, they'd only recently met but...

It wasn't like she had a ton of other options. In fact, he *was* her only option. "I discovered two hundred thousand dollars in my bank account today."

He blinked. "And that's..." A cough. "I'm guessing the money isn't supposed to be there?"

"It's not supposed to be there." Definitely not. Not like it was easy to overlook two hundred grand.

"Call the bank," he told her immediately. "Probably just some kind of mix-up. Maybe you put in a deposit for two hundred dollars and some zeros got moved and—"

"It's not a mix-up. I called the bank. They confirmed that the transfer was legitimate."

His gaze stayed on her. "I'm not following."

That was because she hadn't told him everything. And before she did, maybe they should get the business part out of the way first. "I want to hire you."

Surprise appeared, then vanished from his gaze. "Excuse me?"

"I did more research on Wilde today. It's not just security, not just protection. The firm also does some investigation work, correct?"

"For certain, select clients."

Her hands twisted in front of her body. "I need an investigator." Or, rather… "I need you."

Chase seemed to absorb what she'd said. "You need me because two hundred grand just appeared in your bank account."

"Because…" She sucked in a breath. Her fingers smoothed over her left eyebrow. "Look, can you say that you'll take the job first? And is there like a confidentiality-type agreement that comes with the job?"

"What is going on, Vivian? Is this about your break-in?"

"I think it could be." Her voice went lower. Huskier. "I think I'm being set up."

His gaze sharpened on her. "You're leaving out lots of pieces here. Why don't you just sit down and tell me everything?"

That was the plan. "First agree to the job. I mean, I can pay you. I have two hundred grand just waiting for you." She laughed, but the laughter held a bitter, desperate edge.

"I'll take the job. But we'll talk about payment later."

Relief almost made her dizzy. "And the confidentiality? Can you promise it to me?"

His lips thinned. "Do you trust me?"

"I-I just met you."

"You didn't let that stop you from coming to my door and asking for help. If you trust me—and I think you do—that means you are going to tell me everything, no holding back."

"I don't think that I have a choice." She backed away. Her legs seemed to give out on her as she plopped down on his couch. "I know payout money when I see it. And with the irregularities, God, it's all going to point to me. Someone is setting me up, and if I don't find out who, I'll go to jail. I *can't* go to jail, Chase."

He swore and came to sit beside her. His thigh brushed against hers. "Tell me everything. Now."

Her head tipped forward. "I swear, my life is normally calm and ordered. And there are no break-ins or mystery payouts randomly appearing in my account."

He caught her hair and pushed a lock of it behind her ear. "I got that you went for order. Noticed it in the way everything in your apartment was perfectly in place."

She turned her head to look at him.

"You might have noticed that my shit is still all over the place here." He shrugged. "Don't let that worry you. It just means I like chaos, but I can control it."

"Chaos theory," Vivian heard herself say. "If you can find the order in chaos, then you can start to see patterns."

"Are you giving me new facts to learn?"

She was nervous as hell. She had no idea what she was giving him. "I don't want to go to jail," she whispered.

His jaw tightened. "Baby, you aren't."

Easy to say when he wasn't the one being framed.

"Tell me what's happening," Chase urged her. "Don't leave out any details."

She bit her lower lip. There were things about her job that she wasn't supposed to disclose, but, if she was right—and Vivian feared she was—then people were in danger. "I noticed irregularities. Where I work, I mean. At first, they seemed like glitches. But they were very *specific* glitches."

"Okay, back up. First, you need to tell me where you work. Because you've kind of kept that news from me."

"I work for the CIA." Her voice was so low. Like she was afraid someone would overhear. But it was just the two of them, so she cleared her throat and tried again. "I'm not an agent. I just— I'm a contractor. What I told you before was true. I am a Digital Forensic Engineer. That means I spend my days looking for trouble online. Looking for holes that enemies can use. I stop hackers. I protect our systems." This was so bad. "But that also means that since I'm the one protecting things, I know how to get around every safeguard that's in place."

He didn't speak.

"It looks like it's me." This made her sick. *Sick*. "Data was compromised. At first, I kept going after the trail on my own. I didn't want to alert my boss because..." Her words trailed away.

"You suspected him."

"I suspected nearly everyone at the branch. That was the problem. I had suspicions, but no proof. I'm the new employee. The glitches started after I arrived. All I could do was keep digging. Keep seeing where the trail led me."

"And where did it lead?"

She felt nauseous as she told him, "Agents have been compromised. Undercover assets—their identities are known. Their addresses were found. The material was downloaded, and it's out there."

"*When did this happen?*"

It wasn't a simple matter of when. There was more involved than just an easy timeline. The data was gone. "At first, the glitches were keyed more to just trying to get around the system. I tried to put precautions in place when I noticed the activity."

"Precautions?" His head cocked.

They'd get back to those precautions. The precautions were going to buy her time. "But when I discovered that the data had been taken—I could see the digital footprint, I knew the material was accessed and stolen—then I had to go to my boss. Whether I suspected him or not, I had to follow the chain of command and report what I'd discovered."

"*When* did the breach happen?"

As far as when the data had actually been pulled and not just when the glitches had started... "Last week. Tuesday. I told my boss what had occurred. He said he'd launch an investigation, and then he shut me out. Locked down my access. I was told to report to work each day, but I just sit at my desk and basically do nothing." Her breath expelled in a hard rush. "Then today, that two hundred grand appeared. The CIA is looking for the person who compromised security, and it's going to look like it was me." She had to blink away tears. Tears that she'd fought all day long. "I know you didn't sign up for any of this, but you helped me before." *And you are my only shot.* "You work for a security firm. You're the only person I could think of." She swallowed. Stared into his eyes. "I know a payout when I see it. My father got them for the jobs he took. My mother swore we'd never live on his blood money."

He searched her eyes.

A tear slid down her cheek. A tear she'd tried to stop, but it had slipped out despite her efforts. "I don't want to go to jail. The evidence is mounting—and half of that evidence is info that *I* collected. I turned it in to my boss, and my digital fingerprints are all over the files, but that is only because I was doing my job. I was trying to protect the system." And the agents out there. She'd done everything she could to protect them. Vivian hadn't even told her boss the steps she'd taken for them. *Because I don't know who to trust.*

"You didn't take the intel."

She shook her head. Swiped at the tear. "Absolutely not."

"The money in your account isn't there because you sold out those agents and turned over the material you downloaded."

"*No.* I wouldn't do that."

His hand lifted. His fingertips gently brushed over her cheek. "Are you a good liar, Vivian?"

What kind of question was that? "You don't believe me?" She jumped to her feet. "I'm telling you the truth!"

He rose, too, slowly.

"I don't like lying, Chase. I had too much of that growing up." First from her father. Then her mother. Then—

No, she shut off the thought. Locked it away.

"I told you that I would take the case, and I will," Chase assured her. "But if we're going to find the person who is setting you up, I'm going to have to ask uncomfortable questions. I'm going to have to dig into your life. I'll have to dig into the lives of your co-workers."

"That's a problem." A big one. "The CIA doesn't like it when folks dig into the lives of their agents." Her heart slammed into her chest. "I told my boss that he had to notify all of the compromised agents. That he had to move them. But I don't know if he did. And since my access to the system is shut down, I can't even be sure that more agents haven't been compromised since the breach began."

"We'll figure this out."

He seemed so certain. So calm. Like he handled scenes of international drama and intrigue every single day.

She didn't. She was about to lose her mind.

"Do you think the break-ins at your place are related to what's happening at your work?"

"I'm afraid they are." Her voice seemed so quiet. "I wanted them to be random, but I'm scared they're not."

"If they're related, that means whoever took the data is coming after you. The person wants to harm you." A muscle flexed along his jaw. "It won't happen. You've just hired yourself the best damn bodyguard out there."

Her breath rushed out. "Thank you." She wanted to hug him. Hold tight and never let go. "Um, if we go back to my place, I can tell you more. We can talk and eat and I can—"

"Your place won't work," he cut in quickly.

It wouldn't? Why not?

"Let's go out to dinner," he suddenly told her.

Go out?

"Look, you need to take some time and calm down. I can feel the tension rolling off you."

Because she was freaking the hell out.

"Let's get out of this building. We'll talk about the case in a quiet corner of a restaurant where no one can hear us."

But...no one could hear them where they were, right? And it wasn't as if anyone could hear them in her place.

Then she stiffened. Chase had more experience in this area than she did. Maybe he thought that her place had been bugged? Didn't that happen in spy movies? *All the time.*

But this wasn't a movie. This was her life.

"We'll go out. You'll answer every question that I have. And we'll come up with a game plan." He paused. "You haven't eaten, have you?"

Actually, no. She hadn't. Not all day. Her stomach growled on cue. "I was so nervous that I couldn't eat lunch."

A brisk nod. "Then we're eating and you're telling me everything."

Well, perhaps going out wasn't the worst plan. "I should go change first. Get out of the heels." Slip into some sneakers.

"Sure. Want to meet up in ten minutes?"

"Yes." She smiled at him. A real smile. For the first time all day, Vivian felt as if she could breathe. "Thank you." She stretched up and pressed a kiss to his cheek. "I owe you more than I'll ever be able to repay."

His head turned. He caught her chin between his fingers. Kissed her. Not some light, easy kiss. Hard. Deep. Possessive. "You don't owe me a damn thing," he rumbled against her mouth. He started to let her go.

So she grabbed tightly to him. Vivian kissed him just as hard, just as deeply, and with just as much of a possessive edge. For the first time, she'd found someone who would help her. Someone she could count on. For too many years, she'd felt as if it was her against the world.

This time, it was different. She'd gone to Chase.

And he was on her side.

He spun her around, and her back pressed to the wall. "When I kiss you," his voice was so rough and sexy, "I forget everything else. How do you make me feel this way?" His hands rose to press against the wall behind her. "I think you're dangerous to me."

She stared into his eyes. "I like the way you make me feel."

"Vivian..."

"I want you, and I'm not holding back with you. I hold back with everyone else. You were right. I like control and order. I do everything on my own, but this time, I came to you."

His head lowered toward hers once more. His kiss was almost savage in its need. No, *they* were that way. Savage and hungry. So much for control. So much for order.

Maybe she'd had enough of that. Maybe it was time for his chaos.

Her nails raked over the white t-shirt that Chase wore. Her relationships in the past hadn't been about this wild passion. They'd been careful. She'd chosen safe lovers. Men who were responsible. Stable. And she'd wanted them, but...

Not like this. Vivian didn't think she'd ever wanted anyone like this.

Perhaps she should have been afraid of that forceful, consuming need. She wasn't. She wasn't afraid of Chase. He was there to help her.

His lips slid down her throat. Licked and sucked. Heated desire spiked in her blood. She wondered what it would be like to let go. To strip off her clothes right then and there and just *feel* with him—

"Your case." His voice was guttural. "We need to talk about your case. I have to clear you first."

She blinked. Tried to catch some desperate breaths.

"When you're clear..." His gaze trapped her. "You're mine."

They didn't have to wait. Wanted him so much that she didn't care about the consequences. She'd come to him less than ten minutes ago, practically begging for help...

And, oh, God, now I'm about to beg him to have sex with me.

That wasn't her. "How do you make me feel this way? What are you doing to me?"

His expression was so hard and savage.

"I kiss you, and I want you naked." She wasn't holding anything back with him. *I held back my whole life. He's different.* "I think having sex with you won't be like the way it's been with—"

"I should warn you, I'm finding I'm pretty damn jealous when it comes to you." He leaned forward. Kissed and sucked the skin along her neck once more, right over her racing pulse, and had her heart thundering in her ears. "So how about we don't talk about what sex was like with other people for you? How about we just think about what it will be like for us?" His head rose. His gaze captured hers. "You taste like my favorite vanilla cream. Before I'm done with you, I'm going to taste every single inch of you."

Oh...wow.

"Case first." His chin jerked up. He shoved away from her. Actually, backed up a good foot as if he had to put some distance between them.

She wanted to reach out to him. Because she wanted that so badly, Vivian balled her hands into fists.

"You tell me everything, Viv. I find evidence to clear you, then you're mine."

"And...you're mine."

His eyes gleamed. "Baby, I think I already fucking am."

***

"New development," Chase bit out as he held the phone to his ear. Vivian had gone to her apartment to get changed, and he had used the opportunity to make a fast phone call to his partner.

"You mean the development where our Evil Queen got paid two hundred grand because she's probably getting ready to drop the intel? Because that had to be a down payment and the exchange is probably happening *tonight?* Dude, you know that we went over the two hundred K transfer this morning when the deposit was first made and we tracked it to that account in the Caymans and—"

"She just hired me."

"Uh, you are already *working* the case and the goal is to bring her down."

"She hired me to prove her innocence."

Merik laughed.

Chase didn't.

"It's a trick!" Merik warned. "She's figured out who you are. Vivian knows you're on to her, and she's trying to throw you off the trail."

"Or she's actually innocent, she's scared out of her mind, and she's turning to the one person that she thinks might be able to help her." She'd looked so afraid and when he'd seen the tear sliding down her cheek, he'd wanted to damn well break something.

"The player is getting played," Merik charged back. "Don't buy it! She's trying to distract you while the big deal goes down tonight. What did you she do? Come over? Cry a little? Tell you how desperate she was and that she needed help?"

Actually, yeah. "Don't be a dick."

"I can't help it. It's second nature to me." A pause. "At least you didn't say she tried to seduce you. That would be like every Evil Queen checklist item all wrapped up with a nice, tidy bow."

"She went to her boss. She told him about what's been happening with the intel. Vivian is afraid she's being framed. She even told me about the deposit in her account."

"You are *not* buying her story. Tell me you're not."

"Everything is too neat. Too easy. Don't you get that?" Surely Merik had to see that? "The money being sent to her account was overkill."

"No, it was the final nail in her coffin. The transfer means it's game time. It means the deal is going down tonight—"

"And I will be staying close to her all night long, so if that happens, I'll be there, and we'll catch her in the act." Chase's hold tightened on the phone. "But I don't think that's the way it will play out. I think Vivian needs me. If she's being set up, this isn't going to end with us locking her away in jail. With that scenario, she'll just keep telling the world that she's innocent. She'll keep *fighting* to prove she's innocent."

"Then how do you think it will end?"

Cold settled in his gut. "The real guilty party will have all the evidence leading straight to

Vivian, and then the perp will eliminate her. With her dead, the case ends."

"Fuck." Finally, Merik seemed less certain.

"Exactly. And I don't want to be the man standing around with his thumb up his ass while an innocent woman dies. I'm going to hear what she has to tell me tonight. I'm going to stick to her like glue. Either I'll catch her in the act or I'll stop the real perp from taking her out. But I need to know that my partner has my back. Can I count on you?"

"You know that you can," Merik replied. His voice was flat. Hard. "I'll have your six."

***

Vivian hopped into her tennis shoes and grabbed her purse. She glanced around, knowing that she needed to snag her phone—

It was ringing.

She scooped it up and frowned at the number on the screen. It was a number she didn't recognize. Probably a telemarketer. Talk about bad timing. She almost didn't answer the call.

Almost...

Her finger swiped over the screen as she put the phone to her ear. "Look, I'm sorry but this isn't a very good time for me—"

"You'll do exactly what I say or your new boyfriend dies."

CHAPTER EIGHT

Vivian pounded on the apartment door.

It swung open and Chase smiled—

"It was a mistake. I don't need your help. Everything is fine now."

His smile froze. "What?"

"A mistake," she said again, quickly, even as she swore that she felt a thick bead of sweat sliding down her spine. "Everything has been cleared up. I spoke with my boss, and it's fine. I don't need you any longer."

His brow furrowed. "What's happening?"

"I read a study once that said the average worker makes about one hundred and eighteen mistakes a year. One hundred and eighteen. So, you know, the old expression about everyone making mistakes? It's obviously true." She was rambling. Vivian hurriedly backed up a step. Her words were tumbling out. She had to slow them down. "I made a mistake earlier. I don't need to hire you. The money is gone from my account. I just got a call." She lifted her phone. Held it too tightly. "The situation is under control."

"Bullshit."

Vivian flinched. "I have to go. My boss wants to see me tonight."

"We were going to dinner."

She was backing away from Chase as fast as she could. "Yes, but if I want to keep my job, I have to go, right now. It's a non-negotiable point." Very, very non-negotiable.

"I'll come with you."

"*No!*" She'd yelled. Crap. She had to get herself under control. "Unnecessary. I've got it covered."

His stare was suspicious. "You're lying to me."

Her gaze darted down the hallway. "I am not."

"You are. You won't even look at me."

Her gaze came back to him. "Please," she whispered.

Chase stalked closer to her. "Baby, what is it?"

"I have to go. You have to stay here."

He shook his head. "I thought you wanted my help."

"Yes, but I want you alive more."

"*What?*"

Her hand flew to cover her mouth. *That shouldn't have come out!*

"Vivian..."

She dropped her hand. "Stay away from me. You need to stay away." She whirled and raced toward the stairwell—

"No." His fingers curled around her wrist. He'd moved crazy fast. "You're not going anywhere without me."

She *had* to leave without him.

"You think I can't tell that you're scared? I can. It's like you're broadcasting it in big, neon letters. What happened? You were gone for ten minutes. Less than that. More like eight. You wanted me with you, but now you're pushing me away."

Her shoulders stiffened. "Let go of my wrist."

His fingers uncurled.

"Good-bye, Chase." She took three fast steps away from him.

"Huh."

She stopped. God, no, she knew what it meant when he said—

"You're trying to protect me? That's what this big scene is about?"

She crept forward. She needed to get to that stairwell.

"Did someone make a threat against me, Viv? Because, I assure you, I can handle myself."

She stopped creeping and switched to hurrying.

"I'm coming after you."

She was almost at the stairs.

"You're *not* leaving me behind, Vivian."

She looked back at him. "Watch me." Then she shoved open the stairwell door.

***

"I'll do you one better, sweetheart," Chase muttered. "I'll come after you." Chase whipped up his phone. Had Merik on the line in an instant. "She's spooked, and she's trying to ditch me. Heading after her now. There must be a meeting or she's been threatened or some shit went down." His hand slammed into the stairwell door. Only the door didn't open. He shoved against it again and realized what Vivian had done.

"*Sonofabitch.*" Despite everything, he almost smiled.

"What's happening?" Merik demanded.

"She jammed the door from the other side. Clever." He had to give her that. Chase whirled. "I'm taking the elevator down. It will slow me, so make sure that you have eyes on her."

"I'm not at the building yet! I'm close, but I need more time!"

Fury—and what could have been fear—twisted through Chase. "She'd better not leave before I get down there. We need to track her." *I need to protect her.* He shoved his thumb against the elevator button. *Come on. Come on.*

"How much of a head start does she have?"

"She's probably almost to the ground floor, and my ass is stuck up here." Shit. What was taking the elevator so long?

Ding.

Hell, yes.

"I'm going after her. Get here. *Now.*" He jumped onto the elevator. Pressed the button for the ground floor. He'd seen fear in her eyes. When he'd opened the door, her expression had been unguarded. She'd been afraid. Her lower lip had even trembled before she'd caught herself.

He didn't like it when Vivian was afraid. Not one damn bit.

Ding.

This wasn't the ground floor. The doors opened. Jacob Webb blinked at him. "It's not gonna be bad luck if I get on with you, is it? You're not about to shut this thing down again?"

Chase jabbed the button to close the damn doors and get moving.

"Hey!" Jacob jumped onto the elevator.

"In a hurry here," Chase snapped. "Don't have time for BS."

"Well, someone is grumpy."

"And someone can fuck off." The elevator descended and they finally reached the ground floor. The doors opened. Chase flew out—

"See if I come rushing to help you when you get a busted pipe!" Jacob yelled after him.

Chase ran for the building's main door. He shot outside. Looked to the left. The right and—there. He spied Vivian driving down the street toward him.

He stepped into the street. Waved his hands. "Hell, no, Vivian. Hell, *no!*" Yeah, he was in her fucking path.

She slammed on the brakes. Gaped at him.

He slapped his hands down on her hood. "Get out of the car."

Vivian shook her head.

"Yes."

Cars honked at him. Chase ignored them. There was no way she was leaving him. He didn't move because he knew that if he moved, she'd slam down on the gas pedal and blast away. "We're talking. We're coming up with a game plan."

She threw open the driver's side door. "Are you insane?" Her voice had reached an incredible pitch.

Since she was out of the vehicle—though she'd left it idling—he lifted his hands and took a few steps away from the car.

"You can't jump in front of a moving vehicle!"

He couldn't? "Funny, I just did."

"I could have killed you!"

"Nah, you weren't going that fast. And, besides, I knew you'd stop. You like me."

Once more, Vivian shook her head. "I have to go." She reached for the door handle.

He lunged toward her. Locked his hand around her shoulder and hauled her away from the vehicle and toward him. "Vivian, no—"

The back of the car exploded. The vehicle flew up into the air even as hot flames erupted. The blast sent Chase hurtling back. He tried to keep his grip on Vivian, but she was ripped away from him. He hit the pavement. Rolled. For a moment, he couldn't hear anything at all.

Then he heard the roar of the flames.

The shriek of nearby car alarms because the blast had triggered their sensors.

He could smell smoke. Ash.

He could—

"*Vivian!*" he shouted.

Chase jumped to his feet. Staggered. Shit. He righted himself as quickly as possible even as his gaze flew around the area. He was looking for red hair. He was looking for the green t-shirt she'd been wearing. The t-shirt that had matched her eyes. He was looking for—

She was on the ground.

Chase didn't even remember running to her. One moment, he was searching desperately for her, and in the next, he was kneeling beside her. *"Be okay, be okay, be okay,"* Chase chanted over and over again.

His shaking fingers went to her throat. Her pulse kicked beneath his touch, and he could breathe. He could let out the desperate air that he'd been holding. Then his fingers were flying over her body as he searched for injuries. Broken bones. Contusions—

"Chase?"

Her voice. Scared. Broken.

His gaze whipped to her face.

"What h-happened?"

He swallowed the fear and fury that burned in his throat. "Someone just tried to kill you."

***

"Sorry," Chase rumbled as he stared straight at her. "Stairs aren't exactly an option here."

Here...Here would be...the main building that housed the big, bad Wilde security empire. After her car had exploded—*OhmyGod, my car exploded!*—he'd rushed her away from the scene. Like rushed away as in...gotten her out of there before the cops had even arrived.

And, shouldn't they have stayed for the cops? Wasn't that the normal procedure in situations like this one? To stay, to answer questions, to do an entire interview scene? She didn't know, but running didn't feel right.

He'd gotten her away from that scene and driven them *out* of Marietta. Before she'd known it, they'd been surrounded by skyscrapers and he'd told her that she had to go in at Wilde. She'd followed his orders because this was way beyond her normal world.

No one had ever tried to kill her before. If Chase hadn't gotten her out of the car, if he hadn't jumped in front of her vehicle...

I would be dead.

"Are you feeling claustrophobic, Viv? Do you need me to distract you? Shit, I have never noticed how slow elevators are until tonight." His hands curled around her shoulders. "You're not alone. Everything is okay."

"I-I'm not feeling claustrophobic." She should tell him that he could let her go. She didn't. His warm touch was thawing her ice-cold body. "Why are we here?"

"Because everything has changed. Because they were fucking wrong."

Who'd been wrong? About what? She couldn't follow what he was saying. Wait, had she hit her head? It didn't ache, but she had flown through the air and then landed on the concrete hard enough to rattle her bones.

"The mission goal has to change. Your safety is priority one."

He wanted to protect her. Got it. That brought her back to—"He intended to kill me all along!"

Chase's hold tightened on her. "Who did?"

"Th-the man who called me, right before I came to your apartment. He said if I didn't do exactly what he ordered, I would die." Actually, he'd said Chase would die, too. He'd said that being a former SEAL wouldn't do him any good.

I'll make the fucking SEAL drown in his own blood.

She swallowed. "He lied. He gave me instructions. Told me I had to follow them exactly, but it was all a setup, wasn't it?"

"Hell, yes, it was a setup. From the word go."

"He wanted me in my car. He'd wired it to blow."

A grim nod. "Probably put it on a timer that began as soon as the ignition was started. I figure you were in the car for about three minutes—maybe four—before it blew."

Her eyes squeezed shut. "I think I'm going to be sick." Her stomach was revolting, and her head was spinning.

"Breathe, baby." His voice was low, soothing.

"I am breathing!" Vivian snarled back. Okay, so maybe she wasn't in the mood for low and soothing. She was freaking out. Her breath expelled in heaving pants. "Someone is trying to frame me *and* kill me."

"It's going to be okay."

Her eyes cracked open. "Things don't feel okay."

The faint lines near his mouth deepened. "I'm going to help you. Trust me."

Her stare darted to the control panel. "Just how tall is this building? The Bank of America Plaza in Atlanta has fifty-five stories, and it's considered to be the tallest in the city—"

Ding.

Thank God. Her shoulders sagged.

His fingers were still around her. "Whatever happens, I need you to trust me."

He was being so nice to her. So caring. His care made her feel even worse. "You almost got killed because of me. Have you considered that maybe you should be running away from me?"

Chase shook his head. "Not even for a second."

That warmed her even more—and terrified her. Chase still didn't know that the caller had threatened him. "Can we please get out of this elevator?"

A jerky nod. He released her shoulders. Turned away. But Chase caught her hand in his. Their fingers threaded together as they walked out and stepped onto some lush carpeting. It was late, and Vivian figured the office should have been closed. When they'd arrived downstairs, they'd been greeted by security guards who'd hurriedly opened the doors for them.

She cast a quick glance toward a waiting area and saw an empty desk. Chase didn't even slow as he headed past the desk and toward a big, heavy, wooden door. Vivian cleared her throat. "Uh, Chase..."

"My boss is inside. We've got a crew together. We're fixing this shit."

Fixing it?

At the door, he paused and turned back toward her. "I'm gonna say it again, trust me."

"My stomach is in knots right now."

"You didn't steal the intel."

"Of course, I didn't steal the intel!" How were they back to this?

"The two hundred grand isn't yours."

"No, it isn't." They'd already discussed the money.

"And someone wants you dead because the dead can't talk."

She choked down the lump in her throat. "Typically, no, I don't believe they can. That's a side effect of being dead."

His expression hardened even more. "Then we have to make sure you don't die."

"I would like that very much, yes," she agreed.

A curt nod. "You're getting protection. You're getting *me*."

With his free hand, he opened the door. He strode inside like he owned the place, and Vivian had to follow because he was still holding her hand and—oh, there *was* a crew assembled in there.

Merik stood to the side. He was dressed casually in jeans and a t-shirt. His arms were crossed over his chest and his expression was grim. His dragon looked equally grim.

A man in a white dress shirt, with rolled up sleeves and tousled, dark hair rose from his position behind the massive desk that dominated the office. Vivian figured he had to be the big boss, and yes, as she studied him, she realized he matched the image she'd found online. *Eric Wilde*. The owner of the firm. He looked way more intense in real life than he had in the smiling photo.

A woman sat perched in the chair across from the desk. Her head had turned toward Chase and Vivian, and she studied them with a steady, dark gaze. Her warm olive skin was flawless, and small pearls dotted the lobes of her ears.

Another man stood off to the side, almost slipping into the shadows as he lounged against the wall and watched them.

"Thanks for getting here so quickly," Chase said and she figured he was addressing everyone who'd been waiting. "Because we have a clusterfuck situation going on."

Vivian flinched. *She* was the clusterfuck situation.

"But first..." Chase pointed to the guy lounging in the corner. "Who the hell is that?"

Now Vivian stiffened. She'd figured Chase knew everyone in the room.

Eric Wilde opened his mouth to reply—

"That's classified," the man who seemed to love the shadows replied smoothly. "So sorry. Wait, I'm not really sorry." He rolled one hand vaguely in the air. "Carry on."

"What?" Chase's body stiffened even as he kept a tight hold on Vivian's hand. "Look, this whole case is compromised, and I need to know exactly who I am dealing with before this goes any—"

"I think Vivian should wait outside for a while. We need to go over a few important points," Eric Wilde interrupted. Then he strode around the desk and headed straight for her. "Actually, my apologies." His assessing gaze held no emotion as he stopped in front of her. He smiled, but the smile didn't reach his eyes as he offered his hand to her. "I should introduce myself. I'm Eric Wilde, Chase's boss."

Yes, she'd figured that out.

Eric slanted a quick glance at Chase. "Since my name is on the business, that means he's supposed to listen to my orders."

She pulled her hand from Chase's. Shook Eric's hand. "I appreciate Chase taking my case, even though I tried to fire him earlier."

Eric's brows pulled together. He appeared bemused. "Excuse me?"

"That's why I'm here, isn't it? To go over my case? To figure out who is setting me up?" Her voice cracked a little as she added, "And trying to kill me?"

"That's why you think you're here?" The mocking drawl came from the man in the shadows. "How adorable."

Chill bumps raced over her skin. "I don't like being called adorable."

"No, she doesn't," Chase snapped. "Now let me ask again. *Who the fuck are you?*"

CHAPTER NINE

"What is going on?" Vivian whispered to Chase. Everything felt wrong. She was missing something, she knew it, but she couldn't quite figure out what it was.

His expression seemed tortured. "Baby..."

"So *you're* the lady who survived the car bomb." The woman's voice had Vivian's attention flying back across the room. The lady rose. Moved with grace as she crossed the room. "I believe some Marietta cops I know are looking for you." Her lips pursed. "I'm Detective Layla Lopez, Atlanta PD. You know, it's not considered good form to leave the scene of a crime."

Atlanta PD. "But I didn't do anything! Someone tried to kill me!"

"She wasn't just going to sit in the middle of the street like a sitting duck, Layla," Chase muttered. "I had to get her out of there. For all I knew, someone was waiting to take another hit at her. She needs to be in a safe house, and I have to get her to one, now."

Safe house? Vivian yanked her hand from Eric's and whirled toward Chase. "But if I'm in a safe house, how are we going to trace down the criminals? We have to find them! There is only so much time before they manage to get past the scramble that I put into the coding!"

Chase's brow scrunched. "Scramble? What are you talking about?"

Laughter erupted from the guy who lurked in the shadows. "That's what I was hoping to hear."

Her shoulders tensed as she edged closer to Chase. "I don't think I like him." A guy who laughed at her and seemed to mock her while he hid in the shadows? Nope. Not on her let's-be-friends list.

But then the fellow stepped out of the shadows. He moved toward her with a slow, almost cat-like grace. His steps made no sound as he crossed the room. He was tall, muscled but lean, and clad in dark clothes with his hair swept off his high forehead. His gray eyes gleamed with what *could* have been amusement. A handsome man, if you liked the type. Hawkish nose. Hard jaw. Devil-may-care grin.

The grin was directed at her.

She did *not* like the type.

"How much time will the scramble buy?" He wanted to know.

"Eric, why is this guy in the room?" Chase demanded.

"I think I told you already," the mystery man replied. "Classified." The gray gaze remained on her. "How much time?"

She licked her lips. Calculated. Then decided to hedge with her answer because she didn't know this jerk. "I can't be sure. It depends on how skilled the person is who tries to untangle my knots."

He smiled at her. "Who else knows about your knots?"

"No one. It won't be discovered until the people who stole the data actually try to find the first agent."

"And when they do try," he asked as he tilted his head to better study her, "what happens then?"

"They realize the addresses are wrong. They're all mixed and jumbled together. The street number for one person was mixed with the road for another, and then that road was paired up with a different city, not the real one, and then that city…I tied it to another country. I switched everything around." Was she being clear? Her words were coming out so fast. "It's like when you have all the pieces of a puzzle, but they're not connected to form the picture. The pieces are just in a big, jumbled pile." A long exhale. "That's what I did. I scrambled them into a big, jumbled pile. The data is there, you just have to put it together the right way."

Silence.

All eyes were on her.

"Huh."

She shot her stare toward Chase. "What did you figure out?"

"You scrambled the codes." He nodded. "Because you didn't trust your boss or maybe you didn't think he would believe you?"

Maybe both reasons.

"You wanted a safety net didn't you, Viv?"

"The net isn't for me. When I first noticed those glitches, I put in an extra layer of protection because I couldn't leave anyone unprotected. I wasn't supposed to interfere with the system protocols, but I didn't have a choice." Did he understand? "I told you..." Her voice lowered. "The glitches made me nervous. I had to do something, so I came up with a scramble." Not the right term, but it perfectly described what she'd done. She'd mixed things around. Substituted code. To an outsider, all of the data would seem legit. It wasn't. Not unless you unscrambled it. To do that, you'd need the right code.

Or the right coder.

"They'll realize the truth and want you." This came from the mystery man.

Only she wasn't so sure his identity was a mystery. When someone appeared and started spouting off about things being classified, that tended to shout one thing to her—

He's with the agency.

Just how high up was this fellow in the CIA's chain of command? Her spine stiffened as dread settled in Vivian's bones.

The CIA guy—*had* to be CIA—gave her a broad smile. "Guess it's a good thing they didn't kill you tonight."

Her throat was so dry. "I consider it a very good thing that I didn't die tonight."

His lips twitched. "Then we agree it was a win." He offered his hand. "My friends call me Dex. So do my enemies."

She stared at his hand. "Have we met before?" Because something about him felt familiar to her. She didn't take his hand. This man—he wasn't like Eric. Didn't ooze that open charm and confidence. The same kind of charm and confidence poured from Chase. No, this fellow was different.

Dangerous. Deadly.

Dex lowered his hand. "I may have seen you before. Let's just say you attracted my attention."

"What the fuck does that mean?" Chase demanded as he surged toward Dex.

Eric cleared his throat. "Chase, please escort Vivian to the waiting area. Guards will make sure she's safe while we go over the case."

"That makes no sense." Vivian frowned at Eric. "It's my case. I hired Chase. Why would you kick out the client while you discuss the case?" Who did that? She'd expected more from the Wilde team.

"Uh, Vivian..." Chase began with a cough. "About that..."

Dex laughed. "We do need to clear the air."

Merik was watching silently, though he had edged closer.

And the detective was studying everything with her careful gaze.

"The Wilde agents weren't hired by you," Dex explained to Vivian with a shrug. "They were hired by me. Hired because I wanted them to find conclusive evidence against you."

A dull ringing filled her ears. Vivian shook her head.

"No?" Dex's brows rose. "Not understanding? It has been quite the night for you. Don't worry. I'll break things down. That will help."

"*Don't,*" Chase snarled.

Dex pointed at Chase. "He's not on your side. He's been working for me. Like you, I wasn't exactly sure who I could trust at the agency, at least, not at the branch where you are employed. I, too, wanted a safety net. We must think alike."

The ringing in her ears turned into a dull drumming.

"Wilde was my safety net," Dex added with a careless flick of his hand toward the Wilde boss. "Eric and I go way back, so I knew I could trust him."

I trusted Chase. Chase was going to help me.

"I asked for Eric's best undercover operative. A man who could get in—fast—and make an instant connection with the target."

Vivian flinched. *I'm the target.*

"The undercover operative had to be good at finding weak spots." Dex's words battered at her. "We were working against the clock, and I needed someone who could get to your secrets right away. We were operating under the assumption that you would be selling the intel at any moment, so you can see where time was of the essence."

She forced her gaze to Chase. "He's lying." It was supposed to be a statement, but it came out more like a desperate question. She pressed her lips together so she wouldn't say, *Please, please, tell me he's lying. Please tell me that you haven't been playing me all along.*

But Chase didn't say that Dex was lying. Instead, he just said, "I'm sorry."

Vivian's shaking fingers lifted to smooth over her left eyebrow.

"Ahem." Dex's throat clearing was overly loud and obviously designed to get her attention again. But she didn't look his way. She kept staring at Chase even as her hand slowly lowered.

I'm sorry. That rough apology echoed in her ears.

"Eric sent in his best undercover agent, and Chase's basic job was to find enough evidence so that I could lock you away for the rest of your life," Dex concluded. "But, hey, looks like instead of handling that particular order of business, he managed to save your life. So, again, I'll go back to my previous statement of...this is a win." He paused. "Now that we're caught up on everything, are we all good?"

Good? "Not even close," she managed. She kept staring at Chase. He was gazing at her with his golden eyes, so intent and focused, and an emotionless mask had slipped over his face. "Say something."

"I did," Dex pointed out. "I just told you the important pieces, and now we should really go someplace private so that you can tell me more about this intriguing scramble of yours. The others in this office don't quite have the clearance to hear what you've got to tell me so we need to separate from them." He put his hand on her shoulder.

She stiffened.

"Remove the damn hand," Chase gritted out.

"Oh, sorry, did you not get the memo?" Dex asked, all fake polite. He didn't remove his hand. "I don't need your services any longer. I can take over from here on out."

Ice poured through her veins. She'd thought Chase was perfect. One of the good guys. She should have known those didn't exist, at least, not for her. In some ways, she was too much like her mother. "You lied to me?"

A muscle flexed along Chase's jaw. "Let me explain."

"Yes or no." It was simple.

"I was doing my job."

His job. His job had been to find evidence against her. His job had been to lock her up.

Her gaze darted to the others in the room. They were all studying her with different expressions. Suspicion. Wariness. And the detective—that was sympathy in her eyes.

The sympathy hurt most of all because it told Vivian that this woman—this stranger she'd just met—felt sorry for her. The whole tangled mess was true. Chase wasn't the sexy neighbor who liked her, who wanted to date her, who was charming and easy going. He wasn't there to help. Or to protect.

He'd been sent to destroy her, and she'd been so desperate that she'd fallen right into his hands.

"We need to talk," Chase told her. "Alone."

Vivian shook her head. "No." He couldn't give yes or no answers, but she could.

"*Yes.*" A muscle jerked in his jaw. "I thought you were innocent. Hell, pretty much from the first moment I met you, I thought that. I didn't want to lock you up. I *did* want to help you."

"Ah, yeah..." For the first time, Merik spoke up.

Her head turned toward him. The friend who'd helped Chase move into his place, except he wasn't just a friend, was he? "You're another Wilde operative?"

"Guilty." A wince. "But, I swear, Chase has been spouting off about you being innocent. I could tell he didn't like the mission, but it had to be done. He didn't want to scare you, but he had a job to do."

Scare you. "What do you mean?"

"Uh…" Merik's stare snapped to Chase. "I'm talking about when he had to break the lock on your door that first day. It was just a trick, you know, to make you think that someone had been trying to get inside. The order came from—"

"Me," Dex cut in. "I make no apologies. You needed to know that you were in danger, and the broken lock clearly showed that—"

The last bit of hope that she'd been holding onto faded away. Once more, she found herself staring at the stranger called Chase. "You broke into my apartment."

His Adam's apple moved as he swallowed. "I broke the lock, but—"

She couldn't take any more. Pain was knifing through her. She could barely breathe. And the betrayal, God, it hurt. She broke away from Dex—he'd still had his hand wrapped around her shoulder—and she ran out of the office. She didn't know where she was going. She just could *not* stand there another moment.

She didn't want Chase to see her cry.

***

There had been tears in Vivian's eyes. *Tears.*

"Vivian!" Chase lunged after her.

But Dex grabbed him. "Yeah, that's gonna be a no." He shook his head. "Told you—quite clearly—you are off the case now. I'll go after her and—"

"*I'll* go after her," Layla Lopez shoved past them. "You idiots have done more than enough already."

But she'd had tears in her eyes. "Layla—"

She paused in the open doorway. "You hurt her. I get that you were doing your job. Trust me, I've been there myself. But she felt something for you. You might have been playing her, but to that woman, it was real. Now her pain is real. She doesn't want to talk to you right now. I can help."

You hurt her.

Layla hurried out of the office.

Chase stood there and felt like his own heart had been ripped right out of his chest. It should have been a job. It should have been easy.

Nothing had been easy. Not since he'd looked into a pair of deep green eyes and the whole world had seemed to stop spinning.

You might have been playing her, but to that woman, it was real. "No," he snapped.

"Uh, no what?" Dex wanted to know. "No to you being off the case? Because that's pretty much a non-negotiable point with me."

Chase's gaze cut to him. *Dex.* When the jerk had finally revealed his name, things had clicked for Chase. He knew he was dealing with Dexter Ryan, the guy Eric had told him about before. *Only Eric forgot to tell me what a giant asshat the man is.* "I'm not off the case."

Dex shrugged. "It's nothing personal, truly. If you must know, I recently had to deal with another guy who went off the deep end for a woman, and I've got to say, it was a very eye-opening experience for me." He wiggled his brows. "Hate to say it, but I'm seeing all kinds of warning signs with you. FYI, I am not here to pull you out when you decide to jump in that deep end."

Chase glared at the SOB. "You don't know me."

"Actually, I have extensively read your file." Dex crossed his arms over his chest. Nodded all sage-like. "When my bro Eric came up with the idea of using you, I had to make sure you were the right man for the job."

Eric coughed. "I am not your bro. We are barely friends."

"What?" Dex appeared offended. "Have you forgotten what I did for you? How I saved you?"

"I saved *you*."

A nod. "Because we're friends." The words were light, but his gray eyes were hard on Chase. "You're good at undercover work. Got a long history of success. I knew I could count on you to get close to Vivian, and apparently, you did."

"I'll agree to that," Merik mumbled.

Chase's fury sparked on him. "You didn't help *anything* tonight."

Merik's hands flew into the air. "I was *trying* to help! Look, the woman has to see that you were just doing your job. I *told* her that you didn't think she was guilty. You put your eyes on her, you tasted her brownies—"

"He tasted her what?" Dex asked.

"And you fell hard," Merik continued heatedly. "So hard that I was afraid you weren't seeing clearly. I thought she was tricking you. But then you made me start to wonder. Hell, maybe she *is* as good as she seems."

She is. Only I'm not good. I'm a bastard straight to my core.

"Let's all take a breath here," Dex said as he closed the door. Then put his back against it. His mocking mask had faded, and he suddenly seemed dead serious. "First, let's get this particular stuff straight. Vivian Wayne is not one hundred percent in the clear. I'd say it's looking more like sixty percent she's not guilty."

"Are you shitting me?" Chase snarled.

"I shit you not."

"She was almost killed tonight! Someone broke into her place—"

Dex pointed at him. "I thought that was you—"

"It damn well was not! I jacked up her lock, yes, but that same night, someone else came back. The only reason the joker didn't get inside was because I'd changed the lock. He had a key to her old lock. I chased him off."

"Chased him, but didn't catch him?"

"No," Chase barked. "I didn't." He huffed out a hard breath. "Then there was the elevator. It stopped when she was in it."

Merik moved closer. "It's an old elevator. Building manager said it needed updates. That incident could have been just chance. We don't know that was a deliberate attack on her."

Eric had closed in, too. His brows rose as he assessed Chase. "You think the elevator was deliberate, though."

"Damn straight, I do."

"Why?"

"Because it was what she feared." His hands had fisted.

"I don't follow," Eric said.

"She's afraid of the dark and of tight, enclosed spaces. That's not the kind of shit you find in a file. It's something you discover when you know someone personally." That was what made him so damn nervous. "The perp setting her up? I think he has to be someone she's personally involved with now—or someone she was involved with in the past. Someone who would have a key to her place. Someone who would know her secret fears. Someone who was fucking cold-blooded enough to use her fear against her."

"I'm that cold-blooded." Dex's lips pulled down. "So thanks for the intel. If it becomes necessary, I can put her in a situation where she will be—"

Chase lunged for him. He grabbed Dex's shirt and hauled him forward. "You will not fucking put her in any situation like that! You don't hurt her. You don't scare her. You don't do a damn thing to her, you understand me?"

Dex just stared back at him.

"You aren't hurting her," Chase growled.

Dex smiled. "I don't think you understand just who I am."

"Sure I do." Chase didn't let him go. "You're a prick who threatened Vivian. *My* Vivian. That shit won't happen. You won't hurt her. *No one* will hurt her, do you understand? Anyone who wants to go after her will have to deal with me."

"That's good to know," Dex informed him. "Thanks so much for updating me."

"You are a dick." Chase shoved him away.

Dex casually straightened his shirt. "You might be surprised to hear this, but I get that a lot."

CHAPTER TEN

"When a woman heads to the bathroom in an angry run, it's typically because she wants to be alone." Vivian gripped the edges of the sink and stared at her reflection, but she could still see Layla edging up behind her. "Do you know how many guards I had to pass to get in here?"

"Well, two guards are standing outside of the door," Layla replied. "So I'm guessing...more than two? Because I did catch sight of a third attempting to hide near the potted plant."

"I'm not going to try and escape from the building. I just want a few minutes of privacy." She sucked in a deep breath. "I'm not an idiot. I know I'm not safe on my own. And if I ran from this place, I'd probably either be killed by whoever is setting me up or I'd suddenly look guilty to that Dex jerk, and then he'd send his dogs after me."

Apparently, Chase was one of Dex's attack dogs.

"Who, exactly, is Dex?" Layla asked her. "When I was introduced to him—which happened just a few minutes before you arrived—I got some big spiel about mystery and clearance and he flashed an ID at me so fast I couldn't decipher anything about it."

"I think Dex is a man with a lot of power." The kind of power that could make people vanish.

"Yes, I do, too. And he must be legit because Eric swears that he's known the man for years. He told me that I could trust Dex."

Vivian met the other woman's gaze in the mirror. "I thought I could trust Chase."

"Yes." Soft. "I saw that. You still have tear tracks on your cheeks, by the way. You missed some on the left side."

She scrubbed at the left side of her face.

Layla smiled at her. "All gone."

Vivian slowly turned to face her. "Why are you here?"

"Because the women's restroom is a sacred environment and you didn't want some jerk following you in this place?"

Vivian swallowed.

"Or maybe I'm here because you looked like you could use a shoulder or a hand or, you know, just someone to hear you say that Chase Durant is an unbelievable asshole."

"Chase Durant is an unbelievable asshole."

Layla cocked her head. "You didn't say it like you meant it. Want to try again?"

It hurt to even say his name. "I trusted him."

"I could see that. It might have even been more, right? That was in your eyes. In your body language. When you first came into Eric's office, you were holding Chase's hand as if you'd never let go. Then, whenever you felt nervous or threatened, you moved closer to him." She blew out a long sigh. "Until you realized that he was one of the threats."

"I was a job."

"Yes."

Vivian's chest rose and fell with quick, jerky motions. "You're a police detective."

"Homicide. I'm the lead homicide detective in the area."

Her eyes flared. "I haven't killed anyone!"

"That is excellent to know, but I'm not at Wilde tonight because I think you killed someone. I'm here because Eric wanted someone he could trust to coordinate with the local authorities, and when word hit the radio about your car bomb in Marietta, he knew the PD had to be brought into the loop. If bombs were going to be exploding, if the case was that dangerous and lives were in jeopardy, cops needed to know." A shrug of one shoulder. "I have connections in Marietta. He wanted me to smooth things over."

Vivian wasn't sure that she should ask exactly what those connections were.

"But smoothing things over is very different from protecting civilians. If attacks on you are going to continue, and sorry, but we all suspect they will, then you have to be moved out of the area. Staying in a busy city isn't an option. That would put innocent lives at risk."

"I don't want anyone hurt because of me," Vivian told her quietly.

"I suspected as much. The plan is to relocate you, both for your protection and for the protection of any innocents who might get caught up in this madness and become collateral damage." Layla's gaze turned distant. "I've seen that too much. I'm done with innocents dying."

"I don't want anyone dying because of me. That's the *last* thing I want."

"Yes, I believe that's true, and that's why you'll agree to go to the safe house location, won't you? Because you want this matter sorted out. You want the perps caught. You want to clear your name. And you want to make sure that no one is caught in the crossfire."

Vivian's lashes flickered. "Do you think I'm innocent?"

"Honestly, I don't know enough to say. I do know that you have to be relocated immediately. You have to be secured."

"Secured." Vivian considered the word. "Is that your way of saying I have to be under guard?"

"It will be for your protection."

And it would be to make sure she didn't betray her country.

"If you're worried that you'll be forced to be with Chase again, don't be. Forget that concern. I'm sure Eric has other agents that he will assign for your protection. Dex has indicated that he wants you away from operatives at the CIA, so you will not be near any of them until this situation is contained. You'll be protected by Wilde."

By Wilde, but... "I...won't be with Chase?" Vivian's question slipped out.

Layla's gaze sharpened. "Do you want to be with him?"

"It wasn't real." She had to look past the pain that pierced her. Chase had lied. Yes. The betrayal cut deep. *Everything I was feeling...none of it was real.* Or, at least, it hadn't been real to him. "It's all chemicals. High levels of dopamine and norepinephrine. They're released when you're attracted to someone. They make you feel happy, and dopamine in particular is tricky because it's linked to our mate selection choices. You think it's emotion driving you, but it's not. It's all chemical—"

Layla lifted her hand. "This is an interesting walk that we're taking, but where are we going?"

Vivian pressed her lips together. Now wasn't the time to ramble, but, God, she was so nervous. And scared. Chase would understand her spouting about dopamine. He would—

She turned back to the mirror. Stared at her reflection.

Layla watched her, then said, "If you don't want Chase any longer, then consider your relationship with him over."

***

"You are in my fucking way," Chase snapped.

"Yeah, because I'm trying to stop you from running after the woman who was my chief suspect until about…oh…" Dex looked at his wrist. He wasn't even wearing a damn watch. "An hour ago."

"You mean when someone tried to kill her," Chase corrected. "She was your chief suspect until some bastard tried to blow her up!"

"Yes, that's what I mean. And, of course, there was the little matter of her rushing to you and trying to hire you." He glanced over at Merik. "Appreciate you calling in that news immediately. Helped to speed things up for me. Let me get my head in the right place for the investigation."

Chase whirled toward Merik. "You've been reporting straight to this asshole? Since when?"

Merik raised his hands and held them, palms out, toward Chase. "Look, man, I didn't want to do it." His guilt was plain to see.

"Merik used to work for me," Dex revealed. "I got Eric to put him on the case because I wanted fast communication. A direct line into the investigation. Don't be pissy, Chase. I don't have time for it."

Chase squeezed his eyes shut. "You just called me pissy."

"Yes, I did."

His eyes opened. He focused on Dex. "We need to be clear about a few things."

Dex's brow furrowed. "I thought we were clear. You got close to the target, you did your job—good show. Thanks for a performance well done. But, considering how I believe Vivian is currently feeling toward you, your services won't be needed any longer. Merik can take lead from here on out. She doesn't seem quite so hurt by him."

Hurt. "I never wanted to hurt her."

"The job is over." Dex's voice had turned flat. "I won't be telling you again."

"I'm not leaving her unprotected."

"Uh." Merik coughed. "I'm right here. I know how to keep a person safe. I will look after her, I promise."

I am not leaving her. "I'm not off this case until—"

"What?" Dex interrupted. "Until your boss tells you to walk? Yo, Eric. Tell him to walk."

Chase, Dex, and Merik all turned their focus on Eric.

Eric didn't say a word.

Dex frowned at him. "This is the part where you tell him to walk."

Eric shook his head. "I can't do that."

Dex opened his mouth. Closed it. Opened it again. "Excuse me? Don't you own this company?"

"Sure do." Eric nodded.

"Then you can tell your employee to step aside."

"No."

Dex's hands flew into the air. "Why the hell not?"

"Because from what I can understand, Chase was recently hired—him, specifically—by Vivian Wayne."

Damn, but sometimes... "I straight up love you, man," Chase said to Eric.

Eric shrugged. "My wife says I'm highly loveable, but Piper tends to be biased."

"Stop this crap!" Dex thundered. "Stop playing! This isn't—"

Eric's gaze had gone cold and hard. "I assure you, I don't play when people's lives are on the line. That's not who *I* am." His stare lingered on Dex as if to say...*but I think that's who you are.* "If Vivian Wayne specifically hired Chase, then she's the only who can tell him to walk. Not you. Not me. She picked him, then she can fire him."

Dex laughed. "Oh, is that all?" He was all smirky when he turned back to Chase. "Piece of cake. The next time she sees your ass, she's gonna tell you to get the hell away from her."

"Don't be so sure of that." *You don't know me, and you don't know her.* "Now, either get out of my way or I will move you out of my way."

"You and what army, tough guy?"

"I'm a fucking SEAL. I can handle you on my own." *But you already knew that if you read my files. Eric is right. You do play games.* Chase wasn't in the mood to play. "I won't be telling you again." Chase deliberately threw those words back at Dex. Then he added his own touch as he said, "I'll just knock your ass out and when you fall, my path will be cleared."

Dex grudgingly stepped to the side. "Got to say, with every moment that passes, you remind me more and more of a former agent I worked with. Same control issues. Same tendency to get *over* involved with the ladies in your lives."

"Fuck off." Chase grabbed for the door.

"Yep," Dex's mocking voice followed him. "I'm pretty sure that is exactly what Vivian will say the next time that she sees you."

***

"Is that what you want?" Layla asked when the silence stretched for too long. "You want your relationship with Chase to be over?"

"I don't have a relationship with Chase. He was lying to me and using me." Saying his name caused pain to knife through her. It was okay. She'd get used to the pain. She'd lived with pain before.

Layla's expression turned thoughtful. "When we were in Eric's office, I thought you said something about hiring him?"

She'd been so foolish. "I actually believed he could help me. I asked him to take my case. I wanted him to help me prove my innocence."

"From what Merik said, it appeared Chase *did* believe you were innocent."

"Even innocent people can get sent to jail."

Layla's lips tightened. "Not on my watch."

"Don't suppose you happen to perhaps have the name of an amazing lawyer in case all of this continues to spiral straight to hell and I wind up taking the fall for everything?"

"Is that what you think will happen?"

"I have no idea."

"Chase is a good man."

I asked him to be good. "I wouldn't know." Because she didn't know him. Her head lowered. She stared at the hands she'd twisted in front of her body.

"Ah, now, this is the part where I call bullshit. You have instincts about people. We all do. Chase's instincts told him you were innocent. What did your instincts tell you about him?"

That I'd finally found someone I could trust. That he was different.

He'd been different, all right.

"That's what I thought," Layla murmured. "He went against all the evidence he had, he went against orders, and he was trying to find proof that you were innocent. I know you're hurting, and I'm not saying this because he's my friend—but, he kinda is—Chase isn't the villain. He had a shit hand growing up, something that I don't think he talks about with anyone..."

Vivian's head whipped up. Chase had talked about his childhood with her. But had he been telling her the truth? Or more lies?

She wasn't sure what to believe any longer.

"He grew up hard and, as fast as he could, he left to join the Navy. Flash forward, and he's a SEAL. The man has a hero complex. He wants to make the world safe. He doesn't want to destroy innocent people. Something tells me that he definitely doesn't want to destroy you."

A hard fist banged into the door.

Vivian jumped and spun toward the door.

"I'm coming in there!" Chase yelled.

"It's a *ladies'* room!" Vivian shouted back as her hand flew to cover her racing heart.

"Like that's going to stop me! You can't hide from me, Vivian. We need to talk." Another pound. A stark pause. Then... "Are you decent?"

"No," she yelled back. "I'm running around naked. Do *not* come in."

Layla laughed. "That's gonna make him come running *in* here, you know."

The door inched open. "Vivian?" Chase's voice was way more subdued. "We have to talk. Now."

Layla cocked her head. "Want me to stay?"

"No. I'm good." Lies were getting easier.

The door opened fully. Chase stood there. He looked all tall and strong and sexy and...

Sad? For a moment, she could have sworn something like sadness filled his golden gaze, but then he blinked, and she couldn't read him at all.

Layla sauntered for the door. Just as she stood next to Chase, though, she paused, and glanced back at Vivian. "I get the same instinct about her that you do," she said to Chase.

His jaw tightened.

Layla waved toward Vivian. "Kendrick Shaw."

"I—what?" Her gaze had gotten stuck on Chase. Dammit.

"If the shit hits the fan, if you find yourself behind bars and needing the best attorney out there, Kendrick Shaw is your man. I'd trust him with my life."

Then she walked out.

Chase stared at Vivian for a moment, not moving.

I was starting to trust him with my life.

Finally, Chase spoke. "Yeah, so, the bathroom isn't quite the best place for a discussion. Want to come with me to my office? We can be alone there. You can scream at me in peace."

"I have no intention of screaming at you."

He scraped a hand over his face. "God, I wish you would."

She couldn't figure him out. "I don't understand. Why would you want me to scream?" Vivian didn't move from her position near the sink.

"Because then you'd get out some of the rage that you have to be feeling." He stalked toward her. "I know you're furious."

"I'm not." Was she supposed to be furious?

He gaped at her. Then his eyes closed. "Oh, hell. It's worse than rage." His eyes opened. "You're disappointed."

"I'm not disappointed." *Dumbass.* "I'm…" But she stopped. She'd already revealed more than enough to him. He had enough secrets. All that he'd get from her.

His fingers caught hers. Twined with them as he tugged her toward the door. "Come on. We're going to my office."

She dug in her heels. "You give orders a lot."

He stopped. Looked hard at her. "Can we *please* go to my office so that other people don't burst into the restroom while I am begging your forgiveness?"

"Is that what you intend to do?" Now she was genuinely curious. "Beg? Because I have a hard time imagining that scene."

"Come with me and find out what I'll do."

Not like she could stay in the bathroom forever. Not like she even wanted to do that. "You don't have to hold my hand. I assure you, I can manage to walk on my own."

His gaze fell to their joined fingers. "But I like holding your hand." He sounded uncertain. "I like touching you." His golden stare lifted and pinned her. "I like you."

"Stop lying to me." She didn't wait for him to lead. She yanked her hand away and hurried right past him. Threw open the door. Marched past the guards. *Wait. The guards*. She stopped near one of the guards. If they worked there, she figured they knew Chase so… "Which way to Chase's office?"

The guard pointed to the left.

"Thank you." She strode to the left. Turned down the hallway.

Chase jogged ahead of her and threw open the third door. She went in with her head up and her shoulders straight.

The door closed very softly behind her.

There was a framed photo on the wall. A group of guys with their arms slung around each other's shoulders. Sand was in the background. A desert? Chase's hair was shorter. A much more military-type cut.

"Some of my friends from back in the day," he explained when he caught her staring at the photo. "All retired now. Well, not so much retired as doing other business ventures."

Like he was.

There were no other pictures in the office. There was a baseball and a battered glove on his desk.

"I like to toss the ball around when I'm thinking." He'd obviously followed her gaze.

There were lots of papers. Files. Sticky notes.

"You want to sit down?" Chase offered.

She glanced back at the door. "Where are the others?"

"Probably getting ready to take you away."

Her gaze swung back to him. "Take me?"

"Dex wants to take you to a secure location."

"And I'll go." Because Layla had been right. She couldn't risk someone else getting hurt. "If the person after me is willing to plant a bomb—one that exploded on a city street—I have to leave. I can't have someone getting hurt during an attack that's aimed at me."

He exhaled. "I'm sorry I lied to you."

Her head tilted. "Is this the begging part? Because it doesn't sound like begging." She paced away from him. Fiddled with the baseball.

"I know you're mad."

"I'm not. We went over this. I'm—"

"Hurt."

Her shoulders stiffened.

"You think I don't see the pain in your eyes? Baby, I do."

"Don't."

"Don't what?"

"Don't use endearments. Don't pretend. You had to get close to me because you were undercover. You're not undercover any longer." She spun the ball, sliding it around on his desk. "You don't need to keep pretending with me."

The floor creaked as he moved closer to her. "You think I was pretending to want you?"

She was afraid that he had been. "Just like you were pretending to be my new neighbor. Only I guess being a neighbor wasn't good enough, so you stepped into the role of wanna-be boyfriend."

"There's fucking nothing wanna-be about it."

She stopped spinning the ball. "Excuse me?"

His hand curled over hers. He was right behind her. He'd moved those last few feet silently, and now he surrounded her. She could feel his heat, his strength, and her whole body tensed.

"I wasn't faking," he growled. His breath blew lightly over her neck. "I saw you, and I wanted you."

"Sure. You took one look at me when you were fake moving into my apartment building, and then you instantly—"

"Wanted you in my bed?" Chase finished. "Hell, yes, I did."

"Let go of my hand."

He let go.

She turned toward him. He hadn't moved back. Their bodies brushed.

"The job was in the way," he said. "I wanted you, but I was lying to you. That meant I was a Grade A bastard."

"You are a Grade A bastard." Her quick agreement.

"I am sorry." He said each word clearly, as if he wanted to be sure she understood. "Hurting you wasn't something I wanted. The more time I spent with you, hell, the more I *liked* you."

Her heart ached. "I'm supposed to believe that?"

"Yes."

"Why?"

"*Why?*"

"How do I know you're not lying to me right now? After I left Eric's office, how do I know you and your buddies didn't immediately come up with a new plan? Maybe the new plan involves you continuing to try and seduce me. Maybe it involves—"

"I didn't want to take you to bed while I was lying to you. I wanted you like mad, wanted you more than I'd ever wanted anyone else, but I was holding onto my control." His breath sawed in and out. "Because when I did get you in my bed, I didn't want lies between us. I wanted nothing between us."

CHAPTER ELEVEN

Her gorgeous eyes widened, then narrowed. Or, rather, her eyes turned into tiny, angry green slits.

Shit. He'd said the wrong thing. Made the situation way worse. Just when he'd thought that wasn't even possible.

"I don't remember inviting you into my bed." Her voice was incredibly crisp and cold. Cold enough to ice a man.

"You didn't," Chase muttered.

"Then I don't see the problem."

"I'm the problem. I want you too much."

Vivian looked away.

"You think I was faking my response to you? Ba—um, Vivian," he corrected quickly because he was trying hard not to piss her off. "I'm a good actor, but not that good. When I was in the elevator with you—"

"*OhmyGod.*" She seemed to go pale. Her shoulders hunched.

"What is it?"

Her lower lip trembled as she hauled her gaze back to him. "Did you do it?"

He wasn't following. "Do what?"

"Did you sabotage the elevator so that it would stop?" Her hand gestured to the stack of files on his desk. "Was that fact in there somewhere? Did you read a tidbit about me that told you when I was six years old my father tried to use me on one of his jobs? Only when a security guard came by, my dad told me not to make a sound and he *left* me there." Her breath heaved as her fingers moved up to smooth across the tiny scar that cut across her left eyebrow. "Did you know that? Did you set up the scene in the elevator so I'd be terrified and need you?"

She hated him. Fucking hated him. He could see it now. If she thought… "No." Chase cleared his throat. "I get that you don't have a lot of cause to believe what I tell you, but I swear, I didn't sabotage the elevator. I didn't know anything about your fear of the dark and enclosed spaces. I wouldn't hurt you that way."

"But you broke into my apartment—"

"I made it look like there had been a break-in so that you would need me to…" He stopped. "Fucking semantics. Yes. I'm sorry. I was doing a job. It doesn't make what I did right. Doesn't mean you can hate me less. I did it." He'd learned early on that you took responsibility for your actions. His father hadn't. Everything had always been someone else's fault.

The fact that Vivian was staring at him as if he was a stranger?

That's on me. "I can show you who I really am."

Her hair slid over her shoulder. "What?"

"I'm not your enemy. That's not who I ever want to be. If you believe nothing else about me, know this—"

A hard knock sounded at the door. "Your time is up, Durant!" Dex called. "You're done. We need to move!"

Chase swore. Leave it to that prick to interrupt. "I'm not done!" Chase yelled back.

Vivian's gaze flickered to the door. "What does he mean that your time is up?"

"He wants you moved to a new location."

"Yes, I got that before, but—"

"I'm sure he wants to question you. The bastard probably also wants to use you to catch the bad guy."

A slow nod. "I figured all of that." Her breath came faster. "But why is he saying *you're* done?" Her gaze was steady on his.

"Because Dex figures you don't want me around you any longer. He thinks you'll feel better with another agent."

She seemed to absorb his words. "With one who hasn't lied to me."

"Something like that." Dex pounded again. *Such. A. Prick.* "If he had his way, I'd already be away from you."

"But you're not away from me."

He was standing right in front of her. Her delicious vanilla scent surrounded him, and if he leaned forward, he could brush his lips over hers. "No. When Dex tried to have me removed, Eric backed me up. Said that I wouldn't leave the case, not until *you* fire me."

"*What?*"

"You hired me, remember? Came to my door. Told me you were in trouble. I took the job you offered. So it doesn't matter what Dex says. I don't give a shit if he has the whole CIA behind him. *You* are my client. Eric backs that. I stay with you until you tell me to go."

The door swung open.

"I need a freaking lock on that door," Chase muttered as he turned to glare at Dex. "It would keep the trouble out."

Dex curled his fingers around the edge of the door. "You had five minutes. Time is up."

"We didn't set a damn time limit!"

"No?" Dex appeared confused. "Oh, right. I set it. Mentally. Right after you told me to 'fuck off' and you left. And that brings me to my next point. Ms. Wayne, I understand you are probably quite tired of Chase at this juncture. There are other agents who can now step in to provide for your—"

"No."

Chase whipped his stare back to her. "No?"

"No?" Dex repeated. "Oh, wait, you must not have understood me. I said you don't have to stay with Chase. Or, rather, he doesn't have to stay with you. Actually, in light of the, uh, shall we say...relationship issues...that the two of you have, it's for the best if—"

"Why are you trying to convince me that you should stay with me?" Vivian asked Chase. Her gaze was solemn, her expression torn.

"Because I need to know you're safe." Absolute truth. "Because I'm a damn good agent, though you might not believe that. I will do *anything* to get the job done."

Her thick lashes swept down. "That I believe."

Hell. He'd done it again. Made it worse. "I'll do anything because I believe you are innocent."

Her lashes lifted.

"I'm not lying to you. The more I learned about you, the less the image of you as a criminal mastermind worked for me."

"I could be a criminal mastermind," she mumbled.

"Yes, you could, but you aren't. Because you don't want to wind up like your dad."

She swallowed. "I shouldn't have given you secrets. And he *wasn't* a mastermind—"

"I'm not talking about your biological father, Viv." He'd said this part so quietly. Only for her to hear.

Her eyes widened. "He is not my father." Her voice was just as low as his had been, but pain was there. Thickening her voice. "And he is not part of my life any longer."

"*Still waiting over here.*" Dex's voice was loud while Chase and Vivian's had been soft. "Got things to do. Traitors to catch. I can't just stand in doorways all night."

Vivian's attention darted to him. "What is the plan?"

"My plan? Stage one is to question you. To get every detail from you that I can. Thought you already knew that."

"I mean, how are you going to catch the bad guy?"

"Well, I figure as soon as he realizes that you scrambled the ever-so-important files, he'll be coming after you. He, or sorry, they—I'm not quite sure how many people we are up against yet—will need you. When the perps come after you, I'll be waiting. With Wilde backup, of course, since I'm not exactly sure who I can trust from the CIA branch down here. We'll spring into action. The case will end. Life will resume. You'll write me a thank you card."

Vivian nibbled on her lower lip. "Who will be your Wilde backup?

"Not Chase, so you can stop worrying about that."

Chase took a fast step toward him. "You are not taking her away from me."

"Sure I am. Watch me." He extended his hand toward Vivian. "This chat has been fun, but Vivian, we need to go. Now. I'm sure you were tailed to this location, and since I don't control this building's security, I don't feel the safest here. Let's get moving."

She slipped around Chase.

Shit. She was going with Dex. Chase had burned his bridges with her and— "Don't," the word tore from him.

Vivian looked back.

It wouldn't do any good. It had never done any good. She was going to walk away, but— "Don't leave me."

She was important. He couldn't let her walk away. Couldn't let her face the threats out there without him.

Her lashes flickered.

"I know you're hurt." Not angry, not disappointed, but fucking hurt. He'd hurt her. And if he'd hurt her, then that meant she'd cared. You didn't get hurt when you didn't care. Dammit.

He had screwed up so badly with her. "It won't happen again."

"What won't?" Vivian asked. Her voice was so low and husky.

"I won't hurt you. Not ever the hell again. Protecting you is my priority." Even protecting her from himself. "I'm good at my job, Viv. I can protect you. You can absolutely count on me to do that."

"She's walking away, man," Dex informed him with a long exhale. "That means that even though she may have tried to hire you earlier, she is most definitely firing you now." No small amount of satisfaction was in Dex's voice as he added, "I think that means she is clearly telling you to fuck off—"

"You won't lie to me?" Vivian asked Chase as she broke through Dex's cocky words.

Chase felt his heart stop. "No. I won't lie to you. Not ever again."

"You won't pretend to be someone you're not?"

"What you see will be exactly what you get. Though I can't promise that you'll always like what you see." Full disclosure. *I am an asshole.*

"Uh, let's go." Dex didn't seem so satisfied any longer. "Obviously, I'm not liking what I'm seeing."

Vivian nodded. "Let's go." She was staring straight at Chase when she said those ever-so-important words.

Dex turned away.

Chase hurried toward Vivian.

"Whoa!" Dex whirled back around. "What are you doing?"

"Going," Chase replied. He was at Vivian's side. "She wants me to come with her. So, no, I'm not fired. I'm in for the duration." *Deal with that shit.*

Dex studied him. "We need to talk."

Chase shrugged. "Talk."

"Alone." Once more, Dex turned away. He moved as if he expected Chase to follow—and to leave Vivian behind.

That shit is not happening. "Nope."

And Dex whirled again. "What?"

"I'm working for her. That means I'm not leaving her shut out. Say whatever shit you've got to say, and say it in front of Vivian."

Dex gave him a cold smile. "Fine." His gaze flickered to Vivian, then came back to Chase. "Emotions screw up cases. You fucking got too close on this one. You became your cover, and now you're falling for her." He jerked his thumb toward Vivian. "She's falling for you because you got to her, and the two of you can't see past the lust that's burning between you. That shit is dangerous. I don't need your BS getting in my way while I'm damn well trying to save the lives of a whole lot of good people."

"I can do my job, no matter what." Chase didn't deny falling for Vivian. Because, he had. Fast and hard. But because he'd fallen for her, that didn't mean he couldn't do his job. Just the damn opposite. It meant he'd protect her with his life. There was no way he'd let anyone get to her. "I've got this under control."

"You'd better have. Or she'll pay the price."

CHAPTER TWELVE

"Dex was wrong." Vivian stared out at the lake. The moonlight glistened off the surface. She didn't know what time it was. Hours had passed since the bomb. Dex had grilled her, over and over again, and she'd been taken to a new, supposedly safer location.

They'd left the city. Driven for at least an hour and wound up at a lake-side cottage. The lake seemed to stretch for miles and miles, its dark surface ever so still.

"The guy is a piece of work," Chase said. "But what is it that you think he's wrong about?"

She turned away from the water. Faced him. Chase was on the couch, his body seemingly relaxed, but his gaze was locked straight on her. She was barely standing upright as weariness pulled at her, but there was no sign of fatigue on his face. He was just watching her with that careful, alert stare of his. "He's wrong about you falling for me. About me falling for you."

Chase gave a slow nod. "Huh." His head tilted. "You didn't fall for me."

Now Vivian wrapped her arms around her stomach. "And you didn't fall for me."

"No, I did."

Her body jolted. "What?"

He rose, slowly uncurling his body. "I told you already, I didn't fake anything I felt for you." He took careful steps toward her. "When I touched you, when I kissed you, everything I felt was absolutely, one hundred percent real." He stopped just in front of her. "What about you?"

Her throat had gone dry. "What about me?"

"When I kissed you, how did you feel?"

Like I had never wanted anyone more. Her lips pressed together.

"Don't want to answer? Okay, let's try a different question."

"I've already answered a whole lot of questions tonight." He'd been there for every single one. Listening. Watching. Waiting. "I should go to sleep."

"Answer just one more?"

She nodded.

"Why did you let me stay with you?"

Don't leave me. He'd said those words to her, and they had pierced right through the pain that she'd felt. They'd seemed real. Raw. "Because I wanted you to stay."

"That's not telling me why."

"Because…I feel safer when you're near. Because I do know that you can still do the job. I don't doubt that at all. If anything, I've seen firsthand that you will go to any lengths in order to complete a mission. Means I felt hurt as hell," her words came faster, "but it also means I've seen you in action. I don't have Dex's worries. I don't think you'll be magically blinded by me and not able to catch bad guys. Controlled chaos, I think that's what you said you had before? That you liked it? But I think you were wrong. I don't think there is any chaos in your life. I think everything is carefully controlled. Others don't see it." She brushed past him. "Good night."

"Others don't see it because they don't see me. You do."

She stiffened.

"Dex was right about one thing. I do want you. Might as well clear the air and get that out in the open. I want you more than I've ever wanted anyone, and that desire isn't going away."

She looked back.

"I'm also not pushing. You want me to be hands off, I'm hands off." His hands were currently fisted at his sides. "But I'm not lying to you. I mean that. Not ever again. Ask me anything, and I'll give you the cold, hard truth."

"Fine. Do you think the person who set the bomb will try to kill me again?"

"Yes."

Well, that response was not reassuring. Maybe a lie would have been better.

"Or, rather, he'll try until the perp realizes that he needs you. As soon as that happens, as soon as the scramble is detected, you'll be worth more alive than dead."

"Then the bad guys will try to take me?"

"They *won't* get you. I'm stationed in the house with you. Merik is outside. Two other Wilde agents are on the perimeter. The agents will rotate on watch. You're good here. You're safe."

Wilde agents. Because Dex didn't want others from the CIA getting pulled into the case. *Because he's trying to keep this mess quiet.* And because she knew he didn't trust the others at her branch. But... "Why didn't Dex bring in CIA operatives from other locations? I mean, I get why he doesn't want the people I worked with on the case but surely there are other CIA operatives out there that he trusts?"

"Dex is playing by his own rules on this one, and I think he's keeping information close to the vest. He's hunting for a traitor—"

He thought I was the traitor.

"And until he finds out just how far this mess goes, he told Eric it was better to have a team with no current ties to the CIA. Not the first time that Uncle Sam has come to Wilde for help. Hell, it happens far more than you'd suspect. When the government agencies are investigating their own people, outsiders often do the best work. We don't exactly have the same conflicts of interest."

She absorbed the information.

"Your fingers are trembling," he noted softly.

She looked down. They were. She balled them into fists.

"Adrenaline still pounding through you?"

Yes. "This was the first time that someone tried to kill me."

"The first time is a bitch."

Her heart lurched as she turned to fully face him. "Just how many times have people tried to kill you?"

He gave her a slow smile. One that had her heart doing that lurch thing again. "Do you mean this week?" Chase asked.

"What?"

"Kidding." His smile lingered a moment before it fell away. "I've had more than my share of brushes with death. First in battle, then at Wilde."

That news didn't make her feel better. Not in any way. In fact, it just made her skin feel icy.

"So, speaking from personal experience, adrenaline rushes are hard as hell to come down from. If there is anything I can do to help, I'm here."

Once more, Vivian turned away and shuffled forward. She unclenched her hands. Wiggled her fingers.

"Viv?"

"Adrenaline rushes start in the amygdala," she told him as she wiggled her fingers again.

He laughed.

The response was so surprising that she turned back. "What?"

"I love it when you do that."

She hadn't done anything.

But *he* was stalking toward her. And he was smiling at her—tenderly.

She felt the power of his smile in every cell of her body. *Dangerous.* "What is it that you love?" Vivian asked.

"When you give me your facts. It's sexy as hell."

Facts were sexy? Since when?

"No, correction, *you* are sexy." His gaze was on her mouth. "How do I get back?"

"Get back where?" She was so confused.

"In your good graces. Tell me what I have to do in order to win you back."

"I'm not a prize to be won." Her spine straightened. "Is that how you think of me?"

"No." His gaze lifted. "I don't."

"Then how do you think of me?"

"As someone who changed my world."

That was unexpected. And his stare was *hot*. "You want in my good graces?" Her body felt tense. Tight. "Then catch the bad guy. Clear my name. *Then* we'll talk about good graces."

"Consider it done."

She couldn't stand there with him so close, not without—dang it, she was already leaning toward him. He'd lied to her, hurt her, and she was still drawn to him. Still pulled to him.

What was wrong with her?

Why couldn't she control herself better with him?

Before she could give in to the need that swirled in her, Vivian whirled away and hurried to the room that she'd been given.

***

"Got to ask, buddy, just how much does she hate you?" Merik asked conversationally. He'd come to check in a few moments before.

"Trying to figure that out." Chase rolled back his shoulders as he attempted to push away the tension that had gathered there.

"This is what happens when you lust after a target." Merik nodded knowingly. "Bad things."

Chase stared at him. "Is the stuff you're saying to me supposed to be helpful?"

A shrug. "It is lust, man, isn't it? I mean, you're not like, losing your heart or something?" He laughed, nervously. "God, I can't believe I just said that."

"I can't believe you just said that, either." He glanced over at the clock. "I'm crashing. You trading out with fresh agents for the rest of the night?"

"Yeah, yeah, I got a cabin across the lake. We'll be taking turns on guard duty."

Grunting, Chase headed for the door. "Then I'll walk you out. I want to secure the cabin before I turn in."

Merik gave him a worried look.

"What?"

"You didn't answer me. Is it lust? Or is it more?"

"Get your ass out the door."

"That's still not an answer."

"That's still all you're getting. It's late as hell, and I need to sleep. Go."

"Fine, but if something happens, you know I'll be here in a flash. Always have your partner's back. That's the Wilde motto." He gave a little salute. "See you soon."

Chase locked up after him and set the security system. Then he stood in the middle of the cabin, and his gaze drifted around almost aimlessly. He hadn't been lying to Vivian when he'd talked about adrenaline rushes. They were hell to handle. Chase was still riding out his own wave, though he'd tried hard to act as if he was in control when he was around Vivian.

Control? With her?

Ha. Not likely.

In his mind, he kept hearing the roar of the explosion. If he hadn't stopped her, if he'd been a few moments slower in that elevator or getting out of the lobby, he would *not* have gotten to her in time.

She would have died. He would have gotten to that street and just seen the wreckage. Fire. Vivian would have been gone.

He strode down the hallway toward his room. Maybe it wasn't just adrenaline fueling him. Maybe it was cold, hard fear. But he didn't experience fear a lot, so he wasn't used to the feeling.

Something happening to Vivian? That idea terrified him.

Because she mattered.

He wasn't exactly sure when it had happened. When she'd stopped being a target and become so much more. Maybe it had been when she'd brought him brownies and given him that shy smile? Or maybe it had been the first time he'd heard her rattle off one of her facts for him? When she'd held him in the elevator and battled her own fear?

Chase didn't know. And maybe the *when* wasn't important. She was important, and he would do everything in his power to protect her. This wasn't about the case. Not about the CIA. Not about Wilde. For him, it was about protecting an innocent woman who'd been pulled into a nightmare. From the beginning, his instincts had been screaming that she couldn't be guilty.

He pushed open the door to his room. Vivian was too good, too innocent for something like—

Holy fuck, she was naked in his bedroom. He locked down his body—well, not his dick because that sprang to full, eager attention—but Chase did *not* step forward. If he stepped forward, he'd pounce. He'd take.

He'd devour.

"I was thinking that maybe we should get this out of the way," Vivian said with only a small quiver in her voice. "And then we will both feel better."

CHAPTER THIRTEEN

He wasn't saying anything.

Mistake. This is a major mistake.

Vivian reached for the bed sheet. Pulled it around her body. Chase stood in the doorway like a statue, and he still hadn't said a word. Her confidence plummeted. "I thought you wanted me."

"You're naked."

Well, she *had* been naked. Now she was clutching the sheet in front of her because the silence had stretched too long, and the scene had played out way differently in her head.

"Why are you naked in *my* room, Vivian?"

"I thought it was obvious." As obvious as possible. "I'm here to have sex with you." That sounded clinical and cold, but cold was the last thing she felt. That adrenaline rush he'd talked about? After she'd left him, it had only seemed to get worse. Her whole body was tight and aching and, crap, it wasn't just about adrenaline. She knew that. It was about fear. About being scared that she would be killed. It was about wanting to live. It was about wanting to grab tight to every moment.

No, stop it. It's about him. "Sex is a good way to deal with an adrenaline high." She had zero scientific evidence to back up that claim. She just hoped the statement sounded good when she said it.

His brows shot up. "So you want to use me in order to come down from your high?"

Use him? Vivian faltered. "No, that's not what I meant—"

"Fair enough." He strode across the room. Stopped when he was right in front of her. How was it that she could forget just how big he was? How tall and wide in his shoulders? Chase had a raw power that pulled and pulled at her each time he was near.

"You can use me," he said as he stared down into her eyes. "Use me all that you want." His head lowered.

Her hand rose and pressed to his chest. "No."

Chase stopped. "Change your mind already?" A jerky nod. "Got it." He backed away.

"No."

His head cocked.

"I'm not using you. I'm lying." She bit her lower lip. Everything was so confusing. "I don't know what I'm doing."

"I can clear that up for you. You're standing naked in my—"

"I don't know what I'm doing with *you*. I don't know why I feel this way about you."

"What way?"

Vivian struggled to find words. "Even when I'm hurt, even knowing that you lied, I still want you." More than she'd wanted anyone else. "And maybe, if we have sex, then—"

Chase held up one hand. "Okay. Gonna stop you there." His voice was low. Deep. Almost guttural. "If this is the part where you say that you think if we have sex, we get all that tension out of the way, and then things can go back to normal between us—if you're saying that, you're dead wrong."

Her throat dried even more as she clutched the sheet tighter. "I am?"

"First, there is no normal between us. Never was. I lied to you, and I fucking hate that."

She swallowed the lump in her throat.

"Second, it's not like I'll have sex with you and not want you again. And again. And again." He shrugged. "The way I figure it, I'll have you once, and then get addicted."

That wasn't the experience she'd had in the past. Sex had been good, sure, but it had hardly been anything that she'd call addictive. None of her previous lovers had ever used the word addictive when describing what they'd done. A woman would remember that particular term.

"You want me to help you?" Chase rumbled. "You want me to get you past the rush you feel? You want me to give you so much pleasure you scream?"

She couldn't even talk.

He nodded. "I can do that. I can do all of that without having sex with you. Because we cross *that* line, and there will be no going back for me. I told you, I won't lie again. You need to know that I'm a possessive bastard. Especially where you are concerned. If I have you, I won't be letting go. So before you offer me what I want most, you damn well need to consider what will happen next."

Her breath choked out. "I want you."

A muscle flexed along his jaw.

"I have since we first met. This..." One hand fluttered back and forth between them. "It gets worse the longer I'm with you."

"Worse?" Both of his brows kicked up.

"Stronger. Hotter." She licked her lower lip as her stare cut away from him. "I know I'm not sounding rational. I know I should be running from you, not to you—"

"That's where you are wrong." His voice was low and hard. "You should always run to me. Count *on* me. I will give you whatever you need. Always."

Her heart wouldn't stop racing. "Right now, I need you." As she'd come into his room, as she'd nervously shed her clothes, she'd been thinking...

Just sex. It's just sex. If they got this out of the way, then the tension wouldn't be between them any longer. If they got this out of the way—

He closed the space between them. "It's not about getting it out of the way."

Had she spoken out loud? Horrified, her gaze flew to his. She expected to see anger flashing in his eyes, but...

Only tenderness was in his gaze. "Sex with you is about getting what I want most. Getting it out of the way?" He shook his head. "Hell, no, baby, that's not the way it will go. Not at all."

She wasn't thinking clearly. "I shouldn't have come here." He'd lied to her. Hurt her. *And* saved her life. She kept returning to that part. He had *saved* her. If Chase hadn't run in front of her car—literally, thrown himself in front of her vehicle—she'd be dead.

He'd lied, yes, but...

His lies had saved her. And, God, even she knew the evidence against her looked bad. But Chase was fighting to prove she was innocent. Why? "Why do you care so much?"

His eyes narrowed.

"About what happens to me," she added quickly. "Why didn't you want another agent taking over? Why didn't you walk away? You didn't have to stay with me."

"Yes, I did." His hand rose. His fingers skimmed lightly over her shoulder, sending a shiver skating through her body. "I don't walk away from people who matter to me."

"I'm a target. I don't—"

He kissed her. Her lips were open, and his mouth met hers in a hot, drugging kiss. The kind of kiss that channeled the adrenaline and fear pumping through her. The kind of kiss that made her want to stop thinking. Stop all of the fearful worrying and just *feel*. To simply get lost in him and never, ever let go.

Her hands rose to grab onto his shoulders. His body crowded closer to hers, and the sheet became trapped between them. She didn't care about the sheet. It could fall. She wanted to keep kissing him. To keep feeling. To keep—

"You're not a target. You're my mission. *Mine*," he growled against her mouth. "You always have been."

Then he was lifting her up. Holding her easily. Carrying her a few feet over to the bed and the sheet slipped away from her body. He lowered her onto the bed. Her breaths came quickly as she stared up at him.

"If we go too far, you stop me," he said, as he stared down at her. "All I want to do is give you pleasure. I'm not..." He shook his head. "God, you are fucking gorgeous." He put a knee on the bed. Leaned forward. Trailed his fingers up her side and slowly moved to the tip of one breast.

She bit her lip to hold back a moan.

"So pretty. Can I taste?"

"Yes." Speech was getting hard. Way hard.

His head lowered. His lips curled around her nipple, and she forgot about speech. Her head tipped back against the bedding as need tore through her. His lips and mouth teased her nipple. Licking, kissing, sucking, and her hips jerked upward in instinctive response. She'd never felt like her breasts were particularly sensitive before, but now...

OhmyGod.

He kissed a path to her other breast, and her hands flew out to fist around—she had no idea what. The fitted sheet? A comforter? Didn't matter. He was licking her. Sucking her. And she could feel the faint edge of his teeth in a sensual bite.

Once more, her hips surged up. This time, she hit his jeans. His hips. He'd positioned his body between her legs as they splayed over the edge of the bed, and when her hips arched up, she was riding against him. Need pumped through her. She couldn't hold on to control any longer. She was past that point. Fear, adrenaline, lust—

everything tangled through her. Everything was centered on him. Everything was about—

Chase.

His head lifted. "Vanilla…my favorite flavor."

What?

"Got to taste more."

He was kissing a path down her stomach. Her heaving breaths came even faster. She knew what he was going to do. She *wanted* him to do it. She was desperate to feel his fingers and his mouth.

His fingers touched her sex. Slid between the folds. Stroked her ever so carefully as he moved back, crouching beside the bed.

"Beautiful," he breathed. Then Chase surged forward. He put his mouth on her. Licked and thrust his tongue against her—*into* her—even as his fingers kept working her. The bedding fisted in her hands as her head thrashed because *nothing* had ever felt this good. She could feel her climax thundering toward her, and it had built so fast, faster than it had ever had before.

"*Chase!*" Vivian screamed his name.

He wasn't done. Contractions of pleasure pulsed through her sex, through her entire body, but he wasn't done. If anything, he seemed to grow wilder. His mouth rougher. He kept licking and tasting, and his fingers were stroking her at the same time and she couldn't come down from that first orgasm because—was she coming again? *Yes.*

A second wave hit her, even harder than the first. She couldn't cry out his name this time. She could barely catch a breath. Pleasure didn't pulse through her. It pounded on a wave that seemed to wreck her. Her eyes squeezed shut, her body tightened, and the pleasure blasted through her cells.

Best orgasm of my life.

She wasn't even sure how long it lasted. Time kind of floated as pleasure reigned. When her heart finally stopped thundering and her breath slowed to less desperate pants, Vivian cracked open her eyes.

He was still crouched between her legs. Only his gaze was on her face now and he looked savage. Feral. Wild.

This wasn't the easy-going guy she'd met at her apartment building. That guy had been an illusion. Never real at all. The man she was staring at right now—the dangerous predator who looked at her as if he couldn't wait to pounce—this was the real man. She was seeing him clearly.

And I want him even more than I wanted the handsome, smiling stranger I met in my hallway.

"Have I ever told you..." His voice was a rumble. It pierced right to her core as he continued, "that you taste just like my favorite treat?"

"I..." She couldn't think of what to say.

"When I was a kid, my dad would sometimes take me to the ice cream shop on the corner. On one of the days when he wasn't drunk off his ass."

Her heart squeezed. She pushed up onto her elbows. "Chase—"

"Vanilla ice cream. The best in the whole world to me. Nothing tastes as good." That molten stare of his dropped to her exposed sex. "No, scratch that. You're better. *You're* my new favorite treat."

The way he was looking at her...

"I could eat you right up," he added roughly.

Um, he just had.

He leaned forward. Her body quivered.

But then he rose. Stepped back. "I'm not always a selfish bastard."

She didn't remember calling him one.

"I can prove myself to you. I'm not the monster you think."

Vivian shook her head. She hadn't thought he was a monster.

"I can give. And not take." He carefully positioned her on the bed. Moved her tenderly. Then pulled the covers up around her. "See?" His voice was tight. Hard. "This is me not taking. This is me not being a selfish prick." He turned away.

He was *walking* away.

"Chase?"

"I hope you can sleep better now, Viv. But if you need me, I'll be right down the hall." A rough laugh escaped him. "Though I'll probably be in an ice-cold shower for a bit. *Then* I'll be in the room down to the right."

The room down to the right. That had been the room she'd been assigned when they'd arrived. Merik had taken her bags in there for her. Wait, Chase was going to that room? And leaving her in his bed? "Eighty percent of women have faked orgasms."

He froze. "If you were faking, that was a fucking world-class performance."

"No, I wasn't faking, God, no, that was the best orgasm—orgasms—that I've ever had." Her words rushed out. She was nervous and *that* was why she'd spouted her random orgasm stat. Such the wrong time to share that particular fact.

Chase glanced back at her. "The best?" He smiled. Winked. "And here we are, just getting started."

"Then why are you leaving?"

His eyelashes flickered. "Because you need time. Because you're about to crash. And when you wake up in a few hours and your head is clear and you remember all that I've done, I don't want you to hate giving yourself to me." His jaw tightened. "I don't want you to hate me."

She didn't think she could hate him. "You don't have to leave."

"I do." He nodded. "Because I can't be this close to you, I can't stay in the same bed with you, and keep my control." His voice held a ragged edge. "Trust me, it's barely hanging on as it is. You tasted like my best dream, and I just want more. I want *everything,* and until you're ready to give me that, I need to go down the hallway. I need to take that icy shower. And I need to talk to you in a few hours." His hand moved toward the light switch. Paused. "Do you want me to leave the light on? I know you don't like the dark."

Some of the tension left her body. "The light is on in the bathroom. That will be enough for me." It was kind of him to remember her fear. Kind of him to make sure she was all right. Thoughtful. "I can't quite figure you out."

"I am a man of mystery."

He was leaving. She wanted him to stay.

Chase turned off the light to the bedroom. Pulled the door closed behind him.

"Good night, Chase," Vivian whispered.

***

A cold shower wasn't going to cut it. He needed freaking *ice water* in order to get the job done. But, since he didn't have that on hand, Chase marched through the dark bedroom and went straight for the shower. He flipped on the cold water and let it pound down into the tub.

She tasted better than anything in the world. When she came for me, when she called out my name, no one has ever been so sexy.

His dick was rock hard. All he wanted was to turn around and march right back to the other bedroom. Open the door. Climb into bed with her.

And take and take and take.

Because he was such a greedy bastard.

But he wanted her to see him as more.

She's been through hell. She's going to collapse. Vivian needed sleep. Rest. She didn't need him fucking her for hours, though that was certainly what he wanted.

Chase yanked off his shirt. Kicked away his shoes. Ditched the last of his clothes. Then he stepped under the cold spray of water.

Didn't exactly help. Because when he closed his eyes underneath that spray...

He only saw her.

***

Chase wrapped the towel around his body. He'd stayed in the blasting water for almost ten minutes. He was a little better. Maybe. He flipped off the bathroom light and strode back into the darkened bedroom. He had strong night vision, so the darkness didn't bother him. Never had.

But Vivian doesn't like it. He didn't want her afraid in the dark so he'd tried to make sure she had everything she needed in the other room—

Movement. From the corner of his eye, he saw a shadow shift near the window.

Chase immediately stilled. What in the hell? Was one of the guards checking the perimeter? Odd. Getting this close to the safe house wasn't standard procedure.

The window began to open. *What. The. Hell?*

The window rose, but there was no shrieking alarm. There should have been a shrieking alarm. The cabin was wired, typical for a safe house that belonged to the Wilde company. Eric Wilde designed the security systems, so they were all top-notch. And a window on the ground floor, being opened by an intruder? Hell, yes, the alarm should have been shrieking. It wasn't.

Bad sign.

The shadow eased into the room. Chase could tell the figure had something in his hands as he turned toward the bed.

That's far enough, asshole.

Chase rushed him, hard and fast. He drove his shoulder into the bastard and sent him staggering onto the floor. The man came up instantly, and his arm flew toward Chase.

Knife.

Chase jumped back and avoided the swing of the blade. Then he ducked low and plowed his fist right into the SOB's stomach. Chase heard the other man grunt even as the jerk tried to slice him again.

Chase caught his attacker's wrist. Twisted. As the blade fell, Chase was attacking again. He delivered two fast, hard punches to the perp's face. *He's wearing a mask. A ski mask.* The man staggered back. When he came at Chase again—

I'm done. Chase swept out with his foot and tripped the bastard. The man went down hard, and his head cracked when it slammed into the floor. Chase hit the button on the lamp, and light flooded in the room.

First, he saw the knife. Chase kicked it away. Then...

Handcuffs?

Yes, handcuffs glinted near the side of the bed, and the sight of the cuffs had Chase swearing. If you were coming to kill your prey, you didn't bring handcuffs. You brought handcuffs if...

If you're planning to take her with you.

Chase patted down the bastard. Found a taser. And a syringe. *Fuck.* He ripped off the man's mask. Studied his features. Hell. It was the same bastard who'd tried to break into Vivian's apartment. The guy was still breathing, but out cold. Chase whirled and rushed down the hallway.

Problem. Big fucking problem.

His phone was on the hallway table. He'd left it there earlier, and he grabbed it. His fingers swiped over the screen as he called Merik.

But he only got Merik's voicemail.

He dialed the other agents who were supposed to be there. *No answer.*

Shit.

The door creaked open down the hallway.

He whirled.

Vivian stood in the open doorway. She wore a long, white shirt. One of his shirts—he'd left his clothes in the room she'd been using.

"What's happening?" Her voice was hushed.

The location is compromised. "You have to get dressed. Now."

Her eyes widened. "My clothes are in the room you were using." She hurried out of the doorway and toward the other bedroom. "I'll just get—"

He caught her wrist, but it was too late. She'd already opened the door.

"Chase?" He felt her tremble. "There's a man on the floor."

"He was coming for you."

Her head turned toward him.

"Your location is already compromised." Fast. *Too fast.* "He didn't come to kill you, baby. He came to take you." That meant the bad guys knew about the scramble.

And the fact that Chase couldn't get the Wilde agents outside to answer?

It means trouble. Deadly, dangerous trouble.

He grabbed her clothes. Kept his hold on her wrist and pulled her back to the other bedroom. *His* original room. Chase texted out an alert to his boss, knowing the code-red message would send agents swarming. He didn't try to contact Dex, though, because…

I don't trust him. There was no one at the CIA that he did trust right then.

He yanked on his clothes while Vivian dressed, and he grabbed his weapon. They had to get out of there before—

A bullet slammed into the wall beside him. His head whipped toward the shooter. Some asshole in a black ski mask filled the doorway, and the guy was taking aim again, holding up a gun. One that he'd equipped with a silencer.

Sonofabitch.

CHAPTER FOURTEEN

Once upon a time, Vivian had thought that working for the CIA would be exciting. A real adventure. But with her family's history, she hadn't thought that she'd get past the screening process. Sure, she didn't have a criminal record. She didn't have so much as a parking ticket, but her family's ties were bad, to put it mildly.

So when she'd been called up for the contract job, she'd thought it was her lucky day. Fate's way of giving her a chance. She'd passed the psych evaluations. She'd done all the required training. She'd been close to the action—

She'd never planned to be *this* close.

"He shot at you!" She gaped at the ski-mask-wearing man in the bedroom doorway. A man who was getting ready to fire again.

Vivian leapt at Chase. They slammed together and rolled across the bed before they crashed on the floor.

"What the hell are you doing?" Chase demanded.

She'd thought it was obvious. Vivian shoved hair out of her eyes. "Saving you?"

"I was about to take aim!"

She could see his gun now. She hadn't noticed it before. She'd been more focused on making sure Chase didn't get hurt.

Without another word, Chase surged up. He fired his weapon. Once, twice.

"Fucker!"

That hadn't been a cry from Chase. It had come from the man in the ski mask.

Footsteps pounded as the intruder fled.

"He's running away." Chase caught her arm and hauled Vivian to her feet. "Come on, we have to get out of here before he pulls in his reinforcements."

Reinforcements, as in there were more men in ski masks? "We only arrived a little while ago." She raced to keep up with Chase, but for every step, she could see that he was shielding her with his body. "How did they find us so quickly?"

"Excellent question."

He stopped when the hallway angled. Peeked around the corner. "Clear. Let's get to the car and get out of here!"

"Where are the other Wilde agents? Shouldn't they be here?" Helping? Shooting? Something?

"Another excellent question. And I'm worried about the answer." He kicked open the door for the garage. She wasn't sure why he'd kicked it and not opened it the normal way but—

Then she saw the figure slumped behind the door. "How did you know he was there?" Vivian asked, impressed. When he'd kicked in the door, Chase had knocked out the waiting attacker.

"Lucky guess."

Vivian shook her head. "I don't think it was luck."

He'd opened the vehicle's door. He pushed her inside. "Get in and get down."

She slumped as far down as she could in the passenger seat. The SUV's engine growled to life, she heard the grind of the garage door rising, and Chase whipped the vehicle into reverse. Once they were clear of the garage, he hurtled them forward.

"Coming behind us," he muttered. "Shit. I think there are two of them."

She started to rise and look.

"No! Stay down!"

She slumped back down.

"They want to kill me, but their goal is to take you."

Her heart nearly leapt out of her chest.

"Asshole in the bedroom came with handcuffs. Drugs. A freaking taser. He was going to do anything necessary to get you out of there."

The SUV raced forward, and she knew Chase had the gas pedal shoved all the way to the floor.

"The alarms didn't go off. If you'd been in that bedroom instead of me, if they'd taken you, if you hadn't gotten the chance to call out for help..." His head turned toward her. "If they'd taken you, I would have gone crazy."

"Chase—"

Wham. The sudden, powerful impact tore a scream from her as something slammed into the side of their vehicle. The SUV crumpled. She could hear the horrible sound of metal bending, grating, and then the vehicle was hit again. *Again.*

"We're going in the water. Baby, hold on, just *hold on*!"

The water? Had they made it to the bridge? She didn't—

Her side of the vehicle hit something. There was more grating. More horrible shrieking. She whipped her head to the right just as the SUV seemed to take flight—no, it wasn't flying. The guardrail had given way. The vehicle flipped onto the side—her side—and plummeted into the dark water that waited below.

"Chase!" Vivian screamed.

***

"No, no!" He could see what was happening from a distance. "She's supposed to be alive, dammit! The job changed—those assholes know it!" He yanked out his phone. Called them.

The SUV had gone into the water. Vivian Wayne was in the freaking water. What a clusterfuck.

The call was answered on the second ring. "Get her the fuck out of the water!" he shouted. "We need her alive! What part of *alive* do you not understand, you dumbass?"

Whoop, whoop, whoop.

He stiffened. The sound was faint, but coming closer. And he sure as shit knew the sound of an approaching helicopter when he heard one. "Get out of there." They didn't have time to retrieve Vivian from the water. Not with the cavalry coming in via chopper.

Dammit. This job was screwed in a million different ways.

"What about the woman?"

His hold tightened on the phone. "Did you kill the man with her?"

"No...ah...I don't think so."

You'd better have fucking not. "As long as he's alive, his job is to keep her safe. He'll protect her."

"The fuck he will. If they're both going under, he'll save himself!"

No, he wouldn't. Chase Durant would not leave that water without Vivian Wayne. "Just save *your* ass, all right? Get out of here. Before somebody on the chopper spots you."

"What chopper?"

Dumbass. "Get. Out."

***

The SUV plummeted into the water. Because of those bastards who'd hit them, the SUV was crumpled and crushed in a dozen different ways. Water immediately began to pour into the interior even as the vehicle sank deeper into the icy lake.

Chase yanked off his seat belt. His car door was smashed in, and it sure as hell wasn't like the automatic window control button was working. "Baby, see if you can get your window down."

"It...it won't go."

He turned toward her. The water was rising fast. "I'm going to get us out."

"I think I'm stuck," she whispered.

"We're both stuck, but I'm going to get us out." He yanked open the console between their seats. *Hell, yes.* The small escape device was exactly where it should have been. His fingers closed around it.

"What's that?" Vivian asked as her voice caught on the words.

"Rescue tool. Never leave home without it." An all-in-one device that could cut through a seat belt thanks to a cutter on one side, and on the opposite end, a hard head that angled to a point—one that was perfect for breaking the glass in a vehicle. It was standard Wilde policy to keep such a device in all company vehicles. "This will get us through the window. Now, I need you to take a deep breath for me. I'll break the glass, and then we'll swim the hell out of here." The water was rushing in faster and faster.

"I'm stuck," she said again, even softer this time. "My foot is caught on something. When we hit the railing, the side of the SUV shoved in on me. I-I can't seem to get free."

The water was up to their chests. "I'm going to get you out." The SUV angled forward as it sank even deeper.

She screamed, "*Get out!*"

"Baby, I will, I—"

"*You* have to get out!" She pushed at him. The water surged higher in the vehicle. "Get out now! You can't stay in here with me!"

Oh, he couldn't? *Watch me.* "Where the fuck else would I go?"

"Chase—"

"Don't worry, baby. I can hold my breath for a long time. SEAL, remember?" He gave her a smile, but he wasn't sure she could see it in the dark. "But you take that deep breath for me, okay?" He thrust his hands down toward her legs. She was, dammit, yes, she was pinned. The metal was a mess near her leg. He had to dip his body under the water as he tried to grab her, but, fuck, she was jammed in there. He yanked and yanked, but the metal was like a manacle around her.

I need to move the passenger door. I have to get the door open. The mangled door is what's pushing against her.

His head popped out of the water. Damn. There were only about two inches of unsubmerged space left in the SUV for them to use as breathing room, at least in the front because of the tilted angle of the car. Vivian had stretched her body and craned her head back so that she could keep her mouth above the water and take in gulps of air.

"I'm...still stuck," she said as her voice broke.

"I'm going to get you out. I just need to get that door open first." *But I think I have to do it from the other side. I don't think I can open it from this position.*

"Go," she told him. It sounded like she might be crying. "Please, Chase, *go*."

"I will." The water was about to take that last bit of air space from them. "I'll go and swim around to the other side of the vehicle. I'll get you out." He sucked in a deep breath.

"No, just *go*, I am begging you to leave—"

The water took the last of her words away. Fuck. Chase used the hammer-like end of the escape device and broke the window. He shot out of the window and then kept his hands on the SUV as he maneuvered around to Vivian's side. The water was pitch black, but the SUV's lights were still on. Shining in the dark. He got to her side.

Yanked on the door. It wouldn't give. So he yanked harder. Another try and—

The door wrenched opened.

His hands flew to the bottom of the SUV's passenger side. Without the door there, he could free her and he hauled her foot out. He made sure she wasn't stuck in a seat belt. He grabbed her, locked one arm around Vivian's stomach, and then Chase kicked for the surface. She was limp against him. God, this had to be hell for her. Trapped in the dark. Trapped in the car like that…Her nightmare come true.

She had already been afraid of being trapped. This fucking mess had just upped the ante by a million for her. He kept kicking, kept aiming for the surface. The enemy could be up there waiting but there was no choice. Chase had to get Vivian air. He could stay under the water longer, but she couldn't. He had to take the chance, he had to get her *out*—

They broke through the surface of the water. Gunshots didn't ring out, but hell, they hadn't before because the jerk who'd shot at him back at the cabin had been using a silencer on his gun.

Chase sucked in a quick breath.

She didn't.

Fear shoved through his heart like a knife. "Vivian?"

Still no breath. Her head sagged against his shoulder.

Because she wasn't fucking breathing.

He angled her head, made sure her mouth was open, and he pushed his breath past her lips.

Once. Twice. *Baby, don't you do this to me. Don't you—*

She jerked in his hold.

He lifted his head back just as she coughed up water. "Hell, yes."

She coughed again.

He held her and struck out for shore. *Hell, yes.*

Her arms curled weakly around him. "Chase?"

He pulled her closer.

"You were...s-supposed to go..."

"Not without you. *Never* without you."

***

There were a lot of flashing lights. Red ones. Blue ones. Vivian sat hunched in the back of an ambulance. The EMT had patched up her ankle—it had gotten sliced when she'd been trapped. Luckily, the wound hadn't been too deep. The EMT put a brown blanket around her shoulders, but she was still wearing her soaking wet clothes, so the blanket didn't do much good.

Police had swarmed. So had Dex. She could see him, marching about fifteen feet away as he stormed straight for Chase.

Uh, oh. She stiffened.

Dex grabbed Chase's shoulder and swung him around. "Why the hell didn't you call me?" Dex's bellow easily reached her.

She saw Chase pull back his fist. "Don't!" Vivian yelled.

Too late.

Chase's fist plowed into Dex's jaw. Dex staggered back, but then he caught himself and lunged for Chase.

She ran toward them. *"Stop it!"*

Dex swung his head toward her. His fist froze in the air. "Well, at least she's still alive. Though from what I heard, that's a near thing." His head turned back toward Chase. "She nearly drowned on your watch."

Chase's jaw hardened. "She nearly drowned because this case is compromised. Has been from the beginning. You knew it. You knew the traitors ran deep, that's why you came to Wilde, but you didn't tell us everything. You withheld vital information! And now I've got two Wilde agents on the way to the hospital—" He motioned toward an ambulance that was roaring away from the scene. "And my partner is missing. They fucking took Merik, probably planning to use him as some kind of bargaining tool, all because you don't want to tell me what—or rather, who—you think we might really be up against! *Because you're playing damn games while lives are on the line!*"

A shiver slid over her. "Merik was taken?" She hadn't known that. She also hadn't known about the other agents. "How badly were the agents hurt?" Hurt because they'd been protecting her.

"They're gonna make it."

She stiffened, then glanced over her shoulder. Eric Wilde stood there. She had a vague memory of him jumping out of a helicopter and running toward her and Chase. At the time, Chase had been carrying her out of the lake.

She didn't exactly remember *how* she'd gotten from the submerged SUV to the surface of the water. She'd told Chase to leave. Begged him to go right before things had gone hazy. She'd held her breath. Her lungs had burned. Everything had been dark around her.

Then she'd been in his arms. Holding tightly to him as he swam in the freezing water of the lake. And as they'd neared the shore, Vivian could have sworn that he'd whispered...

"Don't ever leave me again."

Now, Chase stalked toward her. "The doctors need to check you out. You need to get back in the ambulance and get to the hospital."

"I'm okay." Just cold. A bone-deep chill that seemed to start from the inside.

"You're not fucking okay!" he snarled. "You were—" He stopped. Clenched his jaw.

"I was what?" That chill Vivian felt grew worse. A shiver worked over her body.

Chase hauled her against him. Wrapped his arms tightly around her body. "She's freezing!"

"That's because my clothes are soaking wet. So are y-yours." Her teeth were chattering a bit. "But I don't exactly want to get naked in front of everyone so..." So she'd deal with the cold.

The flashing lights sent his face into dark and dangerous shadows every few seconds. "You need to go to the hospital."

"*Ahem*." Dex cleared his throat and closed in on them. "You heard the lady. She's fine. No hospital for her."

Chase sent him a glare. "You don't know what happened. She *needs* the hospital—"

"Sure I know what happened. You two went in the water. *After* you killed the attacker in the house. Very lethal and brutal job, by the way."

Her shoulders stiffened.

"Thanks to the security image you previously obtained from Vivian's building," Dex continued as his voice hardened, "we know the dead man is the same guy who tried to break into her apartment. Obviously, he's a hired thug, not the main player we are after. If you'd left him alive, Chase, then we could have made him reveal his employer's identity to us—"

"I didn't kill him," Chase denied, voice grim. "He was unconscious, but breathing, when I left him."

Dex glanced toward the cabin. "Really?"

"Yes, fucking *really*. I didn't kill him. Maybe the other guys on his team did it—they could have been afraid that we'd make the injured man talk."

"Well, he *was* shot—execution style—in the head."

Vivian jerked.

Chase pulled her closer. "*You're safe.*"

"Forgot you're not used to this kind of thing," Dex drawled as he seemed to assess Vivian. "Would it make you feel better about the man's death if I said that shooting you—execution style—was probably his end goal? You know, after you unscrambled your wonderful code."

"No," she snapped at him. "That does n-not make me feel better!" It made her feel even worse.

"You're alive." Dex gestured to the lake. "Glad I'm not hauling your body out of the lake right now."

Another hard shiver hit her.

Chase's hold around Vivian was fierce. "You are such an emotionless prick."

"Of course," Dex instantly agreed. "Emotions would make it impossible for me to do my job. And, look, while this is a fun chat, we need to get Vivian to a new location ASAP. And, no offense, Eric..." He glanced over at a watchful and silent Eric. "But I have to say that I'm disappointed in your agents. Hardly living up to the hype."

"*She fucking wasn't breathing. This isn't a joke. It's not a game.*" Chase moved to stand in front of Vivian. He put his body toe-to-toe with Dex. "She was trapped in the vehicle. She couldn't get out. She was telling me to *leave* her so that I'd survive."

"Um..." She hugged her blanket—a wet and cold blanket now—tighter to her. "Could you go back to the part about me not breathing, please?"

Chase's shoulders were stiff and his hands clenched as he snarled at Dex, "By the time I managed to pry open her door, she'd been without air for several moments."

Oh, God. She didn't remember him prying open any door. When they'd been trapped, he'd told her to take a breath. She had. Then...

Nothing.

"When we finally reached the surface," Chase continued in a voice that promised hell, "she wasn't breathing at all. I had to fucking breathe for her."

Don't ever leave me again.

"Did you revive her in the water or on land?" Dex wanted to know.

As if *that* part was the important piece of the story.

I wasn't breathing? Her knees were all shaky. "Brain cells can begin dying after just one minute of no oxygen."

Chase's hands were clenching and releasing at his sides.

"After three minutes, that's when the more serious brain damage is more likely. The neurons suffer more severe damage." How far down had the vehicle been in the lake? How long had she been in the water? "After ten minutes, the victim—" *I was the victim.* Her breath panted out. "After ten minutes, permanent brain damage is—"

Chase spun toward her. "Damn well wasn't ten minutes. I got you breathing as soon as we broke the surface."

"So you *did* perform rescue breathing in the water," Dex announced. "Interesting. You have to—"

Eric stepped forward. She saw the movement from the corner of her eye. Had to be from the corner, because she couldn't take her stare from Chase.

"You know he was a SEAL," Eric snapped. "One of the reasons you specifically requested him. Him and not the 'best undercover operative' BS you spouted before. Chase fights hard and dirty, but he can damn well handle things when they go to hell."

Dex had *specifically* requested him? And...

Yes, yes, things had gone to hell.

"I want Vivian checked out," Chase insisted as his stare burned over her. "She needs a doctor."

"The EMT checked her out," Dex said with a sigh. "He gave her the all clear." He took a step around Chase and maneuvered for Vivian. "Now, let's talk about getting you to a new—"

Chase slapped a hand on Dex's chest. Fisted the fabric of Dex's shirt. "That's close enough."

"What?" Dex looked down at his shirt front, then his head swiveled toward Chase. "Move the damn hand."

Chase glared at him. "We'd barely been here any time at all when the enemy team converged. They got into the house, got into the room assigned to Vivian, without making a single sound. If she'd been asleep in there, they would have taken her. The bastard I took out came equipped with drugs, handcuffs, and a taser. If I hadn't been in the bedroom, she might never have made a sound and then what—"

"Yes, well, obviously, you were going to be in her bedroom." Dex sighed once more. "Come on, did you think I was leaving that shit to chance? You wanted her. Any fool could see that, and I knew that as soon as the two of you were alone, it would happen."

"*It?*" Chase thundered.

"Sometimes that kind of attachment can be dangerous, but, other times—as I've recently learned on a previous case—it can be advantageous. Because if you get attached, and you will do anything to—"

Chase slugged him.

Dex took a step back. "Okay, that's the second hit. That's all you get. *No* more. I will hit back."

"I was sleeping in Dex's room," Vivian said, voice soft and still shaky. "He was in my room. I don't think you understand what he's telling you."

"What?" Dex shook his head. "But—"

"*The alarms didn't go off,*" Chase spoke through clenched teeth. "The bad guys came right to us. They knew we'd be here at the lake. Hell, I think they may have just been waiting. It was a coordinated attack, not some last-minute BS. They even knew what damn room she was in, and they went straight in there. Luckily, Vivian was in *my* assigned room, and I was crashing in hers." His head turned as his gaze swept the area, then landed on Eric's helicopter. "We need a ride."

They did?

Chase reached for her hand. His fingers twined with hers. "I'm getting you checked out."

For like the fourth time, she told him, "*I have been checked out.*" The man was worried, obviously. He—

"You were fucking not breathing in my arms, Viv. When I ripped open that car door, your body was floating in the vehicle. Your hair was drifting around you, and you were limp against me. I will *never* forget that moment. I almost lost you. I am damn well going to do everything in my power to make sure that you never, ever slip away again."

Her heart squeezed and she couldn't look away from him as the flashing lights sent his face into dark and dangerous shadows.

"My chopper can take her to the hospital faster than any ambulance can," Eric's voice was low. "After the docs see her, then we'll get her to a new location."

A new safe house? One that wouldn't be compromised?

"Not sure I trust your team," Dex said, seeming to echo Vivian's fears. "And, hey, don't you have an agent to find? Are you guys forgetting that little matter?"

Eric stalked toward him. "I've already got a dozen team members hunting for Merik. You think I would just let one of my own vanish?" Anger vibrated in his voice. "We will find him, and we *will* figure out how this location was compromised."

"Good to know," Dex murmured. His attention flickered back to Chase and Vivian.

There was something about the way he focused on them. *I don't trust him.* She sidled closer to Chase. She *did* trust Chase. With every fiber of her being. Yes, their start had been rocky, to say the least but...

When danger was around her, when the darkness closed in, Chase kept proving that she could count on him. For the first time, she had someone who wouldn't leave her alone to face the dark.

Don't ever leave me again.

She shivered once more. Chase scooped her into his arms and began hurrying toward the chopper.

"I can walk," she told him even as she slipped one arm around his neck.

"I know, but I need to hold you." There was something about his voice. A rough, ragged note that had her pressing even tighter to him.

Chase had saved her. He'd risked his life for her. Vivian's voice was soft as she asked, "Just how long did you stay in the water in order to get me out?"

His head turned. He paused right next to the chopper. But he didn't answer her.

"Thirty seconds is usually how long most people can hold their breath." A general number. A random fact stuck in her head.

"I'm not most people." He put her in the chopper. Secured her in the seat.

"Two minutes is the high end for others," Vivian noted. Normally, her facts helped to calm her. Not this time. *How long did you stay in the water for me?*

He slid into the seat near her. Eric had just jumped into the front seat, next to the waiting pilot. He barked orders to the guy even as Chase handed her a headset.

Their fingers brushed. Tangled. "Was it longer than two minutes?" Vivian pushed.

"I wasn't counting. I just wanted you out."

Her stomach was in knots. "How long did you stay in the water with me?"

His head turned toward her. "Baby, don't you get it? I would have stayed in that damn water as long as it took. *I was not leaving you.*"

The chopper's blades began to whirl.

CHAPTER FIFTEEN

"The doc said Vivian is good to go." Eric stood outside of the private hospital room. He nodded toward Chase. "You saved her. She owes you."

"She doesn't owe me a damn thing." He couldn't get the image of Vivian—so still, so pale—out of his mind. He was still wearing the fucking wet clothes, though they'd gone from soaking to being mostly damp. His freaking shoes squeaked when he walked. The occasional shiver would work over his body. And...

And I am barely holding onto my control.

He'd lost control back at the lake. His fists had flown at Dex, and he had the bruised knuckles to prove it. Or hell, maybe the bruises had come from when he'd knocked out the intruder in the cabin's bedroom.

I knocked him out. I didn't kill him. Someone else had taken care of that part. While Chase had been fighting to save Vivian, some bastard had gone back to the cabin and killed the man Chase had left behind.

The killer had probably been the same bastard who'd taken Merik. "What's the status on Merik?"

"No news yet. His phone was found abandoned. The two injured Wilde agents we recovered at the scene told me that they never saw who attacked them. They were hit from behind. Like you, they had no warning. No alarms blared. None of the motion sensors on the scene were activated." Eric yanked a hand over his face. "Someone disabled *my* tech, and it's not easy to do that."

No, it wasn't. "Inside job," Chase said. It had to be.

Eric's hand fell to his side. "We both know that is what Dex suspected all along. That it was someone within the CIA."

"Dex is holding back on us. He has been, from the very beginning."

"Oh, did someone mention my name?" Dex called as he marched down the empty hospital corridor.

Chase had seen the bastard coming. Eric had made sure the floor was cleared. After all, that was what shitloads of money could do. Get you an entire hospital wing at your beck and call. The Wilde agents who'd been hurt were getting top-of-the-line care. Eric looked after his people, and he damn well didn't like it when they were hurt—or used.

So, this time, it wasn't Chase who lunged for Dex.

It was Eric. Eric caught the guy and slammed him up against the nearest wall.

"Easy…" Dex warned.

"Screw easy. You lied to me," Eric charged.

Dex looked up at the ceiling. Seemed to ponder things. "I neglected to tell you the full truth. That's not technically lying. It's omission, and you didn't have clearance to discover—"

"Screw clearance. My agents are hurt. One is missing. Chase almost died tonight. If he hadn't gotten out of that SUV—"

Dex's gaze angled toward Chase. "He chose not to leave Vivian. Admirable choice, by the way. All stand-up and heroic."

"Screw you." Chase hated that SOB.

"It's truly what I expected you to do. I mean, why else would I allow you to stay with her? Like I said, I saw the personal bond—"

What was this BS? "You said the bond was a weakness that would get us in trouble!"

"I was just pushing your buttons. I knew that if you cared enough, you'd go to any lengths to protect Vivian. That's the kind of dedication that money can't buy."

"You are fucking using me." Another crack in Chase's control. "You manipulated me from the beginning. All along, did you know that Vivian was innocent?"

Eric maintained his fierce hold on Dex. "Answer the question."

"I *hoped* she was innocent," Dex allowed. "But the evidence was pointing against that."

And Chase knew why. "Because she'd been set up."

"It seemed that way. I mean, she was the perfect fall person, wasn't she? Especially with her past."

Yeah, about that... "With Vivian's past—with the ties that she has—how the hell did she get a job working for the CIA?"

"Contract work," Dex clarified with a sniff. "It's a probationary position. Someone pulled strings for her." He looked back at Eric. "I've played nicely for the last few moments because—deep down, way, way deep down—I like you. So, how about you stop being all handsy with me, and let's discuss this thing like gentlemen?"

"You aren't a damn gentleman," Eric snarled back.

Hell, no, he wasn't.

"Are any of us?" Dex wanted to know. "I said *like* gentlemen. We're all wanna-bes."

Disgusted, Eric stepped back and let Dex go. "Who pulled the strings to get Vivian the job?"

Dex made a show of straightening his t-shirt.

"Who, Dex?" Chase demanded.

"Someone with a lot of pull. Someone who believed in her potential. Someone who thought she was more than her past. I mean, not like you can pick your family..." His stare lingered on Chase. "Am I right?"

The sonofabitch knows all about my family. "Just how deeply did you dig into my past before you requested that I be the Wilde agent assigned to this case?"

Dex gave him an innocent smile. "How deeply do you think?"

The hospital door opened to the right. Vivian stood there, wearing green scrubs and with her hair curling lightly around her shoulders. Shadows lined her eyes, and she still looked far too pale.

"You guys were getting loud," she noted softly. "So I thought I'd come join the party. Especially since you were probably talking about me."

"You and Chase's past," Dex agreed with an inclination of his head. "Has he told you all about it yet? About just why he is so good at adopting personas and becoming someone new?"

"I was listening through the door." Vivian moved to stand beside Chase, but her gaze remained focused on Dex. "You are the one who got me the job at the agency."

"Did I say that?" Dex tapped his chin. "Did I say it was me, specifically?"

"Stop your games! I was trapped in that vehicle! And Chase—" Her head turned toward him. "You should have left me," she finished with pain and fear slipping into her voice.

Left her? The hell he should have.

"Promise you won't ever do that again."

His hand lifted, and he tucked a lock of hair behind her ear. "Here's another one of my thirteen secrets," he told her. "I don't make promises that I don't intend to keep."

Her eyes glistened.

"This is so friggin' sweet, but we have some very dangerous perpetrators out there, so how about we move this bit along?"

Chase's gaze swung back to Dex. Dex actually rolled his hand in the air. Such a dick.

"The cabin's location was leaked. We all know that." Dex nodded. His face hardened and all the sly humor vanished as if it had never been there. "I know when I have a traitor working against me. I have one in the CIA right now. It wasn't Vivian, so it had to be someone else at her branch. Or, hell, it could have been multiple agents coordinating together. I just finished another case where an agent's identity was leaked, and, let me just tell you, I don't like this shit. The timeline with that leak and what's happening now worried me."

"Because you were worried, you turned to me," Eric concluded.

"Yeah. I went to an old friend I thought I could trust."

Eric narrowed his gaze. "You're throwing that f-word around again like it's a thing."

"Yes, *friend,* I am. And news flash, the location leak had to come from your people. I didn't tell anyone. We were at *your* office when we discussed plans. Someone on your end spilled her location and maybe even the details about the coding scramble."

Chase waited for Eric to deny the charge.

But Eric didn't.

Eric's gaze did swing to Chase. There were so many emotions raging in Eric's eyes. For once, he didn't look so controlled, either.

"There's a lot of money involved in this play," Dex continued grimly. He scanned the hallway to make sure no nurses or doctors were close, then he added, "Enough money to make people turn on their own mothers, much less prick bosses like you, Eric."

"Thanks so much," Eric muttered.

"And why the hell did you have that homicide detective there?" Dex wanted to know. "Layla Lopez doesn't work for you—"

"Despite my attempts, no, Layla doesn't work for me. But with cars exploding and shit hitting the fan, I thought it was good to keep a law enforcement professional—someone *I* trust completely—in the loop about what the hell was happening."

Dex's brows climbed. "You still feel good about that choice? Or are you wondering if Layla might have decided to trade Vivian for a couple of million dollars?"

Chase heard Vivian inhale swiftly. "That's what the price is for me? A few million?"

Chase actually suspected it was higher, but he didn't want to worry her even more so he didn't say—

"Oh, since you can decode all the names and locations of the agents, I'm sure it's way more," Dex readily told her because he seemed to be in an over-sharing and I'll-terrify-Vivian mode. "There's probably going to be a feeding frenzy over you. Do you really think an attack squad like the one that converged on the safe house goes after just anyone?"

"Stop fucking scaring her," Chase ordered as he took Vivian's hand and gave it a reassuring squeeze. "Stop it now." Dex was getting on his last nerve.

"She *should* be scared." Dex pointed at Vivian. "She should be terrified because there is no one she can trust. With that much money on the table, everyone she meets could be the enemy. She needs someone to have her back, but hell, the team I hired just got knocked out—one of them *taken*—and I'm not sure the others left at Wilde are on the side of the just and righteous. There is no one she can count on in this mess, and she needs to understand—"

"I understand perfectly." Vivian's voice was flat. "I don't need you to break things down for me. My vision is crystal clear."

She looked so fragile in the green scrubs. So heartbreakingly beautiful.

"And you're wrong, Dex," Vivian added.

"No, no, I don't think I—"

"I do have someone I can trust. Someone I can count on to have my back in this nightmare." Her gaze turned to Chase. The green scrubs made her eyes seem even greener than normal. "I trust you," she told Chase.

"Uh, he's the man who lied to you," Dex pointed out. "Did you hit your head in the crash and forget that?"

"He's the man who saved my life. He's the man who fought to protect me. He's the man I trust completely. The *only* person I trust right now." She squared her shoulders. "He's also the man *I* hired to find the people who were framing me, so, yes, we are still most definitely a package deal. Wherever I go, whatever happens next..." Vivian licked her lower lip. "Will you come with me?" she asked Chase.

Like she had to ask. He brought their joined hands to his mouth. Pressed a kiss to her knuckles. "I'd like to see anyone try to keep me from you." A package deal? Hell, yes, they were. He'd be her shadow wherever she went. The people after her would *not* hurt Vivian.

"My chopper is waiting outside." Eric's low voice cut through the silence that lingered a little too long. "Chase, why don't you let me take you and Vivian to a secure location? Me. Not the pilot who was here before. You know I can fly that baby in my sleep. I will keep the new location quiet, no matter what."

Chase knew that he would. Getting to a secure location would be step one. Vivian needed a safe place to rest because she had to be dead on her feet. Dawn wasn't far away. When dawn came, the hospital shift would switch and more people would be swarming into the building.

Time to go.

"The fewer people who know where you are, the better," Eric added.

"So you *do* think you have a leak at your company." Dex pursed his lips. "I'm assuming you'll investigate the hell out of that shit."

"Just like I know you're investigating the hell out of the people who work for you." Eric's retort was immediate.

"Yeah, about that." Chase rolled back his shoulders. "When you do your investigating, Dex, I'd sure as hell recommend that you start with Luc Coderre."

"Luc?" Dex's brows shot up. "I've known him for years. He's a respected operative. He's got a case-closure success rate that is astronomical. He's—"

"He's a suspect. At the top of my list. You also need to double check on the building manager at Vivian's place, too."

Vivian jerked in surprise. "Jacob? Why Jacob?"

"Because of means and opportunity, both for him and Luc. They both came to your place. They were both close to you. And as for Jacob, hell, the man *owns* the building, Viv. He's not just the manager. Wilde discovered that when we were digging. His background seemed like BS to me and—" Chase broke off. He'd seen the faint flickering of Dex's eyes. "Sonofabitch. Is Jacob one of yours?"

"Awkward." Dex coughed. "Technically, yes, he *was* an operative. He's not any longer. While Vivian was still going through the interview process, I wanted eyes on her, so I arranged for her to find a place in his building."

"Still going through the process?" Vivian shook her head. "I had the job."

Chase rocked back onto his heels. He was figuring out more and more of this mess. "You had other plans for her, didn't you, Dex?"

Dex shrugged. Glanced at his watch. This time, he was actually wearing one around his wrist. "This party should get moving along. Can't stay here forever. I've got bad guys to track. Bait to put out. Lives to destroy. You know, my usual morning routine after coffee."

And Chase had to get Vivian out of there. But first, he grabbed Dex's arm when the other man tried to hurry past him. He leaned in close and whispered to Dex, making sure that his voice didn't carry to anyone else, "You use her as bait, and I will put a bullet in your heart."

Dex's head turned toward him. "Is that a promise?" His voice was louder. It was apparent he wanted the others to hear his response.

"Absolutely. Find another option."

"You volunteering?"

"Yes," Chase gritted out.

"Chase?" Vivian touched his shoulder. "I want to get out of here. Can we please just go?"

Dex gave him a hard smile. "I'll be in touch."

"I'm sure you will be." Chase let him go. Then he scooped Vivian into his arms.

"What are you doing?" She wrapped her arm around his neck. "I can walk. I didn't even need stitches on the cut near my ankle. I don't need you to carry me!"

"Yeah, I get that." He did. One hundred percent. But what *she* didn't get... "I need to hold you." He stared straight ahead. Eric had run up in front of him and was holding the door that led to the stairwell. They'd go to the roof. Get the fuck out of there. "I need to hold you because I am barely keeping my control."

"Chase?"

Talking to Dex had been a huge effort. Not driving his fist into a wall had required major self-control. Not hunting down those bastards who'd wreaked havoc at the lake and destroying every single one of them? Well, Chase still planned to do that. But first...

Vivian comes first.

"You're the only thing keeping me in check." His voice was raw. His hold on her too tight as they hurried for the roof. "I need you close." He paused, and his head turned toward her. "Help me to stay in control."

"I'll help you," Vivian promised. She put her head down on his shoulder.

And he could breathe. And he could keep his control.

Just for a little while longer.

CHAPTER SIXTEEN

The view from the top floor suite was killer. She could look out over the city and see for miles. Miles and miles. They'd gone back to Marietta, back to one of the swankiest hotels there. Eric had landed the chopper on the roof of the building. They'd gotten inside with a minimum of contact—no doubt due to Eric's connections—and now she was locked in tightly with Chase.

"Wilde has access to a lot of secure facilities around the US. I thought this one would work well for you because of the views." Chase motioned toward one of the floor-to-ceiling windows that let her see the sunrise. "After you've had a chance to rest and we can regroup, we'll make plans for a different location. This is just temporary. I think it would be better if we got you out of the state. Maybe even sent you to one of the islands that Eric has used before on top secret assignments. Only his inner circle knows about those locations, and you will be safe there—"

"Will you come with me?"

His jaw hardened.

"Or do you plan to send me away while you set yourself up as some sort of lure for the bad guys?"

He stalked toward her. "How did you hear that part?"

"One of my thirteen secrets? I can read lips, and I read yours when you leaned in close to Dex."

Chase stopped right in front of her. "They took my friend. I have to get him back. That means I'll have to do some bad things. Means I'll have to break some fucking rules, but I *will* get Merik back. He's a pain in the ass, but he's my pain in the ass."

"I can help you."

Chase shook his head. "They took him as a way to get to you. That's why you need to be far away. So they *can't* get to you. We remove you from the equation, then we take them down." A muscle flexed along his clenched jaw. "I know you need to crash, but I'm not sleeping in a different room."

Her heart sped up. Was he saying…?

"I'll sleep on the floor next to your bed. If someone manages to get past the security here, then I will be in the same room with you. They will literally have to walk over me in order to get to you."

She turned away from him. Made her way to the bedroom. When she opened the door, a massive bed waited for her. Had to be a king. With what looked like silk sheets. "There's plenty of space." Her head turned toward him. Chase had followed her. "You don't have to sleep on the floor."

"Trust me, I do."

She almost reached for him, but stopped. Scrunched up her nose. "I think I smell like a lake." She was pretty sure she'd swallowed way too much of the lake when she'd been—

No. Stop it. Don't go there. "I need to shower."

He pointed to the bathroom. "I'll be waiting in front of the door."

He was taking his guard duty very, very seriously. She nodded. "That's an option."

A furrow appeared between Chase's brows.

"Or you could get in the shower with me. You're still wearing your lake-soaked clothes." Though Eric had sent them new clothes. He'd ordered clothing from the shop in the lobby and gotten the materials discreetly delivered.

The furrow between Chase's eyebrows deepened. "Did you just ask me to shower with you?"

"Yes, I do believe I did. I mean, if you're going to watch me, you can't very well do it from outside of the door. You don't have x-ray vision. Besides, you do need to shower, too."

"If I see you naked in a shower, I'm done."

"Done?"

"I want to fuck you." Oh, his voice had gone guttural again. Sexy. "I'm riding out a wave of fury and adrenaline, and I'm doing my best to keep my control. But you—without your clothes, gleaming wet in a shower—that will shred the last bit of control that I have. I want you. I *need* you. And you don't want me to—"

"You're wrong."

His blazing gold gaze seemed to burn her.

"You said I don't want you." She shook her head. "I do. I also think it's fine for that control of yours to break. You see, I have this friend, and he recently told me that adrenaline rushes can be extremely hard to handle."

"Huh." A pause. "A...friend?"

"Well, I'm working out exactly *what* he is." Friend was the wrong word. He was so much more. "But he had a rough night. So did I. I happen to think we could both use some help coming down from the rush."

He didn't move. "So that's what this is about? Getting rid of the rush?"

"No." She began to strip. "It's me, inviting you to shower with me. It's me, saying I want you because I do. And then it's you, making the choice about what *you* want." Vivian exhaled. "You don't have to keep your control for me." She stood before him, completely naked. "Because I don't have any control of my own left."

Then she turned and walked into the bathroom. He'd follow her or he wouldn't. She yanked on the water and the spray filled the huge walk-in shower. After she stepped inside, Vivian left the shower door open behind her, just in case—

A warm, strong hand curled around her shoulder. "You're the only thing I want."

He'd stripped. Her gaze slid over him. Took in the broad shoulders. The abs for days. Then going down, down to the heavy, thrusting length of his cock.

"Here, let me help," Chase offered in that rough, growling voice that made her ache even more. He reached for the soap. Lathered it and began carefully rubbing her breasts. Sliding his fingers over her nipples as he put the soap on her with tender, delicate strokes.

Her breath shuddered out as she grabbed for the soap, too. She filled her hands and then was running her fingers over his body because she wanted to touch him. Every single inch of him. His mouth met hers in a hot, drugging kiss even as the shower water pounded down on them. She savored the kiss. Loved it. Got drunk on it. She was pushing onto her toes to get closer and closer.

His mouth tore from hers, and he kissed his way down her throat. Vivian moaned his name and tipped back her head for him. Steam filled the air. The glass doors fogged up.

His hand slid between her legs. She widened her stance, and one long finger thrust inside of her. One, then another.

He stretched her. Filled her. Pulled his fingers out and thrust back inside as he—

"I can't fucking wait." He kissed her again. Drove his tongue into her mouth. Tasted her. "I need a condom. Dammit, I need—"

"I'm covered and I'm clean." Her nails bit into his shoulders. She wanted him then. She kissed him again. Sucked his lower lip. Bit.

"I'm clean." He pushed her back. Lifted her against the wet, tiled wall. Held her as if it was the easiest thing in the world while his cock lodged at the entrance of her body. "I want *in*."

She wanted him in. No more waiting. She wanted—

He sank into her. Drove all the way inside and her nails scratched across his shoulders as Vivian held on as tightly as she could. He filled her, stretched her, and she sucked in desperate gulps of air as her body fought to adjust to him.

"Easy." His hand slipped between their bodies. His fingers rubbed over her clit. Caressed and stroked. "I'm not moving, not until you are ready. God, baby, you are *tight*."

Or maybe he was just super big. Almost too big. But what he was doing with his fingers felt good. No, great.

He kissed her again. Thrust his tongue into her mouth even as he kept working her clit, and she felt her hips rise because she wanted more. Wanted the friction, the force, the driving power of sex.

"That's it. Fuck, yes…"

Her eyes opened. She stared into his gaze, and she saw it—the exact moment when he lost his control.

His stare blazed at her. The gold was so bright and hot even as his expression was locked into savage lines of lust. "Hold on," he ordered roughly.

She was. Her legs wrapped around him in a never-let-go grip.

He drove into her. Pounded into her with hard, powerful strokes, and every single plunge of his cock had her aching for more. Wanting more. Everything. Her hands flew over his slick back. He was driving into her, stretching so deep. He was all she could feel. All that she wanted and she was—

Coming.

Already.

Her sex squeezed around him as she cried out his name. Her right hand flew off him and grabbed blindly for the handle she'd seen on the wall. She gripped it as the pleasure poured through her.

But he wasn't done. Not even close. He sank into her again. Drove into her again, and she felt him coming inside of her. A hot rush of release. Her eyes opened so that she could see his face in that wild moment.

And then, she couldn't look away.

Savage. Powerful. Perfect.

Sexy.

He kissed her. Stayed buried in her even as he stepped out of the shower. Her legs were still wrapped around him. Her arms were now clinging limply to his neck. Sex between them had been...*wow*.

He lowered her to her feet. Grabbed a towel and tenderly patted her dry before he yanked the towel over his own body.

Her toes curled into the plush rug. Now that the crazy haze of passion had cleared, she felt a bit uncertain. Moaning, panting sex in the shower wasn't normally her style. "Did you know that bathrooms can be the most dangerous room in a home?"

Chase stilled with the towel half-way over his chest.

"Each year..." Her voice was husky so she cleared her throat. "ERs get packed with people who have injuries while in the bathroom. Over two hundred and thirty thousand people go to the hospital each year because—"

"I guess it's a good thing we didn't hurt ourselves while we were fucking in the shower."

Her lips pressed together. She nodded.

He dropped the towel. Advanced on her. "I wonder how many people have sex in the shower each year."

Her mind went blank. "I don't know, but I'm sure it's a lot."

His mouth kicked into a half-smile. "Something tells me that it is." His hand lifted. Curled under her chin. "I was right."

She wanted his mouth again. "About what?" Now her voice had gone straight breathless.

"Sex with you—one time with you—was never going to be enough for me."

"It's not enough for me, either," she whispered.

His half-smile was gone. "Good. Because I want you again. Right now."

"Now?" As in...again? Again—now?

"Tell me, what do you think is the most popular sexual position out there?"

"I-I read a survey once that said, um, ahem..." She could feel her face flushing. How was she blushing after what they'd done? "How about I just show you?"

"That would be good." He bent his head. Kissed her. His tongue dipped into her mouth. He seemed to savor her. She was certainly savoring him. She leaned into him before he let her go and rasped, "Very, very good."

Her heart was racing again as she stepped away from him and hurried into the bedroom. All of the curtains were drawn over the windows to block out the rising sun, but the lamp still glowed, giving the light that she needed, and Vivian went straight to the bed. She climbed onto the mattress. Oh, it was nice and soft. Not too soft, though. Perfect for what they needed. She moved toward the pillows. Vivian rose onto her knees and her hands grabbed for the wood of the tall headboard.

"Fuck me."

Her head turned toward the sound of Chase's voice. He stood a few feet away and his face was locked into those hard, tight lines of need again.

"I was about to do just that," she responded seriously. "Um, this position, with you coming in from behind, is rated as the most popular among—"

He pounced. Chase climbed onto the bed behind her, and his hands curled around her hips. "I'm in love with your ass."

Oh. Well, that was nice.

His fingers slid over her ass. Her head was still turned toward him, and from that angle, he could kiss her, and he did. Or she kissed him. Sort of hard to tell for certain. Their mouths met even as her hands tightened on the headboard. Then *his* right hand was moving. Curling around her body. Going between her legs.

Chase's long, slightly rough fingers were sliding over her clit. Stroking her. Dipping into her. Her hips surged back against him. She could feel the long, thick length of his cock shoving against her.

She was more than ready for another round, too. She was—

His hand slid away from her sex.

"Chase!"

"Don't worry. I'm not going anywhere." Then he was angling her hips up. The head of his cock pushed right at the entrance to her body.

She didn't wait for him to thrust. Vivian surged back and took him inside. Her inner muscles were hyper sensitive from before, and when he filled her, she let out a moan. For a moment, she just enjoyed the feeling of having him inside of her.

"You are making me insane," Chase grated. "You feel fucking fantastic." His fingers had clamped tightly around her hips. No, the fingers of his left hand were clamped around her hip. His right hand—

His fingers strummed her clit.

She jerked against him.

And that was it—

There was no control. There was no holding back. This time, it was all about a fierce, wild race toward release. They both knew what the pleasure would feel like. The consuming avalanche, and they wanted it.

His fingers stroked her even as his cock surged in and out. In and out. Her hands gripped the headboard as every single muscle in her body seemed to strain and tighten. The release was close. Already, so close.

His thrusts became harder, nearly lifting her off her knees as she strained to meet him. Harder. Rougher. Deeper.

Her head tipped back. His mouth moved to her throat. He kissed her. Licked her. Bit—

"*Chase!*" The orgasm was even stronger than before. So strong that her whole body bowed up.

"*Dammit, yes. Yes!*" He kept thrusting. Each thrust just drew out her orgasm because the pleasure wasn't stopping. It barreled through her, and she could only hold desperately to that headboard as she shuddered and came. His fingers were still working her clit and pushing her orgasm higher and higher.

"Can't wait," Chase panted out. "You're...too...*good*."

He erupted into her. She felt him coming and slammed her hips back against him. Her inner muscles clamped greedily around him.

"*Viv!*"

***

She didn't want to move. She should move. There was something that Vivian felt like she needed to do, but she was currently content to just be a puddle.

Then the bed—the mattress—shifted.

"I'll be right back. Get some rest, okay, baby?"

Her right eye cracked open. For a moment, she was disoriented. Had she fallen asleep? The last thing she remembered...

Holding tight to the headboard. Moaning out Chase's name. Check. That was what she remembered. Now she was tucked under the covers. Soft pillows were under her head, and she was watching Chase as he padded toward the bedroom door. "You have a tattoo on your ass."

He stopped. "Almost forgot that you like tats." He glanced back at her. Gave a faint smile. "First time you saw Merik, you complimented his ink."

Merik. At the sound of his name, guilt and fear surged through her. Guilt because she'd been having sex while he'd been taken. Tortured? Killed? *Please, no.* And fear hit her because, well, same reason. She feared Merik was being hurt, and it was her fault.

"We're going to get him back," Chase said as if he'd just read her mind.

"I don't want him dying because of me."

"It's not because of you." He turned to face her. "It's because of the bastards who took him. You didn't do anything wrong. They are the ones who are trying to unmask agents. They are the ones who want to hurt and destroy. Not you."

But Merik was the one being hurt.

"Eric is searching for him. I trust Eric completely, and he will not lose an agent. He will get him back." Chase lifted his hand, and she saw the small phone that he gripped. "This is a burner phone that Eric gave me. I'm going to check in with him before I crash with you." A long exhale. "We both need to rest because we don't know what the hell will happen in the next twenty-four hours."

The last twenty-four hours had been pure madness, but one thing stood out in that nightmare. "I'm glad you were with me."

She caught the flash of uncertainty in his gaze before Chase asked, "Does this mean you forgive me for lying?"

"It means I understand." He'd had a job to do. She'd been that job. Vivian pushed up in bed even as weariness pulled at her. "Why haven't you asked me about him?"

His posture didn't change, but she could suddenly feel Chase's alertness. "Him?"

Her hand rose, and she rubbed her finger against her left eyebrow.

Chase's gaze followed the movement.

"I know you have your suspicions about him. He's not exactly a good man. At least, not to most people." Maybe it was the weariness causing her to share this part of her life. She never talked about it—him—with anyone. That had been one of the rules she'd made for herself. Not to talk about him. To keep that part of herself buried but she wanted to share this with Chase. "Another one of my thirteen secrets," she whispered.

Chase waited. The tension grew.

"But you know this secret, don't you?" The way he'd known so much already. Because he probably had a dossier on her. Because he'd seen the background collected by the CIA. Or maybe Wilde had just dug deep and hard on her. "You know that my stepfather is a criminal." That was wrong. Too tame of a description. "No, not just any criminal. You know he's a Russian mob boss."

Chase inclined his head toward her.

"That's another reason why I was a prime suspect, isn't it? Because he could broker the names and identities of all the agents. He'd be able to get me the most money for the intel." She could connect all the dots, too. She knew that she'd been the perfect fall guy—woman—in this mess. "That's the kind of thing that the world thinks he does. He cheats. He betrays. He kills." The same way... "Just like he killed my real father." Her hold tightened on the sheets. "Does that last part count as another of my secrets? I think it does. I'm not so sure it's common knowledge. I mean, it wasn't to me, anyway. I didn't learn the truth about my real father's death until I was seventeen years old." She hadn't learned the truth about her beloved stepfather until then.

And that was when her world had come crashing down.

CHAPTER SEVENTEEN

"Tell me there is news." Over three hours had passed since Chase had last checked in with Eric. Before he'd crashed with Vivian, he'd called his boss and friend, but there had been nothing to report. He was checking in again because Chase needed good news. He needed a lead that they could use in order to find Merik.

"Still nothing." Weariness roughened Eric's voice. "Believe me, I am using every asset I have, and I am not giving up."

No, Eric wouldn't give up.

"But so far, he's hidden."

Because the men who took him wanted Merik to stay that way. "There will be a demand," Chase said. He glanced toward the closed bedroom door. Vivian had been sleeping when he'd quickly dressed and slipped out to make the call. He never slept heavily, and fear for Merik had plagued him. "We both know what they'll want in exchange for him."

"Vivian."

"They aren't getting her." *They will touch her only if I'm dead.* "But we will make an exchange."

"What do you mean?"

"I want you to put the word out—hell, get that SOB Dex to put the word out—that Vivian told me all of her secrets."

The bedroom door opened. Vivian stood in the doorway. A lush, white robe was wrapped around her body, and her tousled curls fell to her shoulders.

Just the sight of her caused his whole body to tense.

I had her. I want her again. I will always want her.

"She told me all of her secrets," Chase continued flatly as he stared into her eyes. "I seduced them out of her."

"Uh, what are you saying—"

"*I* know how to unscramble the code. I know the key."

Vivian took a step forward.

"You know it?" Eric asked.

"Damn straight. I convinced her to trust me completely. While we've been alone here, she revealed every secret she has to me."

Vivian shook her head. Her eyes were huge as she pleaded softly, "Stop."

He didn't stop. He couldn't. "She's not the tool the perps need. I am. If they want a trade, it's going to be me, not Vivian."

"Knew you'd pull some shit like this," Eric groused. "That hero complex will get your ass killed."

Or it will save my friend's life. "Vivian is due for a vacation," he added. He knew Eric would understand exactly what he meant and get to work arranging transport. "The sooner, the better." Which was code for...*Get her to one of your secure islands. I want her away from here before the shit hits the fan. The bad guys aren't touching her. They want to unscramble their data? Then they can take me.*

"I'll be in touch," Eric promised him. "Don't do anything crazy until you hear back from me, got it?"

"Can't make any promises." Not when he felt crazy as hell. Chase ended the call. Tossed the phone onto the couch and shoved his hands into the pockets of his jeans.

Then he waited for the explosion to come.

"You lied." She rushed toward him. Stopped right in front of him. Glared. "You said you wouldn't. You *promised—*"

Damn but she was gorgeous. He caught her hand. Lifted it to his lips. "Ah, sweetheart. That's where you're wrong."

"Do *not* sweetheart me—"

"I promised not to lie to you. I didn't say a damn word about lying to others." So he'd just lied to Eric. It had been necessary.

Tears gleamed in her eyes. "You think I'll let you do this?"

He kissed her knuckles again. "You hungry? Because I'm fucking starving." He let her hand go and turned away. "I ordered room service a few minutes ago. They're doing brunch now. Got some traditional croissants, scrambled eggs, bacon and whatever else was included on the platter. Should be arriving soon."

"Chase."

His shoulders stiffened. "I'm guessing you're mad."

"Mad doesn't cover it. I think you've lost your mind!"

"Nah. Just my heart." He casually strolled toward the window and stared out at the city.

The silence behind him was loud. Then... *"What?"*

"Oh, I think you heard me." He crossed his arms over his chest and turned back to face her. "Come on, as clever as you are, I know you've figured this out."

"I am lost right now."

"Huh."

"You're not lost. You figured something else out. That's what you mean every single time that you say, 'Huh' that way." She bounded toward him. "And you're trying to distract me. You're playing mind games."

"I am playing no game with you." With her, he was dead serious.

"You lied to Eric. He was the one on the phone, wasn't he?"

"I didn't lie. You did share secrets with me."

"You already knew about my stepfather—"

"But it's different when you tell me. Reading something in a typed-up dossier is far, far different than hearing the truth from your lips."

Her lips pressed together.

"You want to tell me more." He knew there was more. After her reveal about being seventeen years old when Vivian learned the truth about her stepfather, she'd stopped talking. Fallen asleep. He'd known she was exhausted, so he hadn't pushed.

But she was awake now. Merik was still gone, and time was running out. "Do you think your stepfather is involved in this?"

"No." She shook her head. Glanced away. "I haven't spoken to him in ten years."

Yes, that was what the dossier had said. "Just because you haven't spoken to him, it doesn't mean he isn't watching you." Chase would bet money on the man keeping tabs on Vivian.

But she gave a broken laugh even as she started to pace. "I wasn't important to Sergei. I was just...there."

I don't believe that.

"He fell for my mother. I once heard him tell a story where he said that he took one look at her, and he was hooked." She turned at the edge of the room. Paced back. "Love at first sight. Crazy, isn't it?"

"Not so crazy." He'd seen it happen.

"He fell for her, and what Sergei wanted, I learned that he got." She paused. Glanced down at the floor. "My mother was still married when they met. Sergei...God, I didn't learn *any* of this until later. Until I was seventeen and standing over my mother's grave." Her breath shuddered out.

He could feel her pain, and Chase hated it. "Why don't you tell me who you *thought* he was...until you were seventeen years old?"

Her head lifted. "I thought he was a man who knew my father. A friend who came to pay his condolences to my mother after my father was put to rest. A man who brought us gifts. A man who got a crew to help my mom with repairs to the house. A man who was kind. He...showed up at holidays. Birthdays. My mother—she thought he was good. Even called him her dream man once."

Sergei the Savage? *Huh.*

"She married him two years after my father died. Sergei spent half of his time in Russia and half here in the US. When he was with us, he acted as if we were the most important people in his world. He'd take my mom dancing. To the movies. He bought her a huge house, and he sent me to a fancy school, and he made sure that I had all the computers and tech and everything that I—" She stopped. "I don't like lies."

Yeah, he got that, and Chase understood how very much he'd screwed up with her.

"Everything he did and said during those years was a lie. My mother had a heart attack when I was seventeen. It was sudden and she'd never had a history of heart issues and, in a blink, she was gone." Her shoulders curled forward. "I was at the gravesite—I'd gone back after the service because I just couldn't say good-bye, and I heard Sergei talking. He'd come back, too."

Chase slowly headed toward her. He wanted to pull Vivian into his arms and hold her tight. But he didn't reach for her. Not yet.

So many secrets. So many lies.

"A man was yelling at him. Saying it was a good thing my mother had never learned the truth about who he was. That she wouldn't have loved a monster. That she would have hated Sergei for what he'd done." Her head lifted. She stared into Chase's eyes. "Sergei told the stranger that he had no regrets. That he didn't feel an ounce of remorse for the murder of my father. My *real* dad. Sergei said some people needed to die, and that he'd been one of them."

"Fuck." That had been cold.

"I must have made a sound. I don't remember, but I must have. I'd been crouched down near the flowers. I'd been on my knees because I was crying and I'd wanted to be close to my mother—"

God, the scene she painted in his mind was wrecking him. "Baby..." He had to touch her.

"Sergei found me. He knew I'd heard everything, and I knew he wasn't my mother's dream man." A tear slid down her cheek. "I thought he might kill me that day."

Sergei the Savage had killed a whole lot of people.

"He didn't. He just stared at me. The next day, he sent me away."

"Boarding school." That part had been easy to discover.

"I haven't seen him since. He went back to Russia, and I learned to live on my own."

So she'd lost her entire family. "You loved him."

Her lower lip trembled even as she swiped away the tear on her cheek. "I learned the truth about him. I mean the *full* truth. Hacking has always been easy for me. As a teen, I never thought that he might be hiding things from me. He was a businessman. Respected. I never even considered using my skills on him."

"But after that day in the cemetery, you started digging into his life."

"Yes." Her lashes flickered. "But you know the rest. You know who he is. *What* he is."

He couldn't hold back any longer. His arms curled around her as Chase pulled Vivian against his body. "Yeah." Yeah, he knew.

She shuddered against him. "Even when I knew, I still missed him."

And another piece of the puzzle that was Vivian slid into place. "That's why you asked me to be a good guy."

Her head lifted. She stared up at him.

"After the first time you kissed me, you said you needed me to be a good guy. It's because he wasn't. You loved him and you found out—"

"That I loved a monster? That I used to laugh at his jokes and try to imitate his accent because I wanted to be just like him?" A nod. "He didn't send me into dark tunnels. Didn't leave me there for so long that I was sobbing and terrified. That I crawled blindly in the dark and banged my head on a sharp screw that jutted out at me." She eased back. Her fingers rose to trace over her left eyebrow—

Shit. The scar.

"I thought Sergei was good because he was good to me. But all along, he was hiding who he really was."

Chase cursed and let her go. "And I did the same thing. That's why you were so hurt when you learned the truth." He took a step back. Hated what he'd done to her. Hated the pain he'd brought. "I am fucking sorry. I hate the way we met. I hate that I lied to you. I hate that—"

"You *are* one of the good guys, Chase."

His chest ached.

"That's something you taught me. Good guys—they lie, too, though, don't they?"

"Baby..."

"They lie when they have to do it. They don't like the lies, but they're trying to protect people."

I would do anything to protect you.

"Like you just lied to your boss. You did it because you want to save your friend. You're willing to trade your life to save Merik."

It's not just Merik I want to save.

"And you're lying to save me," she added softly.

I would lie, steal, or kill to save you. There is nothing I would not do for you. But Chase knew to tread carefully. "Maybe I'm just doing my job. The job was to find the intel. Stop the perps. That's what I'm doing."

She shook her head. "It's personal."

Damn straight it was.

"I've never told another soul about my stepfather. Only you."

He got what a big deal this was for her. "Thank you for trusting me."

"It's not just about trust. I want you to know me. The real me."

"I do." He'd seen her from the beginning. Not the Evil Queen that Merik had dubbed her. Vivian was good. Smart. Kind. Strong.

She was everything he'd ever wanted.

But what he feared he couldn't have.

"I looked guilty because of my stepfather, didn't I?" Her hands twisted in front of her body.

"On paper, yes, that was another nail in the coffin."

Vivian flinched.

"Shit. Wrong word choice. I meant—"

"I know." She held his gaze. "I know. He could be a broker for the intel. He could be my contact. He could have planted me there all along and I..." Her breath expelled. "Why did Dex give me the job? With my stepfather being who he is, I was sure the CIA would investigate and reject me."

The fact that she hadn't been rejected said a whole hell of a lot.

"I wanted to work in intelligence because I wanted to stop the bad guys once I found out what my stepfather had done. He's the reason I started on this path. But he's also the reason I didn't think I could ever have a real chance."

Only someone had given her that chance. Someone who liked to pull a whole lot of strings. "Dex made sure you got the job."

"But why?"

"Because I think he had plans for you." *Still* had plans.

"You don't trust him." Her head tilted. "Even though he's the one who came to Wilde? You think he's hiding things?"

"Oh, I think he's hiding about a million things from us." Before he could say more, there was a knock at the door.

Vivian's shoulders stiffened.

"Probably room service," Chase reassured her as he kept his voice easy and mild. "Go to the bedroom." *Just in case.* "I'll handle this." He had a gun tucked into the back of his jeans, and he moved his hand toward the gun even as he approached the door. He heard the soft pad of

Vivian's steps as she hurried to the bedroom. When he was sure Vivian was clear, Chase glanced through the peep-hole and saw the man dressed in the hotel's uniform. Saw the cart of food with the heavy silver covers over the dishes. *Right on time.* Chase opened the door.

The waiter smiled at him. "Good morning, sir. May I come in and set up breakfast for you?"

"Nah, that's not gonna happen." He shoved some cash at the guy. "I got it, but thanks."

The waiter's brows rose.

"You can go. Really. I got this."

With a nod, the waiter hurried away. Chase watched him until the elevator doors closed, and then he pulled in the cart. The wheels rattled and the silver coverings shook just a little. Chase locked the door—both locks—before he pushed the cart across the room. Then he went back and jammed a chair beneath the doorknob. Overkill? Maybe. The hotel had great security, but he believed in sometimes doing things the old-fashioned way, too.

"Can I come out?" Vivian called.

Chase lifted up the long, white skirt that covered the bottom of the cart. Hell, he didn't know if skirt was the name for that part of the fabric. Whatever the hell it was, Chase pulled it up in order to make sure there weren't any stowaways on the thing.

There weren't.

"Yeah, it's clear," he responded.

The bedroom door opened. She'd changed into a pair of jeans, a loose, green top, and black flats. Her gaze darted from him to the cart, and, as if on cue, her stomach grumbled.

Hell, Chase wasn't sure if that was her stomach or his. He couldn't even remember the last time he'd eaten. He lifted up the silver coverings and offered a plate to her. "Ladies first."

A smile flashed on her face as she hurried toward him. When she took the plate from him, their fingers brushed.

A surge of warmth shot up his hand.

"So that still happens," Vivian noted in her soft, husky voice.

"Yeah, V, it does." He was pretty sure it always would.

"V?" She laughed even as she scooped some eggs onto her plate. "You called me Viv, before…um, when we were…"

He snagged a piece of bacon. "I remember what we were doing." He planned to be doing that same activity a whole lot in the future.

"Now I'm V?" She reached for a croissant. "How'd that happen?"

Because he was comfortable with her. "I like you. I tend to give nicknames to people I like."

The croissant froze in mid-air as her hand stilled. "I like you, too."

That soft confession made him feel as if he'd won the lottery. Like was a good step. It was step one. He'd get to step two as soon as the case was over and she was safe.

Step two? That step was all about getting her to move from liking him to loving him.

Vivian moaned and that sensual sound snapped his attention to her face—and the croissant she was now eating.

"This is incredible! Chocolate chip croissants with some kind of amazing vanilla cream already on top." She took another bite. "Insane." She rushed closer to him. "You should try a bite, especially since you like vanilla so much." Her fingers rose toward his mouth.

Vanilla and chocolate chip? Vanilla was obviously his favorite, followed closely by chocolate chip. Except, well, her brownies had slid into second place in terms of his dessert faves. Still, when a man was offered a bite of food by a woman as sexy as Vivian, he didn't refuse.

His lips parted. Her fingers slid over the edge of his mouth as she gave him the bite. When his lips closed, he gave a quick lick to her finger before she pulled back. Chase heard the fast inhale that she made in response to his sensual lick.

"Delicious," he said after he swallowed.

She took another bite of the croissant. "It is fabulous."

"I was talking about you."

Pink bloomed in her cheeks.

And the words just spilled out of Chase. "God, I fucking love you."

Her mouth parted.

Oh, shit. "What I mean is...I love how real you are. With you, you don't fake reactions. I can tell exactly how you feel."

She hurriedly took another bite of the croissant. She ate in silence a few moments and then asked, "How do *you* feel? Because you can be pretty hard for me to read."

He'd finished another piece of bacon. At her question, Chase glanced up.

Something was nagging at him. Something that just didn't feel right.

"About me, I mean," Vivian added. She reached for another chocolate chip croissant. "Am I just a case to you?"

He stared at the croissants. "I didn't order chocolate chip croissants." He'd ordered plain croissants because they had been part of the platter option. He hadn't been sure what Vivian would like, so going with normal, buttered croissants had seemed the safest bet.

"They probably just did a substitution or something in the kitchen."

"But they put vanilla cream on them." He realized that every single croissant had been carefully covered with cream.

"S-sometimes high-end hotels will do things like…that."

He reached for the menu. Read over the list of items that had been on the breakfast platter once more. No mention of chocolate chip croissants or the fancy vanilla cream.

"Do I matter m-more than just…being a…a c-case?"

"You matter more than fucking anything." He grabbed for the hotel's phone. Then stopped. His head turned toward Vivian. "Your voice is slurring." Stuttering and slurring in a way that she didn't normally do.

Vivian frowned at him. "I don't...th-think I feel so...good." She lowered the second croissant. A croissant that she'd almost completely eaten. She put it on the cart and then staggered, as if her legs were weakening beneath her. "That's...weird."

He lunged for her even as he felt a surge of lethargy sweep through him, too. *Fuck. Fuck.*

Vivian's eyes were fluttering closed. Her body was sagging. She was falling—

He grabbed her right before she hit the floor. He scooped her into his arms. His heart should have been racing. Instead, it seemed to thud ever so slowly in his chest. "V?"

She didn't respond. She couldn't. She was out cold.

He carried her into the bedroom. Put her on the bed and checked frantically for her pulse. When he felt it, his head sagged. *Still there.* Just weak.

She'd been drugged.

He lifted his hand. Saw the tremble of his fingers. They'd *both* been drugged.

The vanilla cream on the fucking chocolate chip croissants. He hadn't ordered them. They'd been sent up to their room deliberately.

Their location had been compromised. The enemy was already in the hotel. No doubt, the perps would be storming in the room any moment. But...

Maybe they don't know that Vivian is here.

No one had seen her this morning. When he'd called in the room service order, he'd ordered the platter instead of requesting specific items that might have given away the number of people in his room. That was a habit, an old trick for when you were trying to keep a client under wraps.

Chase knew the perps would be coming up there any moment. They were just waiting for the drugs to kick in.

But the bastards don't have to take her.

His gaze flew around the room. He had to find a safe place for her, fast.

He heard a thud in the outer room. *Sonofabitch.* The enemy was already there. He turned away from the bed. Nearly fell down, face-first.

The drugs were pumping through him. Soon, he was going to be too weak to protect Vivian.

Unless...

"God, baby, I am sorry." He hauled her into his arms. His knee shoved into the nightstand and sent the lamp hurtling to the floor. His movements were uncoordinated, too rough, and he'd only had one bite of the croissant and vanilla.

She had so much more. Fuck.

He could hear the pounding in the outer room. They were breaking in. Probably had a key to the bottom lock, but he'd flipped the deadbolt, too, then, as a precaution, he'd hauled the chair in front of the door.

Some habits die hard.

He made it to the closet. "I am so f-fucking...sorry." His voice was slurring more. He managed to drag open the closet door. He lowered her inside as carefully as he could.

When she woke up...when she found out that she was in that closet, that he'd put her in there...

Chase pressed a kiss to her temple. "So s-sorry," he said again. He hauled out the burner phone. His fingers were fumbling so badly he almost couldn't send the emergency text. But he managed to get the numbers in—or at least, he thought he did. Then Chase put the phone in Vivian's lap. She could use it for a light when she woke up. *She can use it to call for help.*

He shut the door. The door was on the right side of the room, and it blended almost seamlessly with the wall.

Almost seamlessly.

The dresser was close to the door. Just a few feet away. He put his hip against that dresser and shoved even as he heard wood splintering in the outer room. With his last bit of strength, he heaved that dresser forward a few feet until it blocked the closet door. Until it trapped Vivian inside.

Until it hid her.

An angry voice shouted, "Find them! Hurry!"

He whirled around. Staggered away from the dresser. He couldn't be close to it. Couldn't give away Vivian's location. He saw the bag from the gift shop on the floor, saw what looked like a woman's shirt—

He shoved the bag under the bed and then crashed into the floor as his strength seemed to give out.

"In here!"

Chase lifted his head. Two men in black ski masks filled the doorway. Chase grabbed for the gun that had been tucked into the back of his jeans—

And one of the assholes kicked him in the face. The fucking face. Chase's head whipped around even as the taste of blood filled his mouth.

The gun was wrenched away from him. Not like Chase could put up much of a fight. He could barely move his arms.

"Where is she?"

Oh, one of the guys in the ski masks was crouching in front of him. Chase squinted at him. Blue eyes. The waiter's eyes had been that same bright shade of blue.

"*Where is Vivian Wayne?*"

Chase laughed. Or tried to laugh. A sputter came out. He also thought he might have spat out some blood. "G-gone..."

"Don't fucking bullshit us! We know she was with you! *Where is she?*"

"Eric...t-took her." He was about to pass out. Fuck it. He had to *sell* this shit. "Y-you're...t-too la..." Had he managed to say late? His tongue felt all thick, and he wasn't sure. He—

"Search this suite! Fast! Then we need to get to the roof and get the hell out of here! I'd bet my life this bastard called for backup before we broke through the door."

Yeah, I did. Suck it.

Technically, he'd texted for backup. But that backup wouldn't arrive in time.

"Make sure Vivian isn't here!"

Don't find her. Don't find her. Don't—

The world went black.

CHAPTER EIGHTEEN

Her world was dark. Her eyes were open, but Vivian couldn't see anything.

She felt like hell. Every part of her body ached. Her mouth and lips were so dry, and when she tried to swallow, a bitter aftertaste filled her mouth. "Chase?" Her voice emerged as a weak rasp.

He didn't answer.

Her hands flew out, and her fingers slammed into something. Something on the left. A wall? She patted frantically, moving her hands around and—

I'm surrounded.

Her heart rate kicked up. "Chase?" Still a weak rasp. What in the hell was happening? Where was she? It was so dark, and the darkness seemed to squeeze in around her. It was pulling her in, tighter and tighter, and a scream built up in her throat because she was trapped. She'd woken to her nightmare.

Chase had been with her. They'd been eating. She'd asked him how he felt about her and then—

Then I woke up to the dark. She stood up on shaky legs. Her arm hit something near her head. It swung and clattered into her. *What in the hell?* Her hand swatted, and she touched...plastic? Yes, the object felt like a soft plastic bag.

Her hands kept swatting. Kept touching. Walls were around her. She was closed in. Only a little space to the front and to the back. She couldn't find a handle or a door and—

Her foot slipped over something. Even as she glanced down, a ringing filled the air, and she saw a flash of light.

A phone. A phone was near her foot. She scrambled for it, and the light from the screen bounced around as she lifted the phone.

"I hear ringing!"

Vivian stiffened at the female shout.

"The phone has to be here!"

"Where?" A rough snarl. Male this time. A...familiar voice? "Where the hell is the ringing coming from?"

"I think it's behind the dresser," the woman replied. "Wait! Let me help you move it—"

Vivian gripped the phone tightly. "Eric?" That male voice had sounded like his. She swallowed. "Eric!" Her cry was louder. She shined the light from the phone and finally saw—

A door? Except there wasn't a handle on her side.

But in the next instant, that door was ripped open. "Vivian!" Eric stood there, relief covering his face and he hauled her forward, jerking her into his arms. "Thank Christ!"

She didn't understand what was happening. Vivian peeked over his shoulder and saw a woman with dark hair frowning at her. The woman was leaning over a dresser that appeared to have been hauled into the middle of the room.

Tilting her head, the woman asked, "You okay?" She gave a little wince. "I'm sorry. We didn't know you were in there the first time we did the sweep. Didn't even realize the closet was behind the dresser."

I was in the closet. Vivian pushed away from Eric. Nausea swirled in her stomach and rose to her throat. She put a desperate hand to her mouth even as her temples throbbed.

"Just why *was* the dresser in front of the closet? Who locked you in there?" the woman asked.

As the wave of nausea passed, Vivian took some deep, slow breaths. "I don't...remember." The throbbing in her temples got worse.

"Lace, she needs a doctor." Eric's voice was flat.

"The EMT is in the hallway. I'll get him." The dark-haired woman turned and hurried out.

Eric peered into Vivian's eyes. "You look like you're about to pass out."

I was locked in the closet. In the dark. She grabbed his hand. Held tight. "Where's Chase?"

His lips thinned. "I was hoping you knew."

Her heart squeezed. "We were...having breakfast." What had she been eating? "We were in the—the room out there." She motioned vaguely with her free hand.

Eric put his arm around her shoulders and guided her to the outer room. "Show me," he ordered, "exactly where you were."

A man in an EMT uniformed rushed toward her.

But she shook her head. "The cart is gone." A cart had been there. She was sure of it. "It was right here." She pointed. "Breakfast." The memory was coming back. Stronger. "He ordered the breakfast platter."

The EMT was reaching for her.

"Chase was worried, though...because..." What was it? "Something he didn't order." The nausea rolled through her again. "Oh, God, I think I'm going to be sick." She whirled and staggered for the bathroom.

***

"Drugged." Eric watched as Vivian Wayne was loaded into the back of an ambulance. "I'd bet on it."

The fact that the breakfast cart had vanished from the room? *Not just the room but the whole freaking hotel.* Someone had been getting rid of evidence.

"No security footage from that floor," Lacey Amari said as she strode toward him. "You won't believe this, but the footage cut out right before the food was delivered this morning."

Oh, he believed it all right. Eric glanced up at the building. The top floor was his. No one else ever used it. The suite wasn't really part of the hotel. It had been reserved just for him and for his top clients. Only he'd never actually let any clients use the space before. This was the first time he'd needed this particular safe house.

Except it wasn't so safe.

"Who all knew the location?" Lacey asked.

"I knew it. Chase knew it." That was all. Chase hadn't even known where they were going until the chopper landed.

"Then how were they compromised?"

The ambulance driver was shutting the back door of the vehicle. "We're going with her," Eric said as he shot forward. No way was he going to let Vivian out of his sight. Lacey hustled with him. He'd brought Lacey onto this case because she was someone that he trusted one hundred percent. She was also family, though only a few people in the world knew about that tie. It was a tie Lacey didn't talk about, and because she didn't, neither did he. *Not until she's ready.*

They climbed into the back of the ambulance.

The EMT glanced up. "Only one can ride back here."

They were both going with Vivian. Eric lifted a brow at the guy. A little *try-to-make-me-move* dare.

"I'll ride up front," Lacey announced quickly. "Better for me to see what is around us."

He knew she didn't mean what, she meant who. Lacey would be looking for tails.

While she made her way up to the front, Eric turned his attention to Vivian. She didn't look quite so paper white, but her eyes were huge, and dark shadows lined them. "Feeling better?" Eric asked her carefully.

Her head turned toward him. "Who put me in the closet?"

He suspected the answer on that one, but this might not be the best time to tell her. "You were safe in there. I think if you hadn't been in that closet, then you would have been taken when the intruders burst open the hotel room door."

They'd destroyed the door.

And my security system didn't go off again. One of the bonuses he'd put in place in that suite—it had come equipped with an alarm that should have activated the minute anyone tried to tamper with the locks.

First, the alarm hadn't sounded at the cabin. And now—at his safe house?

"Taken..." Vivian wet her lips as the ambulance drove away from the scene. Her body twisted on the gurney. "Like Chase?" Fear flashed on her face.

He wasn't going to lie to her. There was no point in that. "Yes."

"He doesn't know how to unscramble the code. He was just saying that because he didn't want me to be a target." Her breath heaved out as her words came faster and faster. "They'll realize the truth. If they took him thinking he knew the secret..." Tears gleamed in her eyes. "They'll kill him when he can't unscramble the code."

If they took Chase because they thought he knew the code...*then they would have needed to hear our phone conversation.*

But maybe that wasn't why they'd taken Chase. He considered scenarios. Possibilities. Maybe they'd just taken him *because they couldn't find Vivian*. Because Chase had managed to hide Vivian before the perps got inside the suite.

"I will do anything to help him," Vivian said. "Anything."

The EMT was trying to check her vitals, but her hand shoved past him and she grabbed Eric. She clutched him tightly. Stared into Eric's eyes. *"You can't let them hurt Chase.* If they want to trade him for me, we'll do it. They can't kill him."

And *that* was why the perps had taken Chase. Because they'd found a way to get to Vivian. *Through Chase.* "You offer yourself, you give them what they need, and good agents will die. The men and women you were trying to protect will die."

The EMT was dead silent.

"I can think of something," Vivian whispered. "I can figure something out. A way to save them all." Her gaze darted to the EMT.

Eric knew she didn't want to talk with him there, but he could feel Vivian's mind spinning. He could practically feel it—

"I always loved the story of the Trojan Horse," she said, seemingly to no one in particular. "The people in Troy thought they were getting a gift. They let that present come right in because they didn't see the danger. The peace offering was a lie. A lie in plain sight that led to their downfall."

Eric blinked at her, and he understood her message.

Then he turned his head toward the EMT. "When she's nervous, she likes to share facts."

The young man looked uncertain. "Okay." He drew out the word until it seemed to be a full sentence.

Eric's stare darted back to her. "Chase mentioned to me that you do that."

"Chase knows me well."

"Yes." He nodded. "I think he does." Chase had been on Vivian's side from the very beginning.

Now Eric could see why.

Because he's in love with her, and I think she's in love with him. "We'll get him back," Eric promised.

***

"How long is he gonna be out?"

"I don't fucking know, man! How much of that shit did he eat?"

"Looked like two of them croissants to me. Dammit, we expected him to share the stuff with the woman! How the hell were we supposed to know she wasn't there?"

Chase didn't move as the men who'd taken him had their conversation. He slumped, head hanging forward, shoulders sagging, in the chair. A rope was wrapped around his chest, securing him to the chair's back, but his feet were free.

Bad mistake.

He'd woken a while ago, but had made sure not to let that detail be noticed. He wanted to hear these assholes.

They were the flunkies. The guys doing the dirty work for their boss.

He wanted the boss.

"You think she's going to trade herself for him? Or that Eric Wilde will offer her up for this guy?" One flunkie bastard grabbed Chase's head and shoved it back. The movement was rough and hard, and Chase wanted to kick out with his right foot. Break a knee cap. Maybe some ribs.

He didn't.

He knew the move from his captor was deliberate. A deliberately rough move to see if Chase was awake or faking. He was faking, but those dumbasses wouldn't know it.

Something sharp pressed to Chase's throat. He felt the press of a blade even as wet warmth dripped down his neck. *That fucker just put a knife to my throat.*

"I think it would be easier to kill him now," the gruff voice continued. "Big bastard is gonna be trouble when he wakes up. Besides, Eric Wilde won't know if he's dead or alive. Not until after the exchange." The blade pressed deeper.

Chase got ready to attack. *Change of plans. I'm not going to let this asshole slice me—*

A door opened. "Get the hell away from him!" A familiar voice shouted.

Too familiar.

The blade lifted. "I was just...testing. Making sure he was out."

"Looked to me like you were about to kill him."

He was.

"Might be easier if he's dead," the knife-happy SOB muttered. "Big, bad Eric Wilde won't know until—"

"This isn't just about Eric Wilde. It's about Dexter Ryan. If you think that guy won't have his nose in every bit of this, you're dead wrong. He'll demand proof of life. We have to give it to him. We can't very well do that if our bargaining chip was sliced ear to ear and died in a pool of his own blood."

Footsteps shuffled.

"Get your asses out of here," the familiar voice barked. "Patrol the building. Things are going to get busy very, very soon."

More shuffling. The door closed.

Chase waited. His head had sagged forward again.

Are you the leader? Because you were sure as shit on my suspect list but...

"I knew you would be trouble the moment I saw you," the man said, and there was no accent to his voice. None at all. But he was still familiar. "I could tell by your eyes. By the way you looked at her. You were already getting personally involved from the very beginning."

Chase didn't move.

"Good thing we got you out of the way." A laugh. "With you tied up, not like you can rush to the rescue and play hero. No one else will have the personal connection to her. No one else will be ready to die for her." The floor creaked as he turned away.

Chase waited a beat, waited until the traitorous SOB was almost at the door. "*Non, mon ami...*" Chase let the French roll from him as his head tilted back and he eyed his prey. "*Tu vas mourir.*"

Luc Coderre whirled toward him.

Chase gave him a slow smile. "Sorry. Is my French rusty? Then let me repeat that shit in English."

Luc lunged toward him.

"No, my friend," Chase told him. "Though, really, you're not my friend. More like an asshole enemy, but I couldn't remember the translation for that part. Anyway, *you're* going to die—"

Luc attacked.

CHAPTER NINETEEN

"You were poisoned," Lacey Amari told her. "You should stay in the hospital. That's the *normal* thing to do."

Vivian yanked the IV out of her arm. "Turn around or you're going to get flashed."

Lacey spun around. "You're being difficult. The doctors are still running your tox screen. You were vomiting all over the suite. You could collapse at any moment." Her voice rose with worry as she demanded to know, "*Have* you collapsed? Because I don't hear anything—"

"I'm changing, not collapsing." And there. *Done.* She'd just gotten her clothes back on, and she toed into her shoes. "Now I'm getting the hell out of here."

Lacey turned toward her. "I don't think so."

"Look, you're nice and all—"

Lacey beamed at her. "That's sweet of you to say. Is it because I held back your hair while you vomited in the bathroom? Does it mean we're friends now?"

"I'm leaving. I'm going after Chase." She moved for the door.

Lacey blocked her path. "Major problem with that plan. You don't know where Chase is."

That was a problem. Luckily, Vivian had it covered. "If I go back to my place—just me, no guards—something tells me the bad guys will swarm instantly. They'll take me. Since they took Chase, too, I figure I'll be transported to the same location where they are holding him."

Lacey blinked at her. "That's your big plan? To sacrifice yourself? To give yourself up so that you can save a man you met a few days ago?"

"Yes, that's my initial plan." Again, she moved around Lacey.

Again, Lacey stepped into her path.

"I don't want to hurt you," Vivian told her honestly. "You did hold back my hair, and you seem like a nice person, but I'm going after Chase." No one would stop her.

"What about the agents in jeopardy?" Lacey's delicate jaw hardened. Everything about Lacey seemed delicate. Bone structure, height, build. "You know the CIA men and women you were originally trying to protect? What about them? Are you willing to sell them out now so you can save your new boyfriend? Is that how this works?"

The door opened behind Lacey.

Lacey immediately swung around. Her body tensed. "Who the hell are you?"

Dex frowned at her.

"He's the boogeyman," Vivian whispered. "Super bad guy. You should take him out right now."

Lacey nodded and sprang at Dex—

He caught her hands. "I am *not* the boogeyman." His gaze snapped to Vivian. "Was that shit supposed to be funny? Because I am not laughing."

"No, but you're about to be crying," Lacey promised and she swept her leg under his.

"What the—" Dex didn't get to finish because he slammed toward the floor.

Lacey flew down on top of him. She yanked a knife out of her boot and brought it to his throat.

"*Freeze.*" Dex's voice. Low and lethal. Not at all worried even though he had a knife pressed to his Adam's apple.

Lacey laughed. "Yeah, right. Like I'm going to take orders from some mystery jerk that I just took down without even barely trying."

"I'm not talking to you. I'm talking to Vivian."

Lacey's head whipped up.

Crap. Vivian's hand tightened around the door handle. Just when she'd almost made her escape.

"She was using you as a distraction," Dex explained as he still used that low and lethal tone. "A very good one, I might add. But it's not going to work. I'm not letting her leave."

"Neither am I." Lacey glowered at Vivian. "I thought we were on our way to being besties. I held back your hair."

"I have no idea what that means," Dex muttered. "But, as much as I do enjoy this position, I'm afraid you need to get off me now. Before I have to get physical with you."

Vivian pulled open the door.

"Don't, Vivian," Dex blasted. "The last thing I want to do is explain to Chase why you are dead."

Her shoulders stiffened as she glanced over at him. "Do you know where he is?"

"Nope. But I also know that I can't let you run after him. Can't let you trade yourself and jeopardize the data that was taken." Even though he was still on the floor, his head had turned so that he could stare into her eyes. "Chase wouldn't want you doing this."

"It's not his choice."

Lacey's knife was still at Dex's throat. She'd nicked him. "So are you one of the good guys? Is that what I'm getting from this talk?"

His head turned back toward her. He smiled. "I am the best you will ever have." A sensual note slid into his voice.

"Doubt it." She pressed the knife down harder—

And the next few movements happened really fast. So fast that Vivian couldn't keep track of them all. Dex grabbed Lacey's hand. Wrenched the knife away. Twisted and rolled their bodies, lunged up to his feet, dragged Lacey with him and—

He ended up standing, with Lacey in front of him. One arm was wrapped around her waist while his other hand held a knife to her throat.

"Don't!" Vivian rushed toward them. "Don't hurt her! She's a Wilde agent!"

His nose moved a little closer to her hair. "I figured as much."

"Did you just *sniff* me?" Lacey gasped. "That is weird!" She drove her elbow back into him, yanked on his wrist, and the knife clattered to the floor.

Before Lacey could go in for a bigger attack, Vivian rushed between them. "Stop."

Dex and Lacey were both breathing hard.

"I don't have time for this craziness. Lacey, Dex works for the CIA. Or maybe he's in charge of it. He won't exactly say." Vivian didn't really care right then. *Have to find Chase.* "I do know that your boss will vouch for him, so you don't need to attack or dismember him."

"Pity," Lacey mumbled.

"Yes, I absolutely agree." Vivian lifted her chin. "Chase needs me."

"You were drugged," Lacey reminded her.

"Yes. Doesn't change the point. Chase needs me, and I'm going to him. I will not let him be hurt or killed in my place." With determination, she met Dex's intense stare. "And I don't care *who* you are, you aren't going to stop me." She wasn't going to be intimidated or controlled.

His eyes narrowed.

Good. *Message received.* She turned on her heel, a crisp, almost military-like move...

"You're going to sacrifice innocent agents?" Dex asked.

Why did no one have faith in her?

"You're going to do that in order to save the agent who tricked you into falling in love with him?"

Dex's last taunt seemed particularly cruel. Vivian looked back and let her gaze meet Lacey's. "Maybe I should have let you dismember him."

Lacey's brows rose. "The offer is still on the table."

Dex cursed. "This isn't a fucking game." His hand reached out and curled around Vivian's shoulder.

She caught his hand and twisted, just like she'd been taught during her CIA training. He yelped in surprise. "Do I look like I'm playing?" Vivian wanted to know.

He snatched his hand away. "For the record, I could have attacked you back in a dozen different ways. If you think you can show me one self-defense maneuver and I'll suddenly believe you are capable of fighting off the people who took Chase, you're dead wrong."

"No, *you're* dead wrong."

He frowned at her.

"Chase didn't trick me into falling in love with him. No tricks were involved at all. I fell in love with him because I saw the man he truly is. I know Chase. I love him. And, yes, I will do anything to protect him." When you loved someone, there was nothing you wouldn't do. "But, for the record, I'm not planning to take down the bad guys by using my self-defense moves. You're right. I will be out-trained there."

His stare had turned assessing.

She stepped toe-to-toe with him. "But you know where I'm *not* out-trained? When it comes to tech. To hacking. If those jerks want the data unscrambled, they have to give it to me. They have to put me in front of a computer and let me access it. No other coder out there will be able to get them the data they need because, yes, I *am* that good when it comes to my tech."

"So you'll just hand it over to them."

Was he being a deliberate jackass? "As soon as I start coding, I won't unscramble the tech."

His lips parted, and then Dex smiled. Finally, he seemed to get her plan. "You'll destroy it."

Vivian nodded.

Lacey cleared her throat. "Um, why didn't you just do that to begin with? Am I the only one wondering this?"

"Because then we wouldn't have our traitors," Dex retorted. "And they'd be out there, hiding in plain sight, and another attack would just be in the works. You scrambled it to buy time, didn't you? You were working to find the traitors on your own, but things got blown to hell when they started framing you."

"That was a problem," she allowed. "And when they blew up my car, the problem got a whole lot worse." The initial glitches she'd noticed in the system had put her on red alert. She'd done her best to protect the data and try to draw out the enemies at the CIA. Since she hadn't known who to trust, there hadn't been a ton of options for her.

He nodded. "They had to be taken down, they had to be pulled out of the system, and the only way to do that was to make them think they were getting the data."

Now they were close to unmasking the jerks. "I need backup. I can't do this alone." If she went in alone, then she and Chase could both die. "While I'm working on the data, they'll be distracted. That will be your time to act."

"You want us to tail you," Dex concluded.

"Tail me, bug me, whatever. Just *do* it."

The hospital door opened. They all whirled at the same time. Eric stood there, and he appeared grim as hell. He gripped a phone in his hand.

Oh, God.

"I got a message." He swallowed. His hold on the phone tightened. "They want an exchange."

She'd known that demand was coming.

Dex stalked toward Eric. "Did you get proof of life?"

A curt nod.

Vivian's gaze darted to the phone.

"They want you, Vivian," Eric said. "They get you, and we get back both Chase and Merik. They want—"

"Deal," she agreed quickly. "They'll get me. They can have me right now. Give them a location. Set up the switch." She edged closer to him with a casual glide. "Just do—"

She swiped his phone.

And now she could see the image. The image that was frozen on the screen.

Eric cursed. "You don't have to watch that."

Her fingers were shaking as she got the image to play.

Chase was tied to a chair and slumped forward. It looked as if he'd been tortured. Blood soaked his shirt. He barely appeared to be breathing. Then his head lifted ever so slowly and turned toward whoever the hell had been recording him. "V-Vivian..." Blood dripped from his mouth.

A tear slid down her cheek. "I will trade. I will give myself up and take his place." She looked at Eric. "*Set it up. Do whatever they want.*"

Dex's fingers brushed over her arm. "Just make sure," he said quietly, barely breathing the words into her ear, "that you do what *you* promised."

***

The phone dinged.

Luc smiled as he read the text. Smiled even though he had a busted lip, a black eye, and what Chase hoped were two broken ribs. "Look at that." Luc held up the phone. "Your buddy Eric wants to schedule a meet to swap you for your girlfriend."

No. "I told her *not* to do it. No matter what."

He'd been freaking bleeding all over the place, and he hadn't cared. Luc had told him to deliver a message begging for the exchange. He'd said if Chase didn't do it, he'd cut Chase's throat.

Then cut me, bastard. Cut me. Luc had certainly cut Chase a hell of a lot *before* he'd started filming. Cut him. Stabbed him. What the hell ever.

Chase had stared into the phone's camera, and said, "*V-Vivian. Don't do it. Don't you dare fucking trade yourself for me. They'll double cross you. Kill us both. Don't you do it.*"

"Oh, is that what you said? Sorry. I think I stopped filming right after you called her by name. Thought it would be more meaningful that way." Smirking, Luc sent a fast response on his phone.

That's right, dumbass. Keep using that phone. Eric will be tracing the messages. He'll find you.

Luc glanced up. Frowned. "Why are you looking so smug? Oh, wait, is it because you think the cavalry is coming?" Once more, he wiggled the phone. "Because you think they're going to trace this back to me? To you?" He laughed. "We're steps ahead of Wilde. I know their tech. More importantly, I know how to beat their tech."

If he knew…there was only one way…

Inside man.

As if on cue, the door opened once more. No ski-mask-clad goon swaggered inside. Instead, Merik stood there. His face appeared grim as he said, "Chase, buddy, you look like hell."

Ignoring the pain that coursed through his body, Chase straightened as best he could and replied, "Merik, you sonofabitch traitor, you look like you'll be getting an ass kicking soon."

Luc laughed. "*Mon Dieu,* he's funny."

Merik wasn't laughing.

Neither was Chase. He was making a promise.

Merik didn't move away from the doorway. "Don't worry. I'll take good care of your lady for you."

"Don't fucking touch her!"

"Fine. Then we can make a different arrangement." Merik's gaze slid to Luc. "Once we have the intel, you kill her, and I'll end him."

Luc frowned. "Why wait? He can die now."

"No, can't do it yet. She's going to insist on seeing him. I *know* her."

"But I gave proof of life!"

Big whoop, you sonofabitch. Chase strained against his ropes. When he'd been kicking out and fighting Luc, they'd loosened some. *Just not enough yet.*

"She's in love with him. She'll want to see him." Merik turned his stare back to Luc. "And after she sees you, she'll do whatever we want."

She's in love with him. Merik had sounded so damn confident. "No. You don't know her. You don't understand her."

"Of course, I do. I read all the files on her, just like you did. Hell, I knew about her *before* you did. I was CIA. Worked with Dex. That's how Luc and I met."

"One bloody Paris night," Luc agreed. "For a while, we had the perfect partnership happening."

Merik's gaze hardened. "Then I had to leave the agency. You can only work an angle for so long. But branching out was good. It allowed me to learn all kinds of new things. Like the secrets to Wilde tech. Eric always thought he was so freaking smart. He didn't even notice when I started using tech on *him*. When I bugged *his* devices. Over-confident asshole. But that's okay. He'll fall soon enough. Everyone will."

Chase was staring at a traitor. "I trusted you."

"Yeah, it's a real bitch when people lie to you, isn't it?"

Chase clenched his jaw.

"But, hey, Vivian forgave you, so I figure you'll forgive me, too, eventually." He tapped his cheek. "What am I saying? Of course, you won't forgive me. You'll be dead, and I'll be a rich bastard drinking a pretty drink on some sandy white beach." He turned away. "Come on, Luc. It's time for us to get ready for Vivian."

"*Don't!*" Chase yelled. He struggled against the ropes. "Don't you touch her!"

Merik wasn't looking back. Or stopping.

"*I will put a bullet in your head!*" Chase roared. "Don't hurt her!"

Merik glanced back. "No, buddy, you're wrong." He almost seemed sad. "You'll be the one with the bullet to the brain."

Chase strained against the ropes. More blood poured from his wounds. *Luc stabbed me too many times. Bastard.*

"Damn, that's a lot of blood. Hope you can stay alive until she gets here." He smiled at Luc. "After all, he's our leverage."

No, I'm the man who is going to kill you.

CHAPTER TWENTY

"They're going to take you," Eric told her grimly. "You'll go into the parking garage, and a car will be waiting for you. They'll probably put a blindfold over your head and put you in the back of the vehicle."

Wonderful. More darkness.

"They'll have disabled the security in the garage. If they're smart, they will have multiple vehicles set to leave at the same time. The idea for all the cars is that our team will have to split up as we divide to track them." His mouth tightened. "Their mistake. We won't be dividing up."

"Because I'll be wearing your locator device." Her hand lifted and toyed with her new earrings. They looked like small, sparkling diamonds, but they weren't. They were GPS locators. Eric had said they would allow him to find her no matter where she went.

"Exactly." His gaze swept over her face. "So don't fight them when they take you. Play the role of the scared victim."

She *was* scared.

"They said that they'd trade you for Chase and Merik, but we both know they aren't just going to instantly give them up. They'll probably promise that Chase and Merik will be let go once you unscramble the tech."

"*Ahem.*" Dex waved his fingers. "My cue to cut in." His eyes glittered. "I understand Chase is important to you."

"Yes, he is," she said flatly. "Very important."

"But under no circumstances can the enemy actually get the location and real identities of our undercover operatives. You have to stop that from happening, no matter what else occurs." He held her gaze. "Do you understand what I'm telling you?"

"I understand that I can protect Chase and keep the bad guys from getting the code. That's what I'll do." Chase *and* Merik. She had no intention of leaving either man behind.

"I think she understands," Lacey murmured as she shot a sideways glance at Dex. "Any other words of wisdom you want to impart? Because we're running out of time here."

Yes, they were. The people holding Chase and Merik had sent a location address and a time for the exchange.

After a long exhale, Dex raked his fingers through his hair. "One more thing. And it's bothering me."

Well, that wasn't good.

"Chase wanted me to investigate Luc. So I dug a little more, and I found something. I mean, it could be nothing. Not like it's a red flag waving in the wind, but it's enough that my alarm bells are ringing."

"Oh, for goodness sake." Lacey cocked her head toward him. "Spit it out!"

"Merik used to work for the CIA. I'd used him on several cases and found him to be a solid agent.

When he left, when he said he wanted to step onto the civilian side of things, I referred him to Eric for a job."

Eric crossed his arms over his chest. "I don't like where this is going."

"While I was digging into Luc's past, I cross-referenced some dates and locations. Turns out, even though Merik and Luc were never assigned to work together, they *did* happen to find themselves in the same foreign countries, in the exact same foreign cities, at three different times. At least three. Could be more. I just haven't had time to dig deep enough to be certain."

Her heartbeat sped up.

"That could be coincidence," Lacey said. "Thousands, no, hundreds of thousands of people were probably in those same cities."

Eric seemed to be thinking things over. "During the investigation, Merik never mentioned knowing Luc. At least, he didn't tell me."

"Or me," Dex muttered. "So maybe they don't know each other. Or..." But his voice trailed away.

Or if they do know each other and Merik kept that secret what does it mean? Not anything good, that was for certain. "Where is Luc right now?" Vivian asked.

"He was sent on an emergency mission last night, one sanctioned by his supervisor at the agency. He's supposed to be on a plane bound for Madrid." Dex rolled back his shoulders. "There was no video footage of him getting on the plane. It took off from a black ops site, but I have a friend in Madrid who will let me know if Luc actually steps off that plane when it lands."

Dex didn't trust Luc. And from the sound of things, he might not trust Merik, either?

Dex pinned her with his gaze. "I'm telling you this information because I want to make sure you trust the right people. When you go in there, don't fall for lies or tricks."

Her chin lifted. "When I go in there, I will only trust one person." That had been her intent all along. "I will help Chase, and he will help me." She knew it was time to go. Vivian squared her shoulders and turned away—

"There are lots of variables on an op like this one," Dex's low voice stopped Vivian in her tracks. "You might think you can control things, but the scene can go to hell in a heartbeat."

Her heart squeezed in her chest. "He's my variable."

"Uh, what?"

Vivian glanced back at Dex. "Chase is my variable, and I trust him completely."

He held her stare. "Good." A pause. "Be careful."

She nodded.

"We need to get to that garage," Eric said.

Yes, they did. "Did you know," Vivian said as their little team hurried away, "that there are more than 40,000 parking garages and lots in the US?"

***

Vivian pushed open the stairwell door and slowly walked into the parking garage. The place was massive. Dark. Cavernous. Five vehicles waited in the garage, seemingly parked in random spaces.

Five masked men were waiting there, too. Armed men. As she advanced with slow, uncertain steps, they pointed their guns at her.

Vivian's hands lifted into the air. "I don't have a weapon."

One of the men rushed toward her. He patted her down. Fast and rough. Then he shoved a black cloth toward her.

Her fingers clenched in the fabric. "Where is Chase? Merik?"

"*Put it on,*" the man growled. His voice was low and held no accent.

She lifted up the cloth—the hood—and started to put it over—

"Wait!" Another masked man pointed toward her. "I think my wife would like those earrings." His voice was muffled. "Give them to me."

What?

He approached her. Pointed his gun at her. "Take off the earrings."

"You're really going to rob me?" Vivian licked her lips. "Is that part of the plan? Because I don't think your boss will appreciate this little deviation of yours."

"Give them to me."

"They are family heirlooms. The only thing I have of my grandmother's." Her voice trembled because she was scared. "Please, don't take them."

"Take off the fucking earrings or I will take them off you." He holstered his gun, only to then immediately pull out a knife. "If you don't have your lobes, I'm sure you can still work the scramble just fine." He'd come closer, and she could make out his bright blue eyes.

"I'd rather keep my ear lobes, thank you." Vivian tucked the cloth hood under her arm, and she slowly removed the earrings.

He sprang forward and snatched them from her. "Great. Thanks." He held them up to the light. "Fucking pity." Then he dropped them to the ground and smashed them under his booted feet.

Her breath choked out. "I don't think your wife will like them much now."

"I don't have a wife."

She'd figured that.

"And now you don't have a tracker on you," he added with satisfaction. "So put on the hood and let's get out of here. My boss is waiting."

How did he know about the earrings? Eric had given those to her. Only Eric, Lacey, and Dex had known about the trackers inside them. Eric had said he was deliberately keeping the trackers private. *He'd* been the one who was going to monitor her.

But these jerks knew.

She put on the hood. Someone grabbed her arm. Jerked her forward. Kept moving her and pushing her until her upper thigh hit—a bumper? The back of a car?

"Get in." A rough order.

"This doesn't feel like a back seat," Vivian told him as she struggled to buy time.

"That's because it's not." He didn't tell her to get in again. He shoved her inside. Slammed her down and then laughed before he said, "Heard you don't like tight, dark spaces. Bet you'll be more than ready to cooperate when we finally get you out of here."

They were locking her in the trunk. *Oh, God.* "Where is Chase?" Vivian cried out. "You said you'd exchange him for me! You said—"

"We lied." The trunk slammed closed.

***

"On the move," Lacey reported as she peered through the binoculars. "Five vehicles, and they are heading out now."

Eric's fingers flew over the keyboard, and the same error message appeared again on his laptop screen.

"Eric?" Lacey prompted.

"She's offline." He looked up as the full implications of that truth settled like ice in his gut.

"But...but the cars are moving. She's moving." She'd lowered the binoculars and was staring at him.

"They found the trackers. They disabled them." The only thing that made sense. He and Lacey were alone right then. They'd picked the location deliberately because it gave them the perfect vantage point to see the action below.

Lacey swallowed. "Only you, Dex, and I knew about the earrings."

Yes. "You know what that means." *Dammit.*

She squared her shoulders. Pulled out her gun. "I'm ready."

***

Chase tensed when the delicate figure was pushed into his room. A black hood covered her head, but he would have recognized Vivian anywhere. *"Get your fucking hands off her!"*

The prick in the ski mask just laughed, and then his hand rose to yank the hood off Vivian's head.

Her hair was tousled, her eyes dazed, and when she saw Chase—a wide smile spread across her face. A smile followed immediately by a flash of alarm as she caught sight of the blood covering him. Vivian bounded toward him—

Only to have the prick in the ski mask wrap his arm around her stomach and haul her back against him.

"I told you," Chase snarled, *"get your hands off her."*

"You're not giving the orders, asshole," the man fired back. He kept his left arm around Vivian, and his right hand lifted a gun. He aimed the weapon at Chase. "I could kill you right now."

"And if you did that," Vivian snapped back, not sounding afraid but instead sounding absolutely enraged, "then I would never give you the information that you want. Your boss will be sorely disappointed, and something tells me he will take that disappointment out on *you*."

God, she was beautiful. Her cheeks were flushed. Her eyes were blazing. And the way her voice vibrated with that barely contained fury... "Fucking beautiful."

Vivian's gaze held his.

"Marry me," Chase said.

Her lips parted.

"I need you. Can't imagine the rest of my life without you." He nodded and strained against the ropes once more. They were *almost* to the breaking point.

The man with the gun laughed. "Is this a joke?" His hold on Vivian loosened a little. "Your fool ass is going to die, and you just asked her to—"

Vivian's elbow flew back and slammed into the guy's chest. His breath choked out, and he tried to swing the gun toward her, but he was too close to Vivian, and she was moving too fast. She caught his wrist and pushed it back even as she head-butted him.

The ski-mask-wearing jerk staggered. He caught his balance, and then circled around Vivian. He'd put his back to Chase, and, unfortunately, he still had the gun.

But the dumbass forgot that my legs aren't bound.

"I can't kill you," the man spat at Vivian. "But I can sure enjoy hurting your boyfriend right in front of you—"

Chase kicked out with his right foot, aiming for the spot directly behind the man's kneecap. "No, you can't." Another hard kick to the jerk's other leg. "But I can enjoy hurting you." The man went down with a jarring impact. The gun flew from his fingers. Vivian scrambled for it.

The bastard on the floor shoved up on his arms.

Yeah, you won't be jumping to your feet anytime soon to come at me.

The perp hauled his upper body close to Chase. He shouted, "I will fucking mess you up!"

Chase kicked him in the face. A kick that knocked the man out. "How's that for messing you up?" He leaned forward and felt the ropes strain against him. "I told you to get your hands off her. You should have listened."

"*Chase!*"

Vivian ran to him. Still clutching the enemy's gun, she threw her arms around Chase. "Oh, God, I was so scared."

She felt good against him. Warm and soft and *alive.* "Can you help me with the ropes? I'm almost free." And he didn't know how long they had before more men came rushing into the room. "We don't have much time, and you need to know about—"

"You don't have any time, actually," Luc announced.

Vivian stiffened against Chase, but she didn't let him go.

Over her shoulder, Chase glared at Luc. He'd just entered the room. He held a laptop in one hand, and in the other he gripped a gun.

"Move away from him, Vivian," Luc ordered. "Oh, and be a dear...do drop the weapon while you're at it. *Merci.*"

She eased back. Stared into Chase's eyes.

Don't drop the gun, Chase mouthed. Her body was blocking Luc's view of his face. *Shoot the bastard.*

"Yes," Vivian said.

"Um, yes, you're going to drop the gun?" Luc asked. "Because I wasn't giving you an option. I was telling you to drop the weapon. Or I will shoot *you* in the back. I need you alive, but I don't need you uninjured, Vivian."

She licked her lips and stared at Chase a moment longer. "I will marry you."

He smiled at her. His lip bled more with the movement, but like he cared about that shit.

Luc laughed. "This is so sweet. But you're not going to marry him. Chase Durant isn't going to make it out of this room alive."

She whirled and aimed her weapon at Luc. "You kill him, and I will *never* unscramble the data. You can just put a bullet in me, too, because I won't help you. Ever."

Put a bullet in her? "Uh, Viv," Chase began. "That's…that's not a good plan."

Luc didn't look away from her. His weapon was pointed at Vivian, and hers was pointed straight at Luc. "No, Vivian," Luc agreed. "It's not a good plan. Now follow my orders and *drop your weapon* before I shoot."

"Drop *your* weapon before I shoot," Vivian snapped back. "You should have brought more goons in with you. It was a mistake to come in alone because I am not afraid to fire at you—"

Chase heard a creak behind him. *Fuck me.*

Vivian had stiffened, so he knew she'd heard the sound, too.

"I didn't come in alone," Luc assured her. "I made sure my partner had my back. Chase, you know how great it is when someone has your six."

Chase felt a gun push against his temple.

"In case you're wondering what's happening behind you, Vivian, my partner is currently holding a gun to your boyfriend—oh, sorry, your fiancé's—head. If you don't drop your weapon right now, he'll pull the trigger."

Vivian didn't look back at Chase. "Is he telling the truth?" Vivian's voice shook as she asked the question.

Chase opened his mouth—

"I'm afraid he is telling the truth," Merik assured her. "So drop the weapon or I will kill Chase."

CHAPTER TWENTY-ONE

Vivian whirled around and aimed her gun at Merik. "I didn't want it to be true."

Merik lifted his brows.

"Dex suspected you, but I hoped he was wrong. I know what it's like to be wrongly suspected—*I didn't want it to be true about you.*"

Luc slipped close to her. His hand curled around her gun. "I'll be taking that."

Fighting him right now wasn't an option. He was better trained than she was, and with Merik's gun against Chase's temple...*I can't take the chance he'll be shot.*

Luc took her gun and backed away. She heard the sound of a drawer opening. Closing.

"You're lying." Merik's expression hardened. "No one suspects me."

Vivian's fingers moved to her ear—or rather, her earring-free lobe. "You warned the creep on the floor over there." She jerked her head toward the unconscious man. "You warned him that I'd have a tracking device on me. Not just any device. You specifically told him that the tracker would be in my earrings."

"That's how Eric thinks. Predictable. It's—"

"Eric found the listening devices you'd put in his office, in his car, and even on him. You know, on the watch he always wears. He found them all, and he realized that you were the one who put them there." Eric hadn't, but bluffing seemed reasonable. Merik had betrayed them, and Vivian would bet there *were* listening devices planted everywhere.

"Anyone could have planted those. Could have been—"

"You were sloppy. His techs found a print, and they've matched it to you." Okay, that was a total lie. Since the man had a gun to Chase's head, she was fine with lying to him. No, there was no print. But if she could alarm Merik, then maybe they could get the upper hand in this mess. She needed him unsettled and scared.

Dex *did* suspect him, but there was no direct proof, not yet. *Merik doesn't have to know that, though.* "The final nail in your coffin came from Dex," Vivian continued as she tried to keep her eyes off Chase. When she looked at him, the fear and fury inside of her twisted too much. *So much blood. They hurt him so badly.* "He was able to find connections between you and Luc."

Luc grabbed her arm. "I don't damn well care about Dex." He thrust her into a chair and motioned to the laptop that he'd put on the desk. The room was some kind of old office, and supplies were scattered everywhere. "Unscramble your fucking code now or watch as Chase dies. You do what *I* say. Sergei's precious Russian doll is under *my* control."

Her fingers curved over the keys.

"*Don't,*" Chase bit out.

Her head turned toward him. Yes, she made the mistake of looking at him. The fear and fury twisted so much she could barely breathe.

"Don't sacrifice those people for me," Chase told her. Bruises covered his jaw. Blood stained his lips. "I'm not worth it. Don't you do it."

"I happen to think you are worth just about anything, Chase." Her voice was soft. Certain. Her fingers pressed to the keys as she looked back at the laptop.

"Don't! Baby, no! Don't!"

Her head whipped back toward him just in time to see Chase break through the ropes that bound him. He wrenched forward and the movement yanked his head away from the gun Merik held to Chase's temple. The ropes tore free and the forward momentum had Chase hurtling to the floor.

Her breath caught and she lunged up—

"Sit back down." Luc jabbed the gun in her side. "Unscramble. *Now*. I've got buyers waiting on this shit."

Her gaze cut to Chase. He'd shoved up to his knees and was whirling toward Merik. But, God, Merik was aiming his weapon and getting ready to fire. "No!"

Merik fired. The bullet hit Chase, and he seemed to crumple.

For a moment, Vivian couldn't even breathe. She was stunned. Pain overwhelmed her and her heart seemed to shrivel in her chest. Not Chase. Not him. This wasn't the plan. He shouldn't have been shot. *No!*

What could have been regret flashed on Merik's face as he stared down at Chase. "Fuck, man," he snarled. He leaned over Chase's body.

Chase rolled in a lightning-fast move. He caught Merik's wrist and jerked the other man toward him. The attack unbalanced Merik and had him barreling down on top of Chase.

"*Unscramble!*" Luc's gun jabbed into her side. "*Now!*"

Chase was alive. He was fighting Merik.

Her fingers flew over the keyboard. Code rolled across the screen. Flying faster and faster.

"*You were...my fucking...partner!*"

She heard the thud of fists.

"*Betrayed...all of us!*"

She risked a glance to the side. Merik's gun wasn't in sight. It must have gotten knocked away during the struggle. Chase appeared to be kicking Merik's ass. Her gaze darted back to the screen. More code rushed by her. She was accessing the data and then—

"I see it!" Luc shoved her out of the chair.

Her ass literally hit the floor, and when she hit the floor, her hands splayed out behind her. She'd been right a moment before. Chase *had* knocked the gun away from Merik, and it had slid across the floor during the fight. *Slid right to me.* Her fingers closed around it.

"I can see the new data!" Luc shouted. "It's coming up and it's—"

She saw the exact moment when the screen turned into numbers. Random numbers because the data was now random bullshit.

"Unscramble it! Finish!" Luc's head swung toward her.

"I did finish." She pushed to her feet. He'd put his weapon down next to the laptop. "There is no more unscrambling. It's gone." She was hiding Merik's gun behind her leg.

"You damn—" He grabbed for his weapon.

She lifted up hers. Fired.

Surprise flashed in Luc's eyes as he stumbled back. But he was still trying to lift his weapon. Still trying to fire—

So she shot him again.

He crashed into the wall. Slid down to the floor. When he slid down, streaks of blood were left on the wall behind him.

Vivian stood there a moment with her breath heaving and her body shaking. She'd never shot anyone before. Had she killed him?

An arm locked around her neck, and Vivian was hauled back against a strong, muscled body. The arm squeezed and cut off her air, and Vivian struggled to bring the gun around so she could shoot at her attacker.

"Knew you were going to be trouble," Merik panted in her ear. "From the first day. Evil Fucking Queen coming to ruin everything for me."

She...she couldn't get the gun aimed up at him. Black dots danced in front of her eyes.

"I didn't plan to work with Luc. I wasn't involved in that shit he was running. I mean, yeah, I worked with Luc back at the agency. Back in the day. Had a real sweet operation going once upon a time. But then I started to feel guilty. You can only sell out people for so long before you start to think that shit might catch up with you."

The black dots were stronger. The gun was starting to slip from her fingers.

Where is Chase? If Merik had killed him…

"Everything was going fine until Chase told me to dig deeper into Luc's life. I knew he'd give the same order to the others at Wilde. If we dug too deep, the truth about me and Luc would come out, so I had no choice. I had to go and talk to Luc. Had to team up with him once more. I didn't want things to end this way. Do you really think I wanted to kill my own partner?"

Kill my own partner. Something snapped inside of Vivian. She stopped trying to angle the gun up at Merik. Instead, she let the gun drop so that the barrel pointed to the floor.

"Good. Don't fight any longer. Give in and let go. It will be just like you're going to sleep."

Screw you. She fired the gun. When she'd lowered the weapon, Vivian hadn't been aiming for the floor. She'd been aiming for his foot. And when he screamed, she knew she'd hit her target. Merik let her go even as he howled in pain.

Vivian's body collapsed. The black dots took over her vision, her throat burned, and she struggled desperately to bring air back into her lungs.

"Hey, partner…"

Vivian's heart was drumming madly in her ears, but even over that thunder, she could hear Chase's snarling voice.

Her head snapped up.

Merik had just spun to face Chase. An enraged, pissed-to-hell-and-back Chase.

"You want to kill me?" Chase asked. "You're gonna have to try a whole lot harder." His gaze flickered to her.

I'm okay. She would have mouthed those words to him even if she wasn't.

Merik let out a guttural cry and lunged at Chase.

But Chase—body weaving slightly, blood pouring from him—was ready. He dodged Merik's attack, then drove a fist into Merik's side. Merik's breath left him in a rush, and he slumped forward.

Chase grabbed him, spun him around, and then Chase locked *his* arm around Merik's throat. "You were gonna choke her?" Chase's hold tightened even more. "You were gonna take the breath from Vivian? You were gonna kill her? *You're fucking dead.*"

Merik was punching back at him, but Chase wasn't letting go. They stumbled, their knees hit the floor, but Chase's grip didn't loosen.

Merik's face turned bloodred as it mottled, and Vivian wondered if hers had done the same thing. Merik's wide, desperate eyes flew around the room and locked on her. There was no missing the terror in his stare.

"Ch-Chase..." Speaking was hard for her. Her voice was gone. Barely a rasp. Chase hadn't heard her. He was using all of his strength on Merik. She could see the muscles bulging in Chase's arm.

Merik was trying to get loose, but Chase was too strong. The dragon on Merik's arm barely flexed as his struggles became weaker.

A dying dragon.
Chase was choking his friend, his partner.
The traitor.
She tried to call his name again, but only a gasp emerged from her lips. Vivian hauled her body forward. She crawled to get to Chase because she was so weak. Her hand reached out to touch him.

The door crashed open.
"Fucking freeze!" Dex shouted.
Chase didn't freeze.
Merik's eyes were closing.
"It's...over..." So low. Did he hear her?
"Damn." Dex bounded forward. "Let him go, Chase. I can take over. *Let him go.*"

Chase turned his head toward Vivian. "You're okay?" He didn't let Merik go.

She nodded. A tear slipped down her cheek.

"Baby..." Chase's arm was still around Merik's neck. "Baby, don't cry." His arm began to loosen. "I...hate it when...you...cry..." Chase's body slumped backward.

Merik fell forward even as Chase fell back.

Vivian didn't even try to scream. She couldn't. So she lunged for Chase. His shirt was soaked with blood. He was battered and stabbed to hell and back *and* he'd been shot by Merik.

"*Get an ambulance!*" Dex shouted. "Chase is down and he needs help! That's a fucking lot of blood loss. *Get an ambulance!*"

Vivian's fingers went to Chase's throat. She tried to find his pulse.

But she couldn't.

CHAPTER TWENTY-TWO

"You are welcome."

Chase's eyes fluttered open, and the first thing he saw? Dex. Standing at the foot of his bed. Grinning like some kind of freaking contented cat.

Chase closed his eyes again.

"Nope. Can't do it. I know you're awake. Back in the land of the living."

"Fuck...off." His throat felt dry. His tongue too big and rough.

"That is no way to talk to your brother."

What? Chase's eyes flew back open.

"Blood brother, I guess. Wait. Is that the right term?" Dex's gaze flew to the left.

To the left...Chase's head turned as he followed Dex's stare and—"Yes." Chase smiled. "That's who I wanted to see."

Vivian stood there. The light spilled from the window behind her, and it sent deep red highlights pouring through her hair. Her face was pale, her green eyes worried, and she was—far and away—the most beautiful thing he'd ever seen in his life.

"It took you long enough to wake up," Vivian said. Her hand reached for his.

His fingers closed tightly around hers.

"Ahem. I still didn't hear a thank you," Dex prompted.

"Why is he here?" Chase asked.

"Because I'm your blood brother!"

Chase kept his gaze on Vivian.

Her delicate throat moved as she swallowed. "A blood brother generally can refer to men who are biologically related or the term can also be used to refer to men who have given oaths of loyalty—"

"I'm not related to him."

Vivian shook her head. "I don't think you are."

"Did I give him some kind of oath while I was delirious?" Things had gotten a little foggy at the end. He remembered seeing Merik try to choke Vivian. He remembered attacking the traitorous bastard, and he remembered—

Did I kill Merik?

"It wasn't what you gave me." Now Dex sounded peeved. "It was what I gave you. You have an extremely rare blood type, you know. Good thing I decided to be a donor for you."

Shit. Blood brother. Now he got it. "I have Dex's blood in my veins."

Vivian nodded.

"You're welcome!" Dex called out again.

Chase turned his head to stare at the secretive CIA puppet master. "Is the case over?" He kept his hold on Vivian.

"Yes. Vivian is clear. The bad guys are contained. And none of our undercover operatives were compromised. I'd consider it a very successful op."

Successful? Was the guy crazy?

Dex's attention shifted to Vivian. "Loved the way you performed under pressure. You were able to erase the data and take out Luc Coderre, an operative who has a whole lot of field experience—and kills—beneath his belt. I must say, my suspicions about you proved true."

"You thought she was guilty," Chase reminded the guy.

"I mean my *initial* suspicions. When I first brought her in on a probational basis." Dex's expression suddenly became serious. "I think you'd make one hell of a field agent. I could really use someone with your particular skill set. You see, I recently found myself without a highly skilled hacker at my beck and call. Someone with those talents just doesn't appear every day."

Dex was seriously offering her a job. While standing at Chase's hospital bed.

"I appreciate the offer," Vivian replied, her voice careful. "But someone else actually beat you to the punch. I've already accepted a job with another employer."

"What?" Surprise flashed on Dex's face.

The door opened. Eric poked his head inside. His gaze went to Chase, and when he saw that Chase was awake, relief flashed on his face. "About damn time."

Dex whirled on him. "Did you offer Vivian a job?"

"Absolutely," Eric responded. "I can use her skills."

"I can, too! She was supposed to be working for me!"

"Well, she agreed to work for me. Sorry." Eric didn't sound the least bit apologetic. "Guess you lose this one."

Chase tuned them out. His stare returned to Vivian, and he found her staring down at him. Tears glistened in her eyes. "Get the fuck out," he ordered.

Vivian sucked in a sharp breath.

"Not you, baby." He brought her hand to his lips. Pressed a tender kiss to her knuckles. "Never you. I meant those two guys near the door."

Her gaze flickered to them.

"I need to talk to Vivian," Chase said, voice gruff. "Alone."

"Come on, Dex," Eric announced. "I'll get you a shitty cup of coffee and explain to you how Vivian will be working for *me*."

The door closed a moment later.

Vivian's stare came back to Chase. "I was afraid."

"I'm so sorry. I hated putting you in that closet back at the suite, but there was no choice, and I just needed you to be hidden—"

She shook her head. "No. *No*. I'm not talking about that!" Vivian sat on the edge of the bed. Stared into his eyes. "I was afraid that I was losing you. I don't even know how you managed to fight Merik. You were covered in blood. The docs said the blood loss had been at a near-fatal level."

Yeah, that had been because Luc was a dick who liked playing with knives. Chase didn't want to tell her about that, though. No sense in Vivian knowing about what he'd—

"Don't you do it, Chase. Don't you dare sit there and try to be all stoic and brave with me. I rode in the ambulance with you. I saw what your body looked like when they cut away your bloody shirt. How many times did he stab you?"

The machines near the bed beeped a little faster. "Doesn't matter."

"You hid me in that closet, they captured you, and then they tortured you. You went through all of that for me." Her voice had gone ragged.

His hand lifted. Chase wiped away the tear on her cheek. "I would do anything for you. Haven't you figured that out?"

"*Why?*"

"Because I love you."

Her eyes widened.

"Want another of my secrets?" He wanted to take her pain away. "When you told me the story about your step-dad falling in love with your mother—love at first sight—I completely understood how he felt."

Her head moved in an uncertain shake.

"Because I fell in love with you that fast. You were supposed to be the enemy, but all I wanted to do was make you mine."

Her lower lip trembled.

"I was serious when I asked you to marry me." He forced his own lips to smile. "Figured I might not have another chance, so I had better do it—"

"*Stop.*"

Uh, oh. That anger in her voice wasn't a good sign.

"You think I don't know what you're doing?"

"Proposing?" Chase tried.

Her gaze hardened. "You're not going to distract me. You were tortured, almost killed, because of me."

"No, it was more because my partner was a lying bastard." About that... "Is he dead?" Chase's question was emotionless.

"He's not. He's under guard in a room down the hallway. By the way, turns out that I shot off his pinky toe."

Chase's breath expelled in a long rush.

"Luc survived, too. They're both going to be transferred to jail as soon as they are strong enough. Or, um, Dex will take them some place. I kind of suspect it will be some black ops site and not a typical jail."

Chase suspected the same thing. Those two wouldn't be seen again.

"Eric, Dex, and Lacey took care of the men Luc and Merik had hired when they swarmed in to help us. Those guys are all in custody, and Dex told me they were talking as quickly as they could. They want deals, but I don't think he's offering anything."

No, Dex didn't exactly seem the deal-offering type.

"It's over," Vivian said. "You just have to heal, and then life can go back to normal."

His gaze lowered a few inches. For the first time, he really focused on her throat. And the scarf that she'd wrapped around her neck. Vivian was wearing jeans, a t-shirt, and a scarf. Interesting fashion choice. "Don't you think it's a little warm for that scarf?"

"No, it's quite chilly in hospitals. It's standard for the temps to be somewhere in the range of sixty-five to sixty-nine in ORs. There are lots of health and safety benefits to having a lower temp—"

"Take off the scarf, sweetheart. Show me."

She fumbled. Removed the scarf.

"I am going to fucking kill him."

Her throat was a mottled black and purple.

"His throat looks much worse, and at least I sound mostly normal. Merik can barely croak."

Her voice was huskier than normal. *Because of that sonofabitch.*

"He's also going to be locked up for the rest of his life," she added carefully.

"Uncle Sam doesn't take too kindly to people selling out operatives."

"No." Her fingers toyed with the scarf. "I guess your job is done. You've caught the bad guys."

"Vivian."

Her stare lifted to his.

"I told you that I fell in love with you. I *am* in love with you."

"I think it could be the drugs," she whispered. "I believe they are giving you the very good stuff here."

God, she made him want to smile. "You're my drug."

Her brow furrowed.

"You're the only thing I need. I'm addicted to you, and I don't want to let you go. I'm not delusional. I'm not floating on pain meds. I know exactly what I'm saying." He paused. He wanted this part loud and clear. "I love you."

She twisted the scarf around her fingers.

"Maybe we can start over," Chase said. "Pretend to meet again. I can play the role of the *not*-lying asshole. I can be honest and charming, and maybe you'll find yourself falling for me."

"No."

No, you won't fall for me?

"I don't want to start over."

His heart seemed to stutter and the beeps from the machines went a little crazy. Hell, he'd probably have a nurse rushing in at any moment.

"There is no need to start over," Vivian added. "Because while I like the man I met in the hallway, I love the man who risked everything to help me. I don't need some redo. I just need you."

Had she just said—

She tossed away the scarf and leaned toward him. "I love you, Chase. When I said yes before, when I said I'd marry you back in that crazy-nightmare moment, I meant those words. I wasn't saying yes because I was afraid there wouldn't be another chance for us. I was saying yes because I can't imagine my life without you. I want to be with you. I want to marry you. I want to make this wild thing between us work." She smiled at him. "I just want you."

She was all he'd ever wanted.

"Please kiss me now," he told her. "I am going insane for—"

Her lips pressed to his. His hands closed tightly around her shoulders. She was warm and soft and safe. The case was over. The threats to Vivian were gone.

And she'd just said she would marry him.

"Are you okay?" A woman's worried voice broke through the happy haze around him. "Your vitals are suddenly spiking—"

Chase carefully pulled away from Vivian and glanced at the nurse. "I have never been better," he told her truthfully. *Never. Better.*

CHAPTER TWENTY-THREE

"I don't like loose ends," Chase said.

"This is a huge mistake." Eric crossed his arms over his chest. "There is no good that will come of this. If anything, you'll probably lose your shit and try to kill the man again. You should *not* be in here." He glanced over at Dex. "I can't believe you set up this meeting and actually allowed Chase to be present. You should know better."

Dex stood with one shoulder propped against the cement wall. "I think it's a stellar idea. Chase wants closure. So do I."

"No, you just want more secrets, and you think Chase can help you get them."

"Uh, don't *you* want to know just how much the man compromised you and your company? Aren't you worried about that important matter?"

Eric's jaw hardened. "I've locked down my company. I'm good. Don't worry about me. Merik was the only bad agent at Wilde. An agent *you* sent to me."

Dex winced. "You want me to apologize for that, don't you? Fine. My bad. I'll try not to send any traitors to you again."

The door opened. A shackled Merik shuffled inside. He took one look at the three men there and... "Fuck."

Chase didn't move from his seated position near the metal table. A table that had been positioned in the middle of the small room. "Yes, you are fucked."

The guard prodded Merik toward the table and the empty chair that waited for him. The guard secured Merik's shackles to a lock on the floor. "All yours." He left without a backward glance.

The door clanged shut behind him.

"Is he supposed to do that?" Merik asked. The bruises on his throat had faded. Two weeks had passed since the attack. Chase's stitches were finally out, and he'd finally gotten Dex to set up this...talk.

Interrogation.

Death match.

Whatever.

"I don't think the guard is supposed to leave me like this. I mean, I don't even have a lawyer present." Merik rolled back his shoulders, or tried to. There wasn't much room for movement thanks to the shackles. "Tried to get Kendrick Shaw to take my case, you know, since he is supposed to be the big, go-to man when you need a get-out-of-jail card, but he refused."

"Kendrick doesn't rep traitors," Eric informed him. "He has this thing about liking for his clients to actually be innocent. A character quirk. One I admire the hell out of."

"Um." Merik's gaze flickered to Chase. "You tried to kill me."

"You ever come at Vivian again, and I won't just try." *I'll succeed.*

"It wasn't personal, Chase. I legitimately liked you."

Bullshit. Did Merik even have the ability to tell the truth?

Merik turned his head toward Dex. "If I talk, you gonna give me a deal? That what this meet and greet is about?"

"No. I'm not giving you shit." Dex smiled at him. "This meet and greet is about making sure you understand exactly what kind of nightmare you've entered."

Merik laughed. "Try that line on someone who doesn't know how the game is played. You need me to roll on Luc. He's the big fish. He's the one who set up all the ops that we did back when I was at the CIA. He was the one pulling the strings. I did some of the action, yeah, guilty, but I wanted out after a while. And I really was going to stay out." Now he looked back at Chase. "I was gonna be better." He swallowed. "But then Luc had to become a suspect in this case. He was the one who hired the guy to break into Vivian's place. You were right on that. He wanted to plant evidence at her apartment. When he came by the next morning for their little jogging date and he set off all those alarm bells for you…that's when everything went south."

No, everything went south long before that.

"If Wilde was gonna investigate him, then they'd find dirt on me. All it would take was deeper digging." Merik's focus moved to Eric. "I know how you like to dig."

"You used my own surveillance against me." Eric's voice was flat. Furiously cold.

Once more, Merik tried to shrug. "Surveillance was my thing. It's what the CIA taught me to do. As the saying goes, *'Don't hate the play—'*"

"This isn't a game." Chase slammed his fists down onto the table. "Vivian could have died. You could have compromised a whole lot of agents."

"And if the deal had gone well with Luc's buyers, I could've made a whole boat load of cash. I gambled. I lost."

He was treating this all like a joke.

"I think that is a great start. We're sharing, and that's what deal making is all about." Merik nodded. "What I have given you so far is beginner info. There will be more to come if—"

"You sabotaged the elevator in Vivian's building, didn't you?" Chase remembered how terrified she'd been, and rage poured through his veins.

"Yeah, Luc had learned about her trouble with dark spaces, so I thought I'd use that against her. But, considering what I saw when those doors *opened*, don't you think you should be thanking me for that sabotage instead of being all mad about it?"

Mad? Merik had no clue about how Chase was truly feeling. *I want to tear you apart, asshole. I want to destroy you, and I will.* "Who had the idea of drugging us at the hotel suite?" Chase asked.

Merik hesitated, then revealed, "Luc. He often uses drugs on his prey. Works well for him." A quick bark of laughter. "Actually, I think he learned to use drugs back when he was running some ops in Russia." He tossed a grin at Dex. "You know how the Russians love to use—"

"That's all I need." Dex inclined his head. "I think he's sealed his fate."

"Wait, what?" Merik jerked up his shackled hands. The chains jangled. "We're making a deal here—"

"I never promised you a deal. You just ran your mouth because you're desperate. You should be desperate. You've made a powerful enemy, and he is always going to be coming after you." Dex raised an eyebrow as he looked at Chase. "You want to tell him? Or should I?"

Sweat beaded on Merik's forehead.

I'll tell him. After all, that was the plan. "Dex had already learned that Luc liked to use drugs. Poison."

"Fine, so I didn't tell you anything new yet—"

"We have something new for you," Chase assured him. "Or, hell, maybe it's not new. Maybe you were aware of this all along."

Merik had gone quiet.

"Dex discovered that a while back, Luc took one of his *side jobs*, and he tried to take out the leader of the Russian mafia."

A drop of sweat trickled toward Merik's eyebrow.

"But the poison went to the wrong person, and instead of Sergei the Savage dying, his beloved wife was killed. To the rest of the world, it looked as if she suffered a heart attack. But Sergei knew the truth, and for him, it was always just a matter of time until he found his wife's killer."

"I had nothing to do with that! I wasn't even working for the CIA back then! That was before my time at the agency!"

Merik was cracking. No, breaking. Just as they'd planned. "You knew that Sergei was Vivian's stepfather." Merik had read the dossier just like Chase had. "Luc knew it, too. Making her the fall victim in the data theft was deliberate. Luc hoped to draw out Sergei. He wanted to finish his hit from long ago. And I have to say, Luc was successful."

Merik's eyelids flickered. "Sergei is dead?" Relief flashed on his face.

"No. But Luc is. He was found dead in his cell this morning."

Merik slumped back in his chair. "Shit."

"Looked like a heart attack," Dex drawled. "But my money is on poison. We'll see what the ME discovers."

"Fuck!" Merik's eyes had grown to the size of saucers. "He's gonna come after me?"

"You did try to kill his daughter. I don't think things are going to end well for you." Chase stared at the man he'd thought was his friend. "Not well at all." He rose and stared sadly at Merik.

"You have to help me!" Merik shouted. The shackles jangled again. "Get her to call him off! I will do anything! Give you *any* intel! Don't let him kill me! Don't let him—"

"Told you already," Dex said. "I'm not here to deal." He strolled for the door.

Chase's gaze slid to Eric. Eric was staring at Merik with no expression on his face at all.

"Eric, *please*," Merik entreated. "Don't do this. It's execution. That's not what you do. You don't—"

"You put a gun to Chase's head. You tried to strangle the woman he loves. Why the hell would you think that I would do anything for you now?" Disgusted, Eric shook his head. "We're done."

"*Don't!*" Merik cried. "Please, don't do this to—"

"I believe," Dex interrupted, "that he said we were done. Or, at least, you are."

They shut the door on his shouts. As they stood in the hallway outside of the interrogation room, tension stretched between the three men.

And then...

Dex smiled. "That went perfectly!"

Eric blew out a long breath. He ran a shaking hand over his face.

"I *told* you'd he'd crumble. All we had to do was put the right scenario in front of him. You paint a picture in someone's head—the right picture—and they'll do whatever you want."

Chase sucked in a deep breath. "You're a twisted individual, Dex."

"Yeah, well, *you* are the one who had the idea of bringing up Sergei. I mean, how did you even connect the dots on that one? Damn, man, I am impressed!"

"I connected them because of something Luc said when he was trying to make Vivian unscramble the data." The words had played through Chase's head again and again. "He said 'Sergei's precious Russian doll' was under his control. Weird thing to say. Didn't fit at the time.

But then I considered the drugs we'd been given at the hotel and the fact that Vivian told me her mother hadn't ever experienced any heart problems before her sudden death..." He'd had puzzle pieces. He'd put them together, hoping he might be wrong but...

No, Merik's reaction had confirmed things. *Luc had killed her mother.* Chase would have to tell Vivian. And he'd have to watch her pain.

"The part about Sergei going after Luc was cold." Eric rocked onto the balls of his feet. "What do you think Merik will do when he finds out that Luc isn't dead?"

"I don't really care." Dex's expression reflected his utter lack of fucks to give. "By then, Merik will have talked until he's blue. I'll have all the intel I need from him. I'll have the names of every dirty CIA man or woman that he knows, and I will clean house. I will—" His phone rang. "Who the hell even has this number?" He yanked out the phone. Frowned at the screen. "Excuse me," he mumbled before he turned away.

Eric swung his gaze to Chase. "This news will hurt Vivian."

Yes. "It will also give her closure." It also explained a few things. "She believes Sergei cut her out of his life, but I think he might have been protecting her. Distancing himself from Vivian could have been a way to keep her safe."

"Sergei the Savage." Eric cocked his head. "You're saying...what? Beneath the blood and gore and monster facade, he has a soft spot?"

Maybe. "Even a monster can love."

"*It's not a lie.*" Dex's voice was low, stunned.

At Dex's rather dramatic announcement, Chase squinted at him. "Say again?"

"Luc being dead. Probably being poisoned." He tightened his hold on the phone in his hand. "It's not a lie. He was just found in his jail cell, and I swear, the scene went down exactly as we described to Merik. Looks like a heart attack, but my money will be on poison." He stared at Eric. Then at Chase. "What the hell do you think of that?"

Chase considered the situation. "Huh." His gaze slid to the closed cell door. "I think Merik had better watch his back."

***

When Chase returned to his apartment, he found a vase of sunflowers sitting by his door.

He stopped. Frowned. And bent to pick up the flowers. Okay. That was strange as hell. He unlocked the door and pulled the card from the flowers as he stepped inside.

Make her happy. Take care of her. Love her.
—S.

"Oh, fuck me," Chase breathed. He'd have to check the security camera that he still had installed in the hallway near the elevator, but every instinct he had screamed that freaking *Sergei the Savage* had left those flowers. But sunflowers? What the hell?

A knock sounded at the door. Chase grabbed his weapon because if a Russian mob boss was about to pay him a visit, then he damn well wanted to be ready. But when he glanced through the peephole, Sergei wasn't on the other side.

Vivian was.

He swung open the door and pulled her into his arms. He held her tightly. Far, far too tightly. And he *never* wanted to let her go.

"Hey, not so hard!" Laughter rang in her voice.

He eased up, a little.

"Did you buy me sunflowers?" She pushed against him and peered over at the vase of flowers. A wide smile curved her lips. "How did you know they are my favorites?" She ran to the flowers and touched them with careful fingers. "My mom loved sunflowers. We used to plant them in our garden every spring, and Sergei would be there to help us..."

Her favorite flowers. Of course.

Chase shut and locked the door. "Baby, we need to talk."

But she'd found the card that rested beside the flowers. The card he'd dropped when he rushed to answer the door.

Uncertainly, Vivian's head angled toward him. "Chase?"

He squared his shoulders and went to her.

***

"You bake when you're stressed, and I love that about you. Mostly because I love every single thing that you bake, and if you decide you want to make more brownies, please, by all means, do it. Bake them until you can't bake any longer."

Vivian glanced up. She'd been stirring brownie batter, probably a little too hard, and Chase had snuck into the kitchen. He was right. She did bake when she was stressed, and she'd been stressed ever since he'd revealed the truth of her mother's death to her.

Luc killed my mother. And it looks like my stepfather killed Luc. And my stepfather sent those flowers and—

"I think you might be hurting the brownie batter. While I am not a master baker by any stretch of the imagination, those seem like very vicious swipes."

She put down the batter. "He's a killer."

"Who?"

"Sergei."

Chase nodded.

"He...loved her."

Once more, Chase nodded.

"He...loved me." She yanked off her apron.

"From what I can gather, he still *loves* you. Dex has uncovered intel that shows Sergei had men ready to storm inside and kill Luc when he had me tied up at that old office building. Sergei only pulled back his men because he caught sight of Dex."

So her stepfather was watching over her. She'd thought he'd just left. No, that he'd sent her away. "He didn't think it was safe for me to be with him."

"Baby, he knew it wasn't safe." His golden gaze was so tender. Warm.

"I know what he is," she whispered.

Chase inclined his head.

"And I-I still love the dad I knew." Another of her secrets. She'd lost count of how many she'd given to Chase. The number didn't really matter. She knew that he'd always keep her secrets safe. "What does that say about me?"

Chase slowly walked around the counter. He tucked a lock of her hair behind her ear. "It says you can see good in people, and, baby, that is one of the many things I love about you."

She searched his gaze. "You're not worried because your future father-in-law is part of the Russian mob?"

"The only thing that worries me is the fear that you'll change your mind. You'll realize that you're too damn good for a jackass like me."

"No." She curled her arms around him. "That's not going to happen. I *love* you." With all of her heart because he *was* good. She'd asked Chase to be one of the good guys, and he was. He was brave, strong, determined. *Good.* She knew that he would do anything for her. And she...

She'd take any risk for him.

"I love you, too," Chase told her. His head bent. His lips took hers.

Vivian kissed him back eagerly. She needed his kiss. Needed his warmth and power. After he'd told her the dark news the night before, she'd cried. He'd held her all night long while she'd grieved again.

He'd been there for her, in a way that no one ever had before.

She could count on Chase.

Her body pressed to his. Her lips parted even more. Her tongue darted out to rub against his.

A guttural groan tore from him. "OhmyGod." He kissed her. Harder. Deeper. "You were sampling the brownies. Brownies and vanilla. You taste like my best dream ever."

She laughed. Chase could do that. He could make her laugh in the darkest of times. He held her when she cried. He fought for her when danger closed in.

How could she not love him with her whole heart?

"Chase..." She nibbled on his lower lip. "Make love to me?"

"Baby, I will make love to you forever." He swung her into his arms and carried her to the bedroom.

"Promises, promises," Vivian teased.

"Not a promise." He lowered her onto the bed. Carefully unbuttoned the white shirt that she wore and opened it to expose her bra. "A guarantee." His mouth pressed to the swell of her breast. She arched toward him. His fingers slid under the fabric of her bra, and he teased her nipple. His touch was so careful. Tender. He stroked. Kissed. Licked. He took off her bra and she barely even felt the material slide away. He was taking such good care of her.

Loving her.

Her heart raced, and her hips squirmed against him. "You're being slow."

"That's because I'm savoring you." His hand slid down her body. Unhooked her pants. He eased away long enough to remove her pants and her panties. She hadn't been wearing shoes or socks, so she was naked now, and she waited for him to—

He parted her legs. "Savor," Chase breathed.

His mouth pressed to her sex. He licked and sucked. Took his time as he savored. She was grabbing for the covers and chanting his name and loving every single thing that he was doing to her. Her climax built and built, and Vivian knew there would be no holding back. It was too strong. Too powerful.

He licked her clit. Pushed two fingers deep into her.

Vivian surged toward his hungry mouth as her release poured through her whole body. Pleasure blasted her. The aftershocks of release hummed through her, driving the pleasure higher as her sex clenched around his fingers.

But she wanted more than his fingers inside of her.

She wanted him.

She wanted his control gone.

Vivian's eyes opened. She met his stare. The gold was so bright.

"You are beautiful," he told her. "And mine." He rose over her.

But she put her hands on his chest. "You're mine, too." She slid to the side and pushed him down on the bed. "Every bit of you." She straddled him. He was still wearing his clothes. Jeans and a t-shirt. They needed to go. Her hand trailed down his chest. Her touch was careful because she knew his healing wounds were tender. Yes, the stitches were gone, but she still wanted to be gentle with him. *I never want to hurt him.*

Her fingers eased down and paused at the snap of his jeans. "Body and soul, right?"

"Body, soul, and heart. Sweetheart, you own every piece of me."

Her gaze flew to his.

She could see the love shining in his eyes.

He loved her. No lie. No pretense.

Just as she loved him.

She unsnapped his jeans. Pulled down the zipper. He wasn't wearing underwear, so his cock sprang toward her. Fully erect, long and thick, with moisture already wetting the head.

Vivian had to lean down for a lick.

"Viv!"

One lick wasn't enough. She tried another. And if she wanted a full taste, she needed to part her lips, so she did. Her mouth closed around him, and she sucked his cock into her mouth. Her fingers tightened around the base of his shaft as she worked him. She took more and more. Became greedy for him. Always him.

"Vivian!" His hands locked around her shoulders. "Don't play. I want *in* you."

If that was what he wanted...

She moved up. Went back to her position straddling his hips. His cock shoved at the entrance to her body. Their fingers twined together.

She sank down on him.

He filled her completely, perfectly, and for a moment, she didn't want to move at all. She just wanted to remember this instant. To freeze it in her mind and never forget.

"Baby, I'm about to go crazy," he warned.

She smiled down at him. "Good. Take me with you. Let's be crazy together."

His control shredded. So did hers. His hips shoved against her, and she rode him. She jerked up and down, and each glide had her moaning. A second orgasm built for her, and it came at her so fast she didn't even have time to do anything but—

"Chase!"

Enjoy the ride. That was all she could do. Enjoy.

He tumbled her back onto the mattress. He caught her legs and lifted them high around his hips. He thrust into her, drove deep and strong, plunging into her as her orgasm swept through her. He kissed her, and she felt him come.

His body jerked as he pumped into her, and she held him as tightly as she could.

A wild thunder filled her ears, and Vivian smiled as her heart raced. Sex with Chase was always incredible. No, it wasn't just sex. It was making love. Making love with him would *never* get old.

He'd been right about that. Once for them would never be enough. She wasn't even sure that a million times would be enough. Good thing they had plenty of days—and nights—ahead of them. Forever.

But...her eyes flew open. "Did I hurt you?"

He'd been staring down at her. She caught the faint smile on his face. *He looks so happy.*

At her question, Chase frowned.

"Your wounds," Vivian quickly reminded him. "Oh, God, did I hurt them? Did I hurt you?"

"No, baby. You know the doc said I was all clear. The stitches are gone. I'm fine."

He was better than fine.

Perfect.

Chase slowly withdrew from her. They righted themselves on the wrecked bed, then snuggled together against the pillows.

"I'm so good." He winked at her. "We should totally go for round two."

She was up for that.

"Though I think I should *actually* manage to get my jeans all of the way off. And maybe take off my shirt. You know, do that stuff."

A soft laugh slipped from her.

"I love your laugh." His expression turned serious. "I want to make you laugh and smile every day of your life. I want you to be happy," he continued in his deep rumble of a voice. "Because that's how you make me feel. Happy. Free. Whole. Like there is something good in my world. Something I would do anything to protect." He pressed a soft kiss to her throat. "You're my something good, sweetheart. Always will be." He swallowed. "I...didn't think people stayed."

Tension snaked through her.

"When things get hard, I thought people left."

She knew he was talking about his mother.

"But you didn't leave. You were willing to trade your life for me. You came for me, Vivian."

What else would she have done? "I plan to stay," she promised him softly. "Always." *Because I love you.*

"So do I." His fingers drifted over her cheek. "Always."

She leaned toward him. He slid his head a few inches toward her.

They kissed once more.

But perhaps she should tell him one thing. "I have another secret," Vivian murmured against his mouth.

"Tell me anything."

"I...grew up as an only child."

"Me, too, sweetheart." Another kiss.

"I always hoped to have a big family."

"You're *my* family now."

Just as he was hers. "How do you feel about kids?"

His eyes opened. He stared at her, then slowly smiled. "How many do you want?"

"Three..."

He nodded.

"Is a good start," she finished.

Chase laughed. It was a happy, wonderful laugh that warmed her heart. His mouth brushed over hers again, and he revealed, "I have a secret."

She waited.

"I always wanted a big family, too. A family where there is love and promises kept and a whole freaking lot of vanilla ice cream." He gazed into her eyes. "Wanna know what else I think would be great at that home?"

"What?"

"A field of sunflowers. We can plant them every spring."

Her mom would have liked that. *She* liked that. And... "I love you."

"You can say that as many times as you like. Makes me feel good every time I hear it."

"I love you," she told him again. She kissed him and held tight and knew that, one day, they would have a family. They'd have vanilla ice cream, brownies, and a field of sunflowers. They'd also have laughter. Security.

Love.

Always, love.

EPILOGUE

"Dex, what in the hell are you doing here?" Eric frowned at the man who'd just entered his office. "You know the building is closed. How did you even get inside?"

"Seriously?" Dex lifted his brows. "It's me. Your best friend."

"You are not my best friend. Why do you keep saying things like that? We barely know each other."

"Semantics." Dex strolled across the office and threw his body into the chair across from Eric's desk. "I have a problem."

"You seem to always have problems." Eric flattened his hands on the surface of the desk.

"Yes, but, this time, it's different." He blew out a long breath. "You see, I need a fiancée."

Eric waited. There was no punchline. No laughter. "Um, you do realize that Wilde isn't a dating service, don't you?"

"Of course, I realize that."

"Then why would you come to me for a—"

"She wouldn't really be my fiancée. It would be a cover. I need an agent who can handle herself under some extremely dangerous circumstances. And an agent who just happens to be able to act as if she is completely and utterly obsessed with me." He shrugged. "Shouldn't be too hard to fake that obsession. I am pretty awesome."

"You're insane." Eric pinched the bridge of his nose. "You're making my head ache."

"Dude, you need to learn to manage your stress better."

Eric sent him a glare. "You are my stress."

"Hurtful."

"Truthful."

Dex just stared back at him. "If it helps, I already have a candidate in mind. That can speed things along for you."

"Why can't you use one of your own CIA operatives for this? Don't you have a whole group of spies who could do this job for you?"

"I think one of your agents would be better suited for this mission. I need someone unaffiliated with the agency, if you know what I mean."

He knew Dex was working one of his off-the-books cases. "Who do you have in mind?"

Dex offered him a warm, charming smile. One that immediately had Eric's back tensing. "Who?" Eric demanded.

"I think Lacey Amari would be wonderful for the job."

Eric shot to his feet. "Hell, no."

Now Dex jumped up, too. "Why not?"

"Because you're not risking Lacey!" *Because she's family.* "Because she doesn't even like you. You did not leave the best impression on the woman. There is no way that she'd ever agree to go undercover as your fiancée!" Oh, no. He'd said the wrong thing.

A sly expression stole across Dex's face. "Is that all it would take? Her agreement?"

"Uh...hold on..."

But Dex had turned away. "Got it. If Lacey says yes, then it is game on." He tossed a wave over his shoulder. "Great talk, buddy. Kiss the wife for me, would you? I'll definitely come by for dinner one night soon."

"I didn't invite you for dinner," Eric muttered.

The door closed behind Dex.

Eric slowly sat back down. He didn't have anything to worry about. No way would Lacey agree to be Dex's pretend fiancée for a mission. No way.

His eyes squeezed closed. "This is going to be bad."

THE END

A NOTE FROM THE AUTHOR

Thank you for reading CHASE AFTER ME!

I had such a great time revisiting the world of the Wilde team. I hope you enjoyed Chase's story! The Wilde books have been such a pleasure to write, and I am happy to say that another one will be coming your way. You'll get to learn all of Lacey's secrets in SAY I DO, and you'll see master spy Dex take a very big fall

If you'd like to stay updated on my releases and sales, please join my newsletter list.

https://cynthiaeden.com/newsletter/

Again, thank you for reading CHASE AFTER ME.

Best,
Cynthia   Eden
cynthiaeden.com

Want to read another Cynthia Eden book?

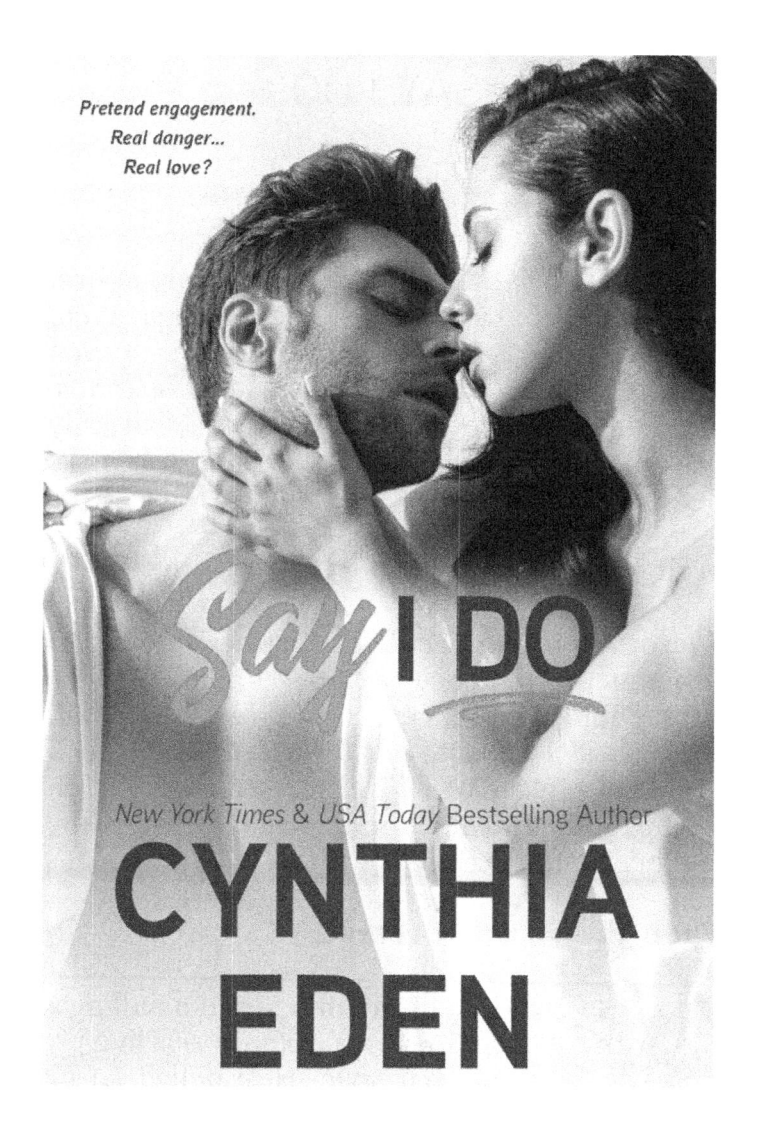

Pretend engagement.
Real danger...
Real love?

Say I Do

New York Times & USA Today Bestselling Author

CYNTHIA EDEN

SAY I DO

She hates him.

Dexter Ryan is smug. Arrogant. Manipulative. And he is also...Lacey Amari's new partner. Well, her partner on *one* case. A case she doesn't even want to take, but when Dex—CIA super operative and all around puppet-master—basically blackmails her, she has no choice. Then he asks her the big question...

Will you marry me?

The proposal isn't real. It's just an undercover assignment. Dex needs Lacey to be his fake fiancée for a case. Not exactly her dream job. But, she'll do it. He wants her to pretend to be head over heels in love with him, he wants her help on a dangerous investigation in a remote ski lodge, and he...*wants* her?

Their desire isn't pretend.

Dex doesn't work well with others and handling a case with a partner in close proximity—as in 24/7 close—isn't his normal style. He's pulled Lacey into the investigation because she is smart and resourceful, and *maybe* because he knows a secret about her that could prove to be very useful to him. After all, Dex uses people all the time. It's his thing. Yet the more he is around her, the idea of using Lacey suddenly doesn't seem like such a good plan. But getting her into his bed? *Stellar idea.*

He wants her, but so do the bad guys.

The attraction between Dex and Lacey burns red-hot, hot enough to melt the snow around them. Except, just as he planned, Lacey's presence draws in the enemy. Now the bad guys are after her, and Dex has to stick even *closer* to her. He's playing the role of the obsessed lover, only it's not just a role. Because for the first time in his life, Dex is falling hard. He's losing *his* control.

He's lied. He's cheated. He's about to give up his heart.
When Lacey finds out the secret he's known, her rage and pain break his heart. Dex has to find a way to make things up to her, *and* he has to stop the enemies who are closing in. Nothing he can't handle. *Maybe.* Dex is a master multi-tasker—most days, anyway. Dex will use every trick in his very large arsenal to win this case. Lacey melted the ice around what the whole world knows is Dex's very, very cold heart, and Dex will fight like hell to protect her *and* to prove to her that even master spies can fall in love.

Author's note: Dex loves playing games. Some would even say he enjoys playing with other people's lives, but this time...it is Dex's life on the line. His life and his heart. The longer his pretend engagement to Lacey lasts, the longer Dex finds himself longing for the real deal. Prepare for lies, tricks, dangerous enemies, and romance hot enough to melt some heavy snow...Dex's story will burn like fire and things will get WILDE.

Learn more about Say I Do.

ABOUT THE AUTHOR

Cynthia Eden is a *New York Times*, *USA Today*, *Digital Book World*, and *IndieReader* best-seller.

Cynthia writes sexy tales of contemporary romance, romantic suspense, and paranormal romance. Since she began writing full-time in 2005, Cynthia has written over one hundred novels and novellas.

Cynthia lives along the Alabama Gulf Coast. She loves romance novels, horror movies, and chocolate.

For More Information
- *https://cynthiaeden.com*
- *http://www.facebook.com/cynthiaedenfanpage*
- *http://www.twitter.com/cynthiaeden*

HER OTHER WORKS

Wilde Ways

- Protecting Piper (Wilde Ways, Book 1)
- Guarding Gwen (Wilde Ways, Book 2)
- Before Ben (Wilde Ways, Book 3)
- The Heart You Break (Wilde Ways, Book 4)
- Fighting For Her (Wilde Ways, Book 5)
- Ghost Of A Chance (Wilde Ways, Book 6)
- Crossing The Line (Wilde Ways, Book 7)
- Counting On Cole (Wilde Ways, Book 8)

Dark Sins

- Don't Trust A Killer (Dark Sins, Book 1)
- Don't Love A Liar (Dark Sins, Book 2)

Lazarus Rising

- Never Let Go (Book One, Lazarus Rising)
- Keep Me Close (Book Two, Lazarus Rising)
- Stay With Me (Book Three, Lazarus Rising)
- Run To Me (Book Four, Lazarus Rising)

- Lie Close To Me (Book Five, Lazarus Rising)
- Hold On Tight (Book Six, Lazarus Rising)
- Lazarus Rising Volume One (Books 1 to 3)
- Lazarus Rising Volume Two (Books 4 to 6)

Dark Obsession Series

- Watch Me (Dark Obsession, Book 1)
- Want Me (Dark Obsession, Book 2)
- Need Me (Dark Obsession, Book 3)
- Beware Of Me (Dark Obsession, Book 4)
- Only For Me (Dark Obsession, Books 1 to 4)

Mine Series

- Mine To Take (Mine, Book 1)
- Mine To Keep (Mine, Book 2)
- Mine To Hold (Mine, Book 3)
- Mine To Crave (Mine, Book 4)
- Mine To Have (Mine, Book 5)
- Mine To Protect (Mine, Book 6)
- Mine Series Box Set Volume 1 (Mine, Books 1-3)
- Mine Series Box Set Volume 2 (Mine, Books 4-6)

Bad Things

- The Devil In Disguise (Bad Things, Book 1)
- On The Prowl (Bad Things, Book 2)

- Undead Or Alive (Bad Things, Book 3)
- Broken Angel (Bad Things, Book 4)
- Heart Of Stone (Bad Things, Book 5)
- Tempted By Fate (Bad Things, Book 6)
- Bad Things Volume One (Books 1 to 3)
- Bad Things Volume Two (Books 4 to 6)
- Bad Things Deluxe Box Set (Books 1 to 6)
- Wicked And Wild (Bad Things, Book 7)
- Saint Or Sinner (Bad Things, Book 8)

Bite Series

- Forbidden Bite (Bite Book 1)
- Mating Bite (Bite Book 2)

Blood and Moonlight Series

- Bite The Dust (Blood and Moonlight, Book 1)
- Better Off Undead (Blood and Moonlight, Book 2)
- Bitter Blood (Blood and Moonlight, Book 3)
- Blood and Moonlight (The Complete Series)

Purgatory Series

- The Wolf Within (Purgatory, Book 1)
- Marked By The Vampire (Purgatory, Book 2)
- Charming The Beast (Purgatory, Book 3)
- Deal with the Devil (Purgatory, Book 4)
- The Beasts Inside (Purgatory, Books 1 to 4)

Bound Series

- Bound By Blood (Bound Book 1)
- Bound In Darkness (Bound Book 2)
- Bound In Sin (Bound Book 3)
- Bound By The Night (Bound Book 4)
- Forever Bound (Bound, Books 1 to 4)
- Bound in Death (Bound Book 5)

Other Romantic Suspense

- One Hot Holiday
- Secret Admirer
- First Taste of Darkness
- Sinful Secrets
- Until Death
- Christmas With A Spy

Made in the USA
Las Vegas, NV
12 April 2022